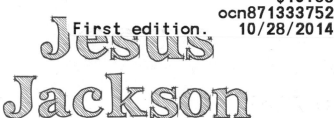

Books by James Ryan Daley

Jesus Jackson

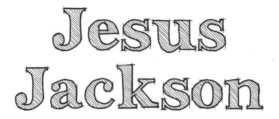

Jesus Jackson

James Ryan Daley

The Poisoned Pencil
An imprint of Poisoned Pen Press

The Poisoned Pencil
An imprint of Poisoned Pen Press
6962 E. First Ave., Ste. 103
Scottsdale, AZ 85251
www.thepoisonedpencil.com
info@thepoisonedpencil.com

Printed in the United States of America

For my girls: Joannah, Antonia, and Emerson—the only three reasons I've ever really found for having one hundred percent, guaranteed, complete faith in anything.

Acknowledgments

Without a doubt, my first thank you has to go to my incomparable editor, Ellen Larson, whose endless enthusiasm, keen insights, and overall editorial brilliance finally helped me turn this into the story that I always hoped it could be.

Thanks as well to the wise and generous friends who read this manuscript in its rough infancy and helped to shape it into what it is today: Jesse Schwartz, Anne Portman, and (of course) Joannah. This would have never happened without you.

Thanks to the publishers, designers, editors, and everyone who works so hard at The Poisoned Pencil for making this all a reality and doing it with style.

I owe a huge debt of gratitude to all of the writers who I've been lucky enough to call mentor throughout my life, especially the immortal Kenny Cook, and indefatigable Xu Xi.

I'm forever grateful to my mother and father for a lifetime of love and support, and to my big brother Jack, who I've never stopped looking up to (even after I outgrew him). To the rest of my amazing family: the Biancaniellos, the Portmans. And to the always-inspirational Spruce Lane Crew: the Davids, and the Benzaks of Rhode Island.

Thanks especially to my two beautiful daughters. Antonia, I often doubt I had a heart at all before you made one for me out of giggles and tears. I owe so much more to you than just this book. Emerson, there is no darkness that you can't brighten, no anxiety you can't melt. I will never be able to express the amount of joy you add to my life, every single day.

And finally, my wife: Joannah. On the day you married me, you promised to always be my lover, best friend, editor, conscience, and biggest fan. After the long journey that led to this book, I might add therapist, caretaker, and drill sergeant to that list. In any case, thank you; everything I am is better because of you.

One

When I first saw Jesus, he was standing like a statue on the fifty-yard line of the high school football field, one arm pointed at the goalpost and the other cocked back—fingers curled around an imaginary pigskin, locked at the ready for a pantomimed hail-Mary in the final seconds of a make believe bowl game. It was a glorious moment to behold…at least, that is, until an invisible opponent rushed his offensive line. Jesus had to fake right, spin left, and duck around a pretend tight end to make a harrowing dash for the touchdown. He hit a few straight-arm blocks, pulled some fancy footwork, and half a second later he was jogging across the goal line, spiking the ball, and moonwalking clear from one side of the end zone to the other.

Now I know what you're thinking, but stop right there. And trust me: This guy was totally Jesus. The long, straw-brown hair, straggly beard, gaunt frame, and clear-bright eyes; he was a dead ringer for the son of God. The only difference, as far as I could tell, between the Jesus on the football field and the one hanging on the cross in the school auditorium, was his clothes. The latter wore nearly none, of course, while this one was done up all dapper in a white linen suit, patent leather loafers, and a wide-collared, pastel pink button-down disco shirt, opened just enough to reveal a tuft of flaxen hair and a sparkling gold chain.

But before I get too far into this story, I need to stop and explain a couple things to you. First, you need to know that this little run-in with the savior was happening on a cold and dewy Saturday morning, at about nine am. It was the first of September—about fifteen weeks after my fourteenth birthday, roughly three months since my last day of junior high, and exactly two hours after my big brother's body was found, lifeless and broken, at the bottom of a sixty-foot ravine behind St. Soren's. I don't want to dwell on this detail too much at the moment (we'll get into it all later, trust me), but I just thought you ought to know. For perspective.

Oh yeah, and another thing: I don't actually believe in Jesus. Didn't then, don't now. Not even a little.

So anyway, I watched the old king-of-kings run a victory lap around the track—arms raised, hair streaming behind him in the wind—but just as I was about to wander off, he stopped again on the fifty-yard line, waved his left hand high over his head, and called out, "Hey, you!"

I looked behind me to see if he was referring to someone else, but no one was there. We met eyes and I pointed to my chest with a shrug.

"Yeah, you," he yelled. "Come on down here, would ya?"

I didn't have anything else to do at the moment (the cops and paramedics wouldn't let me near the ravine), and to tell you the truth, I was happy for the distraction. So I put my hands in my pockets and strolled all the way down the aisle, through the bleachers, and onto the field.

Jesus just stood there, grinning at me more like a salesman than a savior, waiting for me to reach him. And as soon as I stepped onto the grass, he hopped back and began bouncing on his toes, his hands cradling another imaginary football.

"All right," he said, staring down the field. "Go long."

"Excuse me?"

"Go long."

"Why?"

He started bobbing, weaving, dodging pretend defensemen. "It's the fourth quarter. We've got twelve seconds, and we're down by five. Now go *long*."

"But you don't have a real ball."

He shook his head, unimpressed with my logic. "And you aren't a *real* wide receiver and this isn't the *real* Super Bowl, and I'm not about to get sacked by a *real* defensive lineman named the Arkansas Annihilator. Don't be so concerned with *reality* all the time. Just *go long!*"

I realized that I was not about to beat this guy in an argument. And seeing as how my current options were to go long with Jesus or go back to the crowd of cops and detectives and school administrators and weeping parents and one very dead older brother in a ravine behind the school, I decided on the former.

"Fine," I said. "Fine." And I ran.

I didn't run very fast, but it felt good to put my body into action, to pump some blood back through all the numbness. I'd been so still and so frozen since the morning, when I first found my mother in the kitchen surrounded by pancakes and bacon and fruit salad and coffee and pastries and juice (she likes to cook when she's upset), and learned that Ryan had apparently fallen while taking a jog after football practice the previous afternoon. But right then, on that field, I could feel my body begin to warm, the sensation returning (just a little) to my limbs.

The funny thing is, Jesus must have been hiding a real ball somewhere (though I can't imagine where) because when I finally made it down around the ten-yard line and turned to make the imaginary catch, I got smacked clear off my feet by a solid, real, and perfectly spiraling football.

The pass hit me right beneath the rib cage, knocking the wind out of me. I fell hard and gasped for air. My eyes shut while I struggled to catch my breath and when I finally opened them, there was Jesus, standing straight over me, reaching a hand down to help me up.

"Sorry about that," he said, hoisting me to my feet. "I was just trying to make a point."

I rubbed my chest and winced. "I get it. You've got one hell of an arm. You could go pro."

"That wasn't exactly my point." He extended his right hand. "I'm Jesus."

I shook it. "I figured. It's a good look for you. You really pull it off."

Jesus tugged at his lapel. "Well, thank you."

"Aren't you supposed to wear, like…robes, though? And sandals? And, you know, do things more holy then mess around on a football field?"

"No," he chuckled, pulling a business card from his pocket. "You've got me mixed up. I'm not *that* Jesus. I'm Jesus *Jackson*."

He handed me the card. I looked it over. It read:

Jesus Jackson: Spiritual Contractor
100% faith guaranteed!
Call for a FREE ESTIMATE!

Strangely, there was no phone number on the card.

"So, are you going to try to sell me something?"

His face contorted into what can only be described as a very poor attempt at sincerity. "I'd never sell you anything you don't need, of course. And even then, before you paid a dime I'd provide you with a—"

"Free estimate. Yeah, I got that much." In the distance I could hear a siren making its way around the far side of the school. "So what exactly do you do?"

"I'm a contractor. I build things for people, depending on their needs…just not physical things."

"If not physical, then what?"

"Metaphysical, of course."

"Hmm…"

"Gods, to be precise."

"You build gods?"

"Well, not *actual* gods, of course—that would be terribly difficult, and possibly illegal. I build the *belief* in a god. I construct faith." Jesus Jackson put his hand on my shoulder, turning me toward the far side of the field, where a grounds-keeper was laying a piece of sod over some fresh dirt. "Take this guy, Nino Taglione. I'm scouting him as possible client. Nino is fifty-seven years old, and has been working here at St. Soren's Academy since he was twenty-five. He's been married for thirty-five years, and just found out that his wife has been having an affair with Joe Shannon, the custodian for the athletic building, for the past twenty-eight. Obviously, this news has shaken his faith in his wife, but more importantly, it has destroyed his faith in God. After all, how could the same god he's been praying to for fifty-seven years have let him be a such a chump for so long? Right?"

"Um…right."

"Well, that's where I come in."

"You're going to restore his faith in God?"

He shook his head. "Not exactly, that's what priests do…
or rabbis, ministers, or what-have-you…. Restoration is difficult, messy work. I'm going to give him faith in a new one."

"A new…god?"

"Or something like a god anyway. He has lots of options."

I was intrigued. "What kind of…options?"

"Oh, they're endless. It could be a Pantheon of demigods, or
a Divine Force, or a belief in karma and the cycle of reincarna-
tion. He can have a warrior spirit guide, an ancestral apparition,
a guardian angel…he can have a giant bunny named Harvey
with twelve arms and a third eye, if he wants one…so long as
he'll have a little faith in it."

I thought this over for a moment. "But will he ever see the
god you give him faith in?"

"Ha!" Jesus laughed. "No, no. Alas, that's the thing about
gods, they tend to stay out of sight."

"Well if he can't see it, how will he know he's got it?"

Jesus pointed a finger at my nose and flashed his widest
salesman's smile. "Well, you see, I guarantee—"

"One hundred percent faith. Got it."

"Or your money back, no questions asked."

Right then, the siren I heard before came screaming
past the stadium. An image of Ryan in the back of that
ambulance—ghost-white, bruised, bloody, covered in a sheet—
snapped into my head. A wave of dizziness overcame me, and
I struggled to keep my balance. I said, "You know, well…that
all sounds…really great."

Jesus touched his hand to my arm, steadying me. He spoke
softly, "So can I interest you in a free estimate?"

And then—right at that moment, right there, right when
Jesus Jackson touched my arm—it all just became too much:
Jesus and Nino and free estimates for invisible gods and a

dead brother and a magic football and the first real day of high school just three days away.... "No, no, I don't think I need any god right now...I'm sort of an atheist, anyway. But... um...thanks...." And before I even knew what I was doing, I turned and stumbled toward the sirens and the screams and the crowd and the cold, hard, welcoming seat of my dad's car.

Two

Okay, so we've got to rewind here for a minute. I can't really begin with Ryan already dead and Jesus Jackson already trying to sell me his shady services...it just doesn't feel right. So we'll go back a day—twenty-five hours, to be precise—to the morning of the last day in August: the day of the event, the day it actually happened, the day this whole sad, sorry, and absurd story began.

At St. Soren's Academy, the school year officially begins at 8:05 a.m. on the morning after Labor Day. However, the preceding Friday is always bustling on campus, with morning practices for the varsity teams, meetings for the teachers, and, of course, Freshman Orientation—which is precisely where I was at 8 o'clock sharp.

St. Soren's sits at the top of a gradual hill on a small peninsula jutting out into the Atlantic Ocean, with the Sakonnet Creek Ravine forming the border where the school property ends and the rest of the town of Sakonnet begins. The school itself is a great big cinderblock nightmare with a giant concrete cross atop a four-story clock tower, an east wing and a west wing all covered in ivy, and nearly fifty acres of athletic fields stretching from the buildings to the ocean. At first glance, it all has a kind of intimidating grandness, especially when you're looking at it from the last seat on a yellow school bus at fourteen years old, with your hood covering your face, Nirvana blaring in your headphones, and a far-too-tenuous faith in the meaninglessness of everything.

As you may have already guessed, I was hardly excited by the prospect of attending a Catholic high school…not that my opinion was ever really consulted in the matter. Ryan had wound up there (due to a series of a events we'll get to later), he had "thrived" (in my mother's words), so I was going too. End of story.

At any rate, there I was, slumped against the window at the back of the bus, when the driver jerked us to a stop at the front of the school. I turned up the volume, pointed my nose at the ground, and followed the flow of freshmen from the parking lot to the gymnasium, where we were to begin our orientation.

The gym was pretty much like every other gym in the world, with its gleaming wood floor and fold-away bleachers and championship flags displaying the pride and the glory of a hundred old students who just might believe that their records still mean something to someone. The walls were gray-painted cinderblocks reflecting the rows of fluorescent lights shining down from a ceiling that seemed miles above us. There was an old-fashioned, ornate stage cut into the south wall, and above it, a twenty-foot crucifix glared down over the gym in full color and regalia: the nails, the crown of thorns, and a bleeding, emaciated, sleepy-looking Jesus, half-dead in three dimensions.

I had to stop when I saw that crucifix. It had been more than three years since the last time I went to church with my mother, and I'd forgotten just how grotesque a sight it was. It made me smile, a bit, and flush from the almost pornographic brutality of it.

As I stood there, with the rest of the freshman class parting to walk around me, it occurred to me that everyone across the globe, in every church in every city and every town, stared at this exact same image, or one very much like it—and maybe even felt the same brutal rush that I was feeling at this moment. It made me wonder if this rush, this flash of violence and heat, was what some people called the presence of God, or the Holy Spirit, or whatever....

Just as I was having this thought, someone rammed me, at a full hustle, square in the backpack, knocking me flat on my face.

"Jesus Fucking Christ!" I yelled.

Then there was nothing but silence. Great silence. Gargantuan silence. I looked around the gymnasium at the horrified stares of two hundred freshmen, fifty-five faculty, six janitors, two priests, and a nun...not to mention the bleeding, emaciated, sleepy-looking Jesus.

Clearly, I realized, this was no way to start the year.

The only person out of the hundreds who was not glaring at me like I was the son of Satan was the chubby, bespectacled, jittering little Asian kid who knocked me over in the first place. His eyes pleaded with me for help, as if everyone was really horrified at *him* for knocking me over, and I was the only one who could save him.

Unfortunately, such salvation was beyond my power at the moment, but I did manage to wrangle myself to standing, and offer a hand to help him up.

"Thanks," he mumbled.

"Don't mention it," I mumbled back.

And with that, the two of us scuffled off to the top row of

the old wooden bleachers, doing our best to find a place well hidden behind some of the taller kids in the class.

I should probably mention here that while my brother was a veritable athletic god at St. Soren's, none of those sports-related genes made their way into my DNA. On the contrary, I take almost solely after my mother's side of the family, who, though perfectly "fit" by any standards, have the unfortunate tendency to have zero coordination and never grow—male or female—a solid hair's width over five feet five inches.

Needless to say, at fourteen years old, I still had a few inches to grow to reach even that modest height.

The second thing I noticed about the kid who'd knocked me down, other than that he was the only representative of any minority group whatsoever in the class, was that he was also, perhaps, the only person in the room who was shorter than me.

So obviously, I liked him right away.

As soon as the opening prayers began, I whispered, "Hey, sorry about that. You didn't get hurt, did you?"

He had these thin little, oval-shaped, wire-rimmed glasses, and he glared at me through them as if I'd just insulted his mother. He put his finger to his mouth, let out a sharp "Shhh," and then closed his eyes, bowing his head in silent prayer.

"Oh," I stammered. "Right. Sorry. We're…uh…praying."

He glared at me, clearly attempting something like anger, but he only achieved a sort of comical frown. So I laughed (I couldn't stop myself), but I guess I was a bit loud, because the whole row of kids in front of me gave me the same angry stare…which just made me laugh even harder, until a teacher pointed a menacing finger right at me, and I bit my lip to stop.

After the assembly, they released us to our homerooms, and as the mob of freshmen walked through the halls, I got to take my first real look at my classmates. The only thing different about this group than the one at my old school were the uniforms—plaid skirts for the girls, khaki slacks for the boys, and SSA-emblazoned Oxford button-downs for everyone—but even these couldn't hide their utter sameness to everyone else I'd ever met from every school everywhere.

They all sickened me a little, so I turned up my music, pretended to be looking at something important on my phone and made a beeline for room 209, trying not to think about how I was now sure to spend the next four years of my education the same way I'd spent every other one of the past nine: alone.

Room 209 was the homeroom for students whose last names fell between Roberts and Turkleton. It was a science room, and there were posters of Einstein and Newton beside the chalkboard, shelves filled with Bunsen burners and beakers, and a row of shiny new silver computers on a long, black table by the window. Once inside, we were all arranged alphabetically into rows, with myself sitting firmly between Wendy Spooner and, quite fatefully, my new little Asian friend.

He seemed downright frightened to see me (or else just frightened in general), so I leaned over, extended my hand, and said, "Sorry, man. For…you know…back there. I'm Jonathan Stiles."

He eyed my hand cautiously. "Henry," he said, finally taking it. "Henry Sun. And I'm not religious."

"Um…okay," I said, unsure how to interpret this. "Well, you looked like you were praying pretty hard back there in the gym."

"I was respecting the opinions and authority of my high school," he whispered.

"Alright, alright. Whatever you want to call it."

"All religion is unbound by empirical data and therefore inherently unscientific and therefore absurd." He sounded like he'd been practicing this for months.

I couldn't help being amused by his earnestness. "If you say so, man. I just think it's stupid."

He glared at me again, as if trying to work out whether I was mocking him or not. "Well, yes. But it's only 'stupid' because it can't be proven through observation and the scientific method."

"I guess," I replied. "Did you need observation and the scientific method to prove to you that the Tooth Fairy wasn't real either?"

"Well, no."

"What about the Easter Bunny, or Zeus, or SpongeBob SquarePants, for that matter?"

Henry blushed a bit, stifling his laughter. "Of course not."

"Right. Because that would be stupid."

He took a beat. "Essentially, then, we agree…right?"

"Right. So we can be friends."

Henry let an awkward, unpracticed smile make its way across his face, as if it hadn't occurred to him that I'd ever want to be his friend, or that anyone would ever want to be his friend. "Good," he said. "Okay. Yeah, good."

After homeroom they gave us a tour of the school, which was followed by another assembly (this one thankfully less eventful than the last) before they freed us for the day just after lunch. Nearly nauseated by all of the praying (made tolerable only by sharing snickers with Henry), I decided to take a little tour of the woods behind the school, having been told once by my brother that this was where the upperclassmen went to smoke, drink, make out, and engage in all of the other activities that just might make St. Soren's bearable.

Henry followed me for about fifty paces beyond the milling crowd of freshmen before asking where I was going.

"Exploring," I told him.

"Umm…why?"

I turned around to stare at him, wondering how sustainable our friendship would turn out to be. "Why not?"

"But what about the bus…," he began, though I'd already turned to walk away. If we were going to be friends (and I hoped we would), he'd have to step up to a little mischief, and fast.

In all honesty, I expected to make my little exploration alone. But to my great surprise, a little further along, I heard the shuffling of Henry's gargantuan backpack come speeding up behind me. "So what's back here?" he asked.

"I don't know. I think it's where everybody does drugs."

Henry stopped so fast he almost tripped over his feet. I'm positive that if I told him we were going to attend a virgin sacrifice by a Satanic coven, it wouldn't have elicited such a horrified response. "You're…going…to…."

"I'm joking," I lied. "Relax. This is just where the upper-classmen hang out."

His attitude didn't change; not much, at least. Whatever small amount of his trust I'd earned was, at this point, all but lost.

"Whatever," I said. "Go back and wait for the bus, if you want."

Henry clenched his jaw, clearly upset by my challenge. But he was unable to stand up to it. "So, there're no drugs back there?"

"Come on now, man, there are drugs everywhere in this corrupt world of ours. Are you coming or not?"

After a moment more of consideration, he dropped his guard and followed me. We both smiled as he matched my pace across the lawn, neither of us aware in the slightest of what we were getting ourselves into.

So let me preface this next scene by saying that, at this point, my general view of humanity was that it was all a useless, phony, hypocritical cancer upon the Earth, providing nothing of any good to anyone, while it went about causing endless pain and suffering to every living species on the planet, itself included. Out of the six billion of us walking around on this wretched stretch of sand, there was only one exception in my mind: Ryan.

It didn't matter that I hadn't actually seen very much of him in the past few years (since he'd started St. Soren's, he just seemed to get caught up in the whole high school thing). I mean sure, he was my older brother, and I loved him. But more importantly: I trusted him. I *knew* him. So when Henry and I stepped into the hostile situation we were about to find in those woods, it was Ryan that I first thought of. It was Ryan that I hoped would save me.

This was how it happened:

About twenty feet inside the tree line we rounded a small stone wall to find a group of four football players, padded and uniformed and covered up and down with grass stains and dirt, standing in a little clearing and looking nervously all around. At their feet, just a few yards from me and Henry, was a textbook—a math textbook; trigonometry—on top of which was piled a small (though significant) dusting of white powder.

We stopped in our tracks. To be honest, my first instinct was just to smile and keep walking, as if nothing were odd about the whole scene. But Henry, being the spaz that he was, made the intelligent and judicious decision to scream like a little girl, yell, "Shit! Drugs!" and run madly back toward the school.

Then everything started to happen very fast. One of the football players—this hulking blond giant with squinty little eyes—yelled, "Get him!" which caused a different hulking giant to literally pick Henry up and throw him in the dirt, while yet another one started frantically dumping the coke (or whatever) into a tiny plastic bag.

I tried to make a run for it, but someone screamed, "Alistair, look!" to the squinty-eyed blond one, who promptly jumped at my legs, taking me out below the knees.

And then, a second later: there he was—Alistair—his face mere inches from mine. His hands were on my throat and he was growling: "This all never happened, you understand? You were never here, you never saw this, you've never seen me before—get it? get it? get it?"

I was struggling to breathe. I jerked my head to the left and saw Henry getting similar treatment, but from an even bigger asshole.

"Yeah," I tried to whisper. "I get it. Sure."

Alistair was enraged, furious, and scared. His eyes were bloodshot and dilated and jerking all around. His whole body shook as if possessed. He screamed, "What?!? What?!?! Do you get it? Say it louder, if you get it! Say it louder!"

Well, I could barely breathe at that moment, so being loud was not an option.

And it was right at this point that I first thought about Ryan. He was a football player, after all; he'd know these kids; he could help me. Silently, I wished for him to appear. I pictured him strutting through the brush, in full football gear, as big as the biggest one of these guys (Ryan was over six feet tall—nearly a foot taller than me). He'd kick the first one right off of Henry, smack the second to the dirt, throw the third against a tree, and then take Alistair by the neck....

A few seconds later, just as I felt myself coming dangerously close to losing consciousness, my wish came true…sort of.

Ryan did come strutting through the brush, in his full football gear…but not the way I hoped. He was stumbling more than strutting, dazed and flushed as if he'd just been crying or running or both. And he was scratching furiously at his right nostril.

He squinted at me, confused, mumbling, "Now what the fuck is this, Al?"

Alistair leaned back, revealing me to my brother. He said, "A couple of little shit freshmen. The Chinese one was about to run for a teacher."

It seemed to take a moment for Ryan to figure out who I was, and that Alistair was getting ready to beat me senseless. But as soon as he did, Ryan pounced. He jumped on Al, ripping him off of me and throwing him to the ground. He started swinging his fists into Alistair's face and stomach and ribs and throat. Al flailed his arms, trying desperately to block and push Ryan away. And then the biggest one of the shitheads—who had been holding down Henry—jumped right into the middle of it, yanking at Ryan's hair and his jersey and his neck. Ryan pushed Alistair's face into the dirt and stared straight into my eyes. He said, "Jesus, Jonathan. Take your little friend and get the fuck out of here."

These were the last words my brother ever said to me.

 Three

It's strange. For the rest of that day, I went over and over what happened back in those woods, but I never once thought about the worst and most shocking part of it all: the moment when Ryan first appeared in the brush, scratching his nose, stumbling and red-eyed like the rest of them. Somehow, that image temporarily vanished from my memory. There was just me, getting pummeled, and then Ryan coming to save me. That was all I remembered. Or at least, that was all I allowed myself to remember. Ryan had no guilt, none at all. Not in my mind.

In fact, it didn't occur to me that Ryan, my steadfastly health-conscious and anti-drug brother, was snorting cocaine *at school* directly after football practice until the next day…until well after I learned of his death at the bottom of the ravine. Until, to be exact, about two hours after I left Jesus Jackson on the fifty-yard line of the football field.

This is what happened:

After saying good-bye to Jesus Jackson, I stumbled in a daze from the football field back to the crowd of people by the ravine. It was about a five-minute walk, and all the while I felt nauseous and weak-kneed and dizzy, as if each side of my brain were trying to get me to do something different, and my body just wanted to give up and fall over.

My parents were standing next to a police car, parked just at the entrance to the path that ran into the woods. They were talking to a uniformed cop. My father had his arm around my mother—a sight I hadn't seen since their divorce three years prior. Dad looked haggard (which was to be expected), but my mother, more disturbingly, was completely composed. Her hair was blown-out, her makeup perfect, her tailored "weekend driving suit" (just a pair of khaki pants and a khaki shirt with big collar) clung to her, as always, without a seam so much as a centimeter out of place.

At any rate, when I finally reached my parents, the cop was giving them a rundown of what needed to happen over the next few days: an autopsy, an investigation ("just a formality," he assured them), and he highly recommended counseling, at least for me.

My mother dismissed him with a wave. Then she whispered (as if I weren't standing right next to her), "We'll take him to Saint Christopher's. He hasn't been to church in ages, anyway, and they have a very nice young priest there."

My father removed his arm from her shoulder. "Priest? His brother just died and you want to send the kid to a priest?"

I hate it when my dad calls me "the kid" (which he does *constantly*), but at least he was arguing my side of things, so I left it alone.

My mother, acting as shocked as she always did by my father's blatant disregard for everything holy, shot him the evilest of her evil stares. "Of course, church. Maybe at least this will finally shake some sense into the boy."

I hate my mother calling me "the boy" even more than my father calling me "the kid."

"Sharon, I don't want to hear another word about it," snapped my father.

My mom was about to slap him, or so it seemed, but the officer intervened. "Let's just take it easy, folks," he said. "This is a hard time for everyone. Just focus on making it through the day, okay?"

My parents agreed begrudgingly. The officer continued, "We'll be finishing up here in the next hour or so and when we're done, one of the detectives will be able to give you some more information down at the station."

The officer, seemingly satisfied that no one was about to erupt into a fistfight, gave a brief nod and walked away.

An hour and a half later my father and I were in the waiting room of the detectives' wing at the police station, my mother having gone home to cook, or clean, or pray (or more likely, all three).

I found myself surprised by the atmosphere of the station: It felt more like a doctor's office than the kinds of dirty, bustling police stations you see on television. It was just a boring old office building with white fluorescent lights and dull gray cubicles and men in ties and women in suits and all of them walking around with coffee and paperwork and very pleasant expressions on their faces. I mentioned how strange I thought it was to my father. He was jittering almost spastically in his seat—shifting his weight around and shaking his legs and tapping his phone over and over on the armrest—but he just shrugged, saying, "What do you expect? It's the suburbs."

After a few more minutes of waiting, a secretary called him into some room somewhere in the back. I watched them walk through the maze of cubicles, wishing I could go with him, but only because I didn't really want to be alone in that waiting room.

I sat there for almost an hour, strangely unable to think about Ryan, or my family, or much of anything. The only thing I could focus on was Jesus Jackson, and how strange it was that he was out there all alone, playing imaginary football in a white linen suit. For a moment I tried really hard to imagine what kind of a god I would choose, if I were to take him up on his offer. But I couldn't come up with anything. It just seemed so pointless. I mean, why have someone make you a god if you know it's going to be fake, right? But then again, if you have one hundred percent faith (as was his guarantee) would it really matter that it's fake? At least someone would know why the fuck I was sitting in this goddamned waiting room.

I thought about all this, just sort of zoning out in my head for what felt like hours. When I finally looked up, I saw my father and this other man staring down at me, all furrowed brows and concerned frowns, as if they'd been standing there for a while.

"Oh. Hey," I mumbled.

"This is Detective Conrad," said my father. "He's, uh… working on the case. On, you know, Ryan's…."

I acknowledged the man. "Hey."

The detective sat down in the chair next to me, which made me a little uncomfortable. He seemed like a nice enough guy, but I'd never really done too well with figures of authority. He said, "How are you doing, Jonathan?"

The question took me by surprise. No one had really even noticed me since that morning—except Jesus—and now that someone had, it seemed so silly. Maybe I was just numb, or in shock, or confused, because the only thing I could think to say was, "What do you mean? I'm alive. I'm fine."

He paused, took a breath, and continued. "Now Jonathan, I've explained everything we know so far to your father, and he can fill you in on the details, but before you go I just want to ask you a few questions, okay?"

"Sure."

The detective exchanged a glance with my father, then continued. "Have you noticed anything strange about Ryan lately?"

"No," I replied, not really understanding what he meant by "strange."

"Did he seem happy, normal, upbeat over the past few weeks?"

"I guess. Ryan's always a pretty upbeat guy."

"When was the last time you saw Ryan?"

And then it happened. The whole thing just came flooding back to me. Alistair, the woods, the drugs—everything. It's amazing, and almost ridiculous, that I hadn't thought about it until that moment, but I swear that I hadn't. I was about to blurt it all out, too—tell them everything. But just as I took a breath to speak, something stopped me. And maybe it was just some kind of guilt, or loyalty, or a habitual reaction not to rat out my brother (especially to a cop), but what really stopped me was the one single, absurd, yet irrepressible thought: *Ryan will kill you if you tell them.*

Of course, I knew, logically, that Ryan would never have the opportunity to "kill" me again…but I couldn't shake the thought. *Ryan will kill you, Jon. And he will never forgive you.*

"I don't know. Yesterday morning, I guess."

"And did he say anything unusual to you?"

"No. I don't think he said anything to me at all."

"Now, according to his teammates, Ryan went for a run after practice, and headed off toward the trail behind the school, alone. Is this something Ryan did often, as far as you know? Go running by himself after a full practice?"

"I…um…guess so. He liked to run."

The detective put a hand on my shoulder. "And you're sure he hasn't been acting strange lately? Even a little?"

"No," I said, sort of truthfully (other than the drugs, he hadn't been). "Not that I've noticed."

Conrad seemed satisfied with my answers. "Okay, then, Jonathan. That's really all I need to know."

"So…what happened?" I asked.

He looked at my father, then back at me. "Well, it seems that the trail Ryan had taken was still wet from the morning's rain, and he lost his footing somewhere along a three- or four-foot stretch that follows right by the edge of the ravine."

The tears began to well in my father's eyes. He squeezed my shoulder, but I couldn't really feel it.

The detective continued: "Really, if you want my opinion, this was an accident waiting to happen. Now I'm not saying you should go sue the school or anything, but it's safe to say they owe you more than just an apology. There should be some kind of barrier along that trail. I mean what happens when one of the other athletes decides to take a jog…?"

My father didn't seem to be paying attention. The detective squinted over his eyeglasses, waiting for a response, and I nodded comprehension for both of us.

"The good news is, the school already told us they'll be putting up a fence. Now, I'm no lawyer, but that seems to me to be at least a partial admission that something was wrong in the situation."

My father finally composed himself enough to speak. He said, "So that's it? You don't need anything else from us?"

Conrad rose to his feet. "Yeah, that's it," he said. "The only thing left is for the medical examiner to do an autopsy. In a week or two we'll get a report back, just to make sure there was nothing unusual."

"Unusual?" said my dad, turning his eyes sternly on the detective.

"It's just a formality, sir. We have no ulterior suspicions at all. He was probably just low on blood sugar, or lightheaded, or..." The detective paused. "Or maybe God just thought it was his time to go."

This seemed to annoy my father, the claim that God was somehow responsible for all of this. And honestly, it annoyed me, too. Why did people always feel the need to corrupt life's purest moments—whether joyous or tragic—with their own obnoxious beliefs?

Ryan was dead. That was the only truth. Ryan was dead and Ryan was dead and Ryan was dead and Ryan was dead. Ryan was dead and there was nothing I could do about it... but not because God, Harry Potter, the Tooth Fairy, or any other damned fictional character killed him.

Here's the crazy thing, though: I never once, while I was in that police station, stopped to question Detective Conrad's judgment. Maybe it was because I was so overwhelmed by my own existential dilemmas, maybe I was in shock, or maybe I was just too damned sad. But it never once occurred to me just how ridiculous his theories were. Of course something more sinister was afoot than *low blood sugar*. I left Ryan in the midst of a drug-enraged fistfight! Any of a hundred dark and terrible sequences of events could have led to his flying over the edge of that cliff—any of a thousand, even—but certainly it was no accident; I should have at least put that much together. If there was one thing I should have ruled out it was fucking glucose.

Four

I was only nine years old when Ryan told me there was no such thing as God. At the time, it didn't seem like such a strange thing to do; I was even grateful, for a little while. After all, he was just being honest, just looking out for me, just trying to show me the truth through everyone else's lies. But now, looking backing on it, I'm not quite so sure. I think maybe he should have known better; maybe he should have kept it to himself; maybe he should have known that one day he might not be there to help me cope with the consequences of such a loss.

I hadn't thought about that day for years, and I probably never would have if it hadn't been for Jesus Jackson, and his curious offer to "build" me some faith. So when my dad dropped me off after our trip to the police station, I found myself sitting on the floor in Ryan's room, thinking back on all of those times we spent talking about gods, about the universe, and about what really happens when you die. It was somehow so comforting and yet so painful at the same time. I loved recalling our endless deep, philosophical conversations, but there's a darkness about those memories, too. I don't know—maybe it's because our little club wound up ending so abruptly. Or then again, maybe it's because, in the end, we never found any answers.

At any rate, this is how it happened:

It was a lazy summer weekend, a Sunday, and I was playing in the backyard, pretending to be a ninja and getting grass-stains on my church clothes. Ryan called me over to the side of the house, next to the garage where no one could see us from inside. He was twelve at the time, and it was a very clear aspect of our relationship that I did what I was told or suffered the consequences. Besides, I sort of worshipped him.

"Sit down," he said. He looked serious, and a little sad. "We have to talk."

I sat Indian-style in the dirt, staring up at him with great attention. I remember assuming that he was about to send me on one of his usual missions—hide a broken vase, steal five dollars from our father's wallet, return a basketball to the neighbor's garage—but it was nothing so innocent.

Instead, Ryan took a knee, looked me straight in the eye, and said, "Jonathan, I hate to be the one to tell you this, but the whole God thing? It's a big lie."

My first thought was that Ryan must be taking drugs. You see, our mother was a devout Catholic, had raised us as devout Catholics (I had just received my first communion, and was about to begin serving as an altar boy—a fact that nauseates me to this day) and she was always drilling into us her lunatic notion that any lapse in churchly duties would lead instantly and inevitably to drug addiction and death (usually from either a car crash, an STD, or both). Her typical response, for example, to one of us complaining that we didn't feel like going to church every day of Easter week was a long string of reprimands, followed by something like, "…and the next thing you know you'll be addicted to the drugs, crashing some god-awful sports car and have a disease you'll get from one of those tramps up by the gazebo!"

So I asked Ryan point-blank. "Ryan, are you addicted to the drugs?"

"What?" he said, caught off guard. "No. Listen, Jonathan, you can't always believe everything Mom tells you. That's kind of the point. She's been telling you that there's a god, but it just isn't true."

I was still confused. "But Rye, if there's no god, then who do Jesus and the Holy Spirit sit next to all the time in heaven?"

He shook his head and swirled the dirt with his finger, seeming to find my naiveté profoundly sad. "No, Jon-Jon. There's no Jesus, either, and no Holy Spirit. There are no saints and no angels and no heaven or hell or devil or any of that stuff."

Now you've got to understand, Ryan had a history of getting me to believe some pretty tall tales—that our father was a Russian spy, that the scruffy-bearded guy down the block was really Wolverine in disguise, that if I ate too many Blow Pops my brain would turn blue—but I could tell he was being serious about this. There was no mischief in his eyes; no sense of fun or amusement at all.

But I just couldn't quite make sense of it all; not yet. "So then who is the guy on the cross at the church? And who is the priest always talking about the whole time?"

"It's all just made up, Jon. It's not real. It's just a story. It's fiction."

It wasn't until he spoke that last word—fiction—that I began to grasp what he was really telling me. You see, I had some major issues with the whole fiction-versus-reality line when I was little. Until I was almost seven, I just assumed that everything I ever saw or heard was true: every story, every movie, every cartoon—everything.

It's not that odd, really, when you think about it; no one ever told me differently. I just assumed, naturally, that at one point in real space and time Sam I Am had been really pushy with his favorite breakfast, that Sesame Street was an actual place with a humorous assortment of improbably fluffy residents, and that somewhere under the ocean, probably near Florida, there really was an absorbent, yellow, porous little sponge named Bob, living in a pineapple and doing his darnedest to be employee-of-the-month at the Krusty Krab.

It all began to fall apart, however, with Santa Claus. Ryan (of course) had told me, in very much the same way he had just told me about God, that Santa Claus wasn't real, and that neither were the Easter Bunny or the Tooth Fairy. At first, my parents tried to deny it all, but once I started ranting about how I couldn't deal with Santa being fake because that would mean that Batman and SpongeBob and Harry Potter probably weren't real either, they knew that there was a problem.

I won't get into all of the messy details that followed, but let's just say that there was a long talk, a lot of me crying and screaming things like, "You lied to me!" and at the end of it I was left with some very sensitive issues about the whole "fiction-versus-reality" thing.

So when Ryan told me that God, and all the other stuff that went with God, actually fit into the "fiction" category, I didn't doubt it for a moment.

We sat there for a long time in silence. Ryan was swirling endless spirals into the dirt, and I was just staring off into a sky that was now created by nobody. Finally, I turned to my big brother, and said, "Thanks for telling me."

"No problem. I thought you should know."

"How did you find out?"

He told me to wait a second and ran into the house. When he came back he was holding a King James Bible in his hand. "Just read this," he said. "It makes it pretty obvious."

I ran to my room, opened up to page one, and started to read. It only took me about half a page to see what Ryan was talking about. I mean, the whole creation of everything in the universe in a week was sketchy enough, but as soon as "God" created a woman out of Adam's rib, I decided I had read enough. That kind of nonsense wouldn't even fly on Power Rangers.

So I decided right away to confront my mother. I would tell her all about this "no God" thing, and she would either summon up some irrefutable proof of his existence, or crumble (like she had with Santa Claus) behind a long string of nonsense about how he would exist if I just really really believed in him.

I found her in the kitchen, cooking. I stood in the living room for quite a while before I worked up the courage to go in, torn and conflicted and on the verge of tears. I wanted so bad for her to tell me that there was a god and that Ryan was just being silly, but I also wanted her to tell me the truth... and I just didn't see how she could do both at the same time.

Finally, mustering all of my strength, I turned and stood in the doorway, glaring at her with my hands on my hips. I whispered: "Why did you lie to me about God?"

She looked up from her casserole. "Excuse me?"

"You lied to me. God isn't real." Then I lost the battle against my emotions, and the tears just started to fall.

She rushed over, picked me up and sat me on her lap. "What do you mean? Of course God is real."

"Then why can't I ever meet him? Why does nobody ever see him except in pictures? Why does he have so many crazy powers that no people could ever really have, just like Santa Claus and Dumbledore?"

She was clearly taken aback, and remained speechless for a few seconds. Finally, she stammered, "It's just…different. With God you…you have to have faith."

I was skeptical. "What do you mean?"

"Well faith is when you believe something is real, even though you can't see it, or touch it, or hear it…because you know it's real…or…because it is real."

That was all I needed to hear. She might as well have told me to clap if I believed in fairies. I got up off her lap, and as I moped out of the room, I turned my head slightly and mumbled under my breath, "I used to have faith…in Batman."

Ryan had taken off somewhere on his bike, so I waited for him on the front stoop of our house, my face in my palms, elbows on my knees. He didn't come home for nearly an hour, and as I sat there, sweating and crying under the hot July sun, the ramifications of this absence of a god began to dawn on me: If there was no god, then no one was watching me when my parents weren't around. No one was keeping track of me when I was good or when I was bad. I could do whatever I wanted, and there would be no consequences.

On the other hand, though, no one cared if I lived or died. No one would protect me and my family from a car crash, or a disease, or a robber. No one would fend off a hockey-mask-wearing serial killer at summer camp, or hear me when I wanted a new bike for Christmas…and Christmas, what about that, anyway? I could barely handle there not being a Santa Claus, but no Jesus either? What was left? Did it even have a point anymore? Did any holiday have a point anymore? Or worse—did anything have a point anymore? Was I just going to live my whole life with nobody watching or caring what happens to it, just to die someday, and....

Oh, crap.

After some more consideration, I decided I liked it better when there was a god. So when Ryan finally came around the corner, I told him so. "I think there has to be a god," I said. "I think I sort of need one."

Ryan turned his face to the sky. "Yeah, I've been thinking the same thing."

"But there isn't one...right?"

He sat down beside me. "Well, at least not the one that everyone's always talking about. He just doesn't make sense."

"Yeah. I guess not."

Ryan put his hand on my back. "But I have plan."

"What kind of a plan?"

He smiled mischievously. "We're going to get a new one."

"A new what?" I didn't like that smile.

"A new god!" he said, clearly trying to cheer me up. "A better one."

"Oh." I sighed, disappointed. "So it'll just be make-believe too."

"Oh no. Ours will be real."

"What are you talking about? If we make it up, it will be fiction. That's how fiction *works*."

"Sure, if we make it up," he said, squeezing my shoulder. "But if we discover it, then it will be real."

"Discover it? You mean, like, find it?"

"Exactly. The truth has to be there. We just need to find it."

"But how do we do that?"

"Leave it up to me," he said, tousling my hair. "I'll start poking around on the Internet tonight."

I sat there next to Ryan for a long time, quietly thinking about everything he had said. It did make some sense, after all—people discovered things that were real all the time: Columbus discovered America, Benjamin Franklin discovered electricity, and people were constantly discovering things in the ground like new types of dinosaurs and old buildings and ant colonies. And besides, if you were going to discover the truth about God, the Internet did seem like the logical place to start.

"Okay," I said finally. "What do I do? I want a job too."

Ryan stroked his chin a few times. "Well, for something like this, I think there's only so much you can figure out online. Why don't you go around to some of the other churches in town, maybe even some of the synagogues too? See if you can find anything useful."

I liked this idea a lot. It sounded important. "Okay," I said. "I'll probably start tomorrow. Right after breakfast."

Five

Tuesday was the first day of classes; a dark day, to say the least.

My mother woke me at six a.m. with a sun-dried tomato and smoked salmon frittata, fresh squeezed orange juice, and home fries, brought to me on an oak serving tray before I even had a chance to silence my alarm clock.

"Jon-Jon?" she said, knocking politely at the door. "Jon-Jon, are you awake?"

"No," I groaned.

She giggled. She always giggles at my humor, no matter how lame it is. "You're such a goof," she said. "You've always been such a goof, since you were two feet high."

That's another thing she always does—refers everything in my life back to when I was "two feet high." I rubbed my eyes and squinted at her. "What did you make?"

"Nothing special, nothing special at all. Just a little break-fast, if you're in the mood, and I don't want you to feel as if you have to eat it all, because you don't." She set down the tray beside my alarm clock, and sat down on the edge of the bed. Her smile stretched her face like a drum skin. She was wearing a bright yellow sweater and her hair was held back with a glaring pink headband. Everything about her screamed

HAPPY-HAPPY-HAPPY…but her eyes gave her away.
There was something manic and crazed in them. She said,
"You don't have to eat anything at all if you don't want to. You
don't have to go to school if you don't want to, you don't even
have to get out of bed if you don't want to."

I checked out the frittata. It was beautiful, of course. Everything she makes is always beautiful, and almost half of it is
edible, too. She'd been on this insane caretaking kick since I
got back from the police station. She was a terminally over-
involved mother to begin with, but the combination of my
brother's death, and the fact that she had so completely broken
down in the hours succeeding it, had heightened her moth-
erliness to near explosive proportions. She'd been absolutely
attached to me for the past twenty-four hours—helping me
off with my coat, making my bed, getting me water and Advil,
and cooking cooking cooking—and frankly, I'd had enough.

"I don't know," I groaned. "School will be rough. Everyone
will be talking about Ryan, and—"

"Well," she said, cutting me off. She jumped to her feet in a
burst of energy. "If you do stay home we can just sit on the sofa
and watch TV all day! Or better yet: movies. Just download
whatever you want and I'll pay for it. Anything at all. And I'll
make you some brownies and a nice lunch and we'll make a
fire in the fireplace and just do whatever it is you want all day."

"Um, great. But I kind of feel that Ryan would want me—"

"Or," she cut me off again, "we could go to the *mall*. Would
you like that? We could go shopping…for…video games? Isn't
there a new X-Station or something that just came out? I can
buy you that. Or a new phone! Yes, that phone of yours is just
ancient—you were just telling me that last week, weren't you?
It doesn't have enough memory or doesn't do some kind of

app or something? How about that? We'll get you the latest and greatest. Whatever you want."

Now I'd be lying if I said that I didn't consider (at least for a few seconds) how much I could benefit from my mom's current state of mind. I'm fairly certain that I would have wound up with a new phone, laptop, and half the stock of the game store (not to mention her brownies, which are always amazing). But the thought of spending the next eight hours on the receiving end of my grieving mother's mania was just more than I could bear.

I sat up in my bed. "I think I'll go to school," I said. "It's what Ryan would want."

She was clearly upset, and her frenzied excitement seemed to fade almost instantly, with the realization that she would be spending the day alone. But in her usual style, she swallowed her disappointment, pulled her smile even tighter and said, "Just like I told you: whatever you want!"

Thankfully, I was spared the torture of taking the bus on that morning. My parents had planned on making my brother drive me most days, and I think they decided that the bus would be too much of a reminder of what I'd lost. So my father came to drive me, honking twice as he pulled up in front of the house. My dad's car—a jet-black 2011 Porsche Boxster convertible—was like everything else about him: loud, fast, and slightly uncomfortable. I don't think I can recall a single moment with the man, and certainly not in his car, when I'd felt completely at ease. He's short, like me (Ryan got the tall genes from my mother) with a bald spot and a thick black beard, and he just has this way about him—a kind of frenetic nervousness, as if he's eternally late for some imperative appointment, but can't quite remember why—that infects everyone around him. My mother, of course, just says that he's crazy.

She also says that he's a heretic—or heathen, blasphemer, infidel, idolater, etc.—all of which, honestly, are fairly accurate descriptions…and also the main reasons why I usually enjoy his company.

I closed the door and settled into the hard leather without so much as a hug or a hello. He hit the gas and the car screeched out of the driveway, leaving my mother's worried face worrying in the window.

After a minute, he said, "You know she hates that you're going to school today."

I nodded, silently.

"She just thinks it's like, some sort of abomination, or catastrophe, like a big middle finger in the face of the holy fucking spirit or something, you know?" He lit a cigarette and puffed at it furiously. He rarely smokes anymore, so when he noticed my look of disapproval (I can't stand the smell), he took one last long drag, and threw it out the window. "Sorry, sorry! You kids these days…you're so healthy, so damned good! You probably spend all of your time drinking mineral water and watching yoga videos on the Internet or something. When I was your age, we—well never mind. Forget it. Forget I said anything. And don't tell your mom I was smoking. She always says I'm corrupting her perfect boys."

"Sure," I said, as an image of Ryan, stumbling through the bush, dazed and high, flashed across my mind. "No problem."

"Anyway, I told her, you know, of course, after all, that if you want to go school, you should go to school! However you wanted to mourn, you should mourn, and there isn't a damn thing she can do about it. I mean, your brother just died like forty-eight hours ago and she's going to try to tell you how

you should feel about it?" He glanced at me sideways, a hint of
concern shooting across his face. "I'm sorry, that was insensi-
tive, wasn't it? I know it was, you don't have to answer that. I'm
sorry, but this has just been…this has just been…" He choked
up, coughed miserably, and jerked the car to a sudden halt on
the side of the road. "Where do you think Ryan is right now?"
he asked, almost pleadingly.

"Dad," I said, not really getting what he was asking. "He's
dead."

"I know that. I mean, of course. I mean, where do you think
he is *now that he's dead?*"

"Oh."

"And I want to know where *you* think he is. You, you, you—
not your mother or your damn Catholic school or whatever.
Where do *you* think he is?"

I had no idea what to say to him. Ever since Ryan died, I'd
either been thinking obsessively about that very question, or
else I'd been completely and utterly numb—and the numbness would set in right when I started to imagine some kind
of an answer.

And my reaction right then, right there on the side of the
road, in my father's flashy little sports car, was exactly like that.
I felt this great wave of—I don't know; grief, I guess—that just
began to crest and overtake me, and then: nothing. Pure numb.

In my numbness, I turned to my father and said, "He's just
dead. He's nowhere. He's just dead."

"Okay," he said. "I mean, good. I mean, if that's what you
feel then that's great. Or, it's not great, of course, it's very very
sad, and miserable, but at least it's yours. I mean, at least you're
not one of them." Then he wiped his eyes on the lapel of his
blazer and tore back into traffic.

Six

All of the numbness in the world could never have prepared
me for what I found when we pulled into the parking lot at St.
Soren's. The normally imposing front steps of the school—a
fifteen by thirty-foot mass of solid concrete—had been trans-
formed into a multimedia, rainbow-colored shrine to Ryan:
purple chalk hearts encircled the letters, "RIP RJS" written in
bright baby blue; construction paper tears flowed out of papier-
mâché crosses and real flowers sat next to plastic flowers that
sat next to homemade pink tissue flowers that stood beside
poster-sized pictures of my brother on the baseball field, or the
basketball court, or the football field or the golf course. Ryan's
likeness was created a thousand times over in oil on canvas
and acrylics on plywood and crayon on poster-board, and on
and on and on, and all around all of this were hundreds upon
hundreds of three-by-five note cards, taped to the steps and
tacked to the posters and stuck in the cracks and the crevices
in the granite—and on each of these cards were little letters
and messages and poems for Ryan about missing him and
mourning him and praying for him and about not being able
to believe that he was dead.

I stepped out of my father's car and wandered, zombie-like,

right into the middle of everything. I began reading some of the notes and messages and prayers—each one more personal than the last—growing more and more confused with every second. You see, none of these people were Ryan's friends; at least, they weren't friends that I'd ever heard of. Since he was a little kid Ryan only had three friends that I ever knew—Bryce Michaels and the twins, Derek and Clay Hodge. There was also his girlfriend, Tristan, but I didn't see a note from her anywhere. Was he really this popular? Was there really this much that I didn't know about him?

Apparently there was quite lot I didn't known about Ryan. You see, within moments of my wandering up those massive concrete steps, I was surrounded by a cacophony of whispers, which quickly swelled into a chorus of murmurs and mumbles, until a frail little, red-haired, blood-shot-eyed girl, wearing neon green earrings and red leather boots (an odd combination for mourning, but there it was), walked up and put a hand on my shoulder.

She said, "You're Jonathan, right?"

I nodded, unsure of whether admitting my identity was a good idea, or the worst one.

The girl smiled a bit, as tears welled in her eyes. "Your hair," she said, tousling the top of my head. "It's just like Ryan's." And then she hugged me, sobbing into my shoulder.

I nearly panicked. I mean, what was I supposed to do? Do I hug her back? This stranger? Do I gently push her away? Do I just stand there and let her cry? What?

Before I could make a decision, though, I was promptly robbed of all options, when no less than ten or twenty more students—male, female, upper and lowerclassmen alike—joined in, surrounding me with a huge, sobbing, wailing group hug.

It occurred to me at that moment that it was perhaps a little strange that I had yet to shed a single tear since Ryan's death. For a second I considered this, in an oddly rational way. If there were ever going to be a good time to cry, this was certainly it—surrounded by Ryan's friends and acquaintances, all mourning, literally standing on a memorial to his death.

But in the end, no tears came; no sobs swelled within my chest. I just stood there, feeling awkward and out of place, still shocked by the scale of Ryan's popularity, until the majority of the kids slowly slipped away, leaving only me and the red-haired girl standing amid the shrine.

She looked at me with an overly earnest, grossly empathetic face. "I'm Carrie. We've met before. Ryan took me to a dance freshman year. I came over your house in a purple dress afterwards, with some other people. Do you remember?"

"A little," I lied, hoping to shorten the conversation.

"I also had Theology with Ryan last year." Again, she started tearing up. "At least we know he's with God now. At least we know he's home…." Her tears turned into sobs, which let forth a torrent of wails.

I took the opportunity to run—as fast as I could and with my eyes on the ground—all the way to my locker.

Inside, the whole school was awash with more posters, pictures, and collages of my brother. Many of them were splayed with the most horrifying and absurd of religious propaganda: "Save me a seat in Heaven, Ryan!" or "You are now our guardian angel!" and "Rest with God, Stiles" and perhaps the worst, "Say Hi to Jesus, Rye!"

All this, for a kid who rejected Christianity when he was twelve; the very person who told me that the Bible was a work of fiction.

The hypocrisy of it was nauseating. Ryan hated their religion (he had proved that to me in more ways than one) and yet here, St. Soren's Fucking Academy had beatified him in construction paper and glitter less than two days after he died.

When I finally got to my locker, Henry was standing right beside it, staring at the black dial of his padlock in deep confusion. I mumbled a "Hi, Henry," as I fumbled through my own combination and opened the door. My locker was empty, but I still felt like I had to stare at it, like I was searching for something important. It was almost like if I could stare in there hard enough, I could pretend to be inside, where no one would see me.

I was not able, however, to ignore Henry for very long. He was right there, at the corner of my eye, staring at me. His lips were pursed as if to speak, but nothing was coming out. After a few unbearable moments of this, I couldn't take it anymore. I said, "What is it?"

"I just…," he stammered. "I just…"

"You just what?"

"I just…I just wanted to say how sorry I am, um…about your brother."

"Oh," I murmured, staring back into my locker. "Thanks."

"Okay," he replied. Then he began to walk away.

I called after him. "Hey, Henry."

"Yeah?"

I didn't quite know how to phrase what I was about to ask him. We'd only known each other about six hours, and most of that in the silent boredom of orientation. But what I needed from him was too important to let go, so I just said it, as plainly as I could: "Could you, like, hang around me today? I don't know anyone here, and they all know me, and I just can't handle having everyone come up to introduce themselves. I figure, if I'm talking to you, maybe they'll stay back a bit more."

A look of sincere honor came over Henry right then. He said, "Yeah, okay. Okay, sure. You mean, all day?"

"Well, I don't want you to miss class, but…as much as you can."

"Okay," he repeated. "Okay, sure."

And with that, Henry and I were inseparable. It was a little strange at first; I'd never had a "best friend" before. In grade school and junior high I was always a loner; I would talk to people, sure, and play kickball with the kids on my block, but I never really hung out with any one person so consistently. My mother used to beg me to make more friends, even wondering aloud sometimes if there was something psychologically wrong with me. I don't think there was, though—I just never liked anyone's company enough to want to bother with it every day. And besides, before he started high school, Ryan and I were so close that it didn't feel like I needed any other friends.

Anyway, it actually turned out to be kind of nice, just hanging out with Henry. We had five out of seven classes together and, being that our names were Stiles and Sun, we almost always got placed next to each other. And by the end of the day I was sure I knew Henry better then I'd known almost anyone in my life (which, admittedly, is not saying much).

Here's the thing about Henry: he's a really smart kid, but he has the social skills of a rock. Seriously, it's like his parents kept him locked in his room looking up quadratic equations on the Internet from birth until two weeks before orientation. Almost every time a teacher asked the class a question, he'd know the answer, write it down in his notebook, but never raise his hand. On the rare occasion when a teacher called on him by chance, he'd stumble over his words so badly that the right answer on his page came out sounding like a wrong answer, spoken in a foreign language. The teacher would sigh and Henry would wince and someone else would get it right, while Henry silently berated himself beneath his breath.

And, maybe worst of all, he was the only person in the whole school, besides the eighty-year-old third-floor janitor, who wore the official St. Soren's cardigan (I had thankfully learned from Ryan that next to streaking through the cafeteria, there was nothing more embarrassing you could do at St. Soren's than wear that awful sweater).

At any rate, throughout the better part of that day, Henry did a pretty good job of keeping me away from the constant stares of the curious minions, all hoping for a thrilling peek at the tragic Dead Kid's Brother. For the most part, he would just get real close to me, frowning with grave seriousness, while whispering nonsense until the intruders turned away. This worked great in class, moderately well in the halls (I still had a few people coming up to say they were sorry, though only briefly), but it all fell to pieces right after homeroom, when we ran into Alistair outside the library.

Henry was talking about something or other—blabbering on in his mumbly, almost incoherent way—when he suddenly stopped short, in the middle of a sentence. His face melted into dread.

"What is it?" I asked.

His terrified stare was all I needed to see. I snapped my head around and sure enough, there was Alistair St. Claire, striding straight toward us. He came across a little less menacing than he had on Friday (the absence of hard drugs and football padding helped), but still dangerous-looking enough to scare me nearly breathless.

I thought about running. I thought about cowering inside the nearest locker, or garbage can, or even behind little Henry. After all, without Ryan to protect me, what was to stop him from picking up right where he left off?

Obviously, though, that's not how it went down at all. Alistair approached quickly and stopped with a stomp. He had these narrow blue eyes and piss yellow hair that made him look, in that moment, like some sort of an evil surfer ghost. One of the dickweeds who had been in the woods with them on Friday was a few feet behind him, hands in his pockets, staring at Henry.

I braced myself for danger, for peril, or least some kind of menacing threat, but instead—and I swear this is true—he took a deep, trembling breath, and quietly began to cry. His broad shoulders heaved and his little eyes teared and he let out a loud "Haw—uh-HAW" in a high-pitched squeal. I felt like I'd start laughing if I wasn't still so terrified.

I turned back to Henry. He shrugged, squinting suspiciously.

Alistair said, "I'm so sorry, man. So, so sorry."

Not knowing what else to do, I placed an awkward palm on his shoulder. But I didn't quite have the will, courage, or the intestinal fortitude to offer any condolences.

Then out of nowhere, Alistair pulled me into a great big, sobbing bear hug. I almost screamed, but he was squeezing me too tight to breathe. I wanted to push away, to make a break for the door, but then he whispered something in my ear—four sentences; *the* four sentences that set everything in motion.

He said, in as clear, eloquent, and unremorseful a voice as I have ever heard from anyone, "Whatever you *think* you saw, it didn't happen. It won't bring him back. It won't change a thing. Ryan's a hero in this school, and you do not want to destroy that." Then he pulled back a bit, met my eyes. "Do you?"

What else could I say? I mumbled, "No," and looked away.

And with that, he pushed himself off of me, waved to his shithead friends, and said, loud enough for everyone to hear, "At least he's home now, with Jesus."

Then Alistair took off strutting down the hall. After a few steps, though, he stopped. He turned back around. "Oh yeah," he said. "The first game is on Saturday, so Friday night we're having the pre-game party up at the radio tower. You should really come…and bring your little friend."

I stood frozen, unsure how to respond, until Alistair turned again and strode lazily away.

"Wow," said Henry, once they were all out of sight. "It looks like things might be okay with him now."

"I don't know about that," I said, still trying to make sense of it all. "I really don't know."

Seven

Shortly after my run-in with Alistair, I was walking down the hall before biology class, when this cold, bony hand clutched at my shoulder. I snapped my head around, startled by the grim-reaper feel of it, to find Ms. Lucy LaRochelle, principal of St. Soren's. Her face was clearly attempting to convey something sort of like sympathy, but it was only managing an emotion more akin to constipation.

"Jonathan," she said, taking my hand in her icy palms. "I'm so sorry. So so sorry."

I tried to avoid her gaze. "Um, thanks."

"Ricky was such a treasured member of our school community. He meant so much to us all."

"Ryan."

"Excuse me?"

"His name is Ryan."

"Oh yes," she said, not missing a beat. "Ryan. Well. At any rate, there's someone I'd like you to meet."

"Right now?"

She flashed her yellowed dentures. "Yes, now. Please follow me." And she started to walk at a brisk pace down the hall.

I followed her to the end of the main hallway. The glare off of the beige-painted cinderblock expanse was blinding as her shoes clicked and squeaked toward the rusting metal door in the distance. She led me down a flight of stairs and into a dark basement hallway with mud-colored walls, flickering fluorescent lights, and the faint smell of onions lingering in the air. Ms. LaRochelle continued on ahead of me, unfazed by our horror-show surroundings, until we finally came to a wooden door, marked, "Sheldon Finger, B.A. School Psychologist."

Oh, shit, I thought.

She opened the door, revealing a thirty-something, blonde-bearded man, sitting alone in a comically small office—five, maybe six feet square at the most—dressed head-to-toe in pastel blue, bright yellow, and khaki. "Mr. Finger," said Ms. LaRochelle. "This is Jonathan Stiles."

The khaki man leaned forward in his chair. He extended his hand, the overemphasized empathy on his face so brutally effortful that I had to look away for fear of laughing or throwing up. I shook his hand weakly, staring at the motivational posters papering his wall: pictures of beaches and sunsets and puppies, espousing such philosophical gems as, "You can do it!" and "Dedication!" and "Believe in your dreams!"

I said, "Hi."

"Hi, Jonathan," he purred. His voice was soft and slimy, and made me feel kind of gross. He turned to Ms. LaRochelle. "Thank you, Lucy." She nodded and quickly left, closing the door behind her.

Then there was this incredibly long pause. Just silence, as he sat there staring at me, as if I were the one that was supposed to get this thing started.

Finally, he said, "I'm very sorry for your loss, Jonathan."

I nodded. "Mm-hm."

Another pause. "It's tragic."

"Mm-hm."

And another pause. "So," he said at a last, "would you like to pray before we get started?"

Really, at this point, after the morning I'd had…after the day and the weekend and the life…really, there was only one option left for me: I panicked. It was just too much. Having to come talk to this lunatic was bad enough, but pray with him? Fuck that.

"I think I'm going to be sick," I blurted out, only half pretending.

"Oh my." He seemed shocked, and a little scared. "Well, you should…you should…."

"I have to go to the nurse."

"Yes. Yes, of course."

I didn't wait for him to say anything more or write me a pass. I just bolted through the door, ran back through that dank, disgusting hallway, up the stairs, past the infirmary, and busted out the great big oak doors at the front of the school.

 Eight

Outside, everything was the opposite of that awful basement; it was all bright sun and cut grass and quiet breeze, and it felt good. I decided to wander a bit to calm myself down. I made my way around the perimeter of the school, over to the football field. I walked past the bleachers and up to the edge of the field, when I noticed that someone was jogging on the far side of the track. He looped around, came closer, and it wasn't until he was about a hundred yards away that I realized who it was: Jesus Jackson, running laps in a velvety white track suit, white high-top sneakers, and a white Nike headband.

He reached me a few moments later. "Hey, Jonathan!" he said, continuing to jog in place. "What's shaking?"

I was a little surprised to see him there, but too grateful for his presence to ask any questions. Strange as it may seem, after the insanity of my first morning at St. Soren's, Jesus Jackson seemed like the most normal person I had encountered all day. "Not much, I guess."

He glanced at his watch—a flashy gold digital, covered in what appeared to be diamonds (but I suspected were really rhinestones). "Shouldn't you still be in school?"

"Technically, I'm at the nurse right now."

"Gotcha." His feet slowed to a stop, and he bent down into a stretch. "Is everything all right?"

"Not really."

"Kids giving you a hard time?"

"No, it's…you know that kid, the one whose face is plastering the front of the school, whose name is soaped onto every car in the parking lot?"

"Your brother, right?"

I paused. "How'd you know?"

"Well, you were the only kid standing around with the police on Saturday."

"Oh yeah. Right."

He placed both palms flat onto the grass, exhaling sharply. "School's been tough today? You feel like everyone is staring at you?"

"Everyone *is* staring at me. But that's not what's bothering me."

"What is?"

My first instinct was to drop it, like I did with everyone else. Just assume that everything was innocent and easy, and go on with my life. But I couldn't. Not with Jesus Jackson. Not after that morning.

"There's something not right about Ryan's death."

He snapped upright, pulling one foot up to the back of his leg and leaning forward. "There's a lot not right about it. He was so young…"

"Well, yeah. But I mean, there's something *strange*. Something fishy."

"Fishy?"

"Yeah, fishy."

Jesus arched his body, reaching his arms towards the sky.

"As in, what people are saying happened isn't really what happened? That kind of fishy?"

"Yeah.

"Interesting. What makes you think it's so fishy?"

"Well, there's this kid Alistair. And he got into a fight with Ryan, and there were drugs involved…it's a long story."

Jesus stopped stretching. He put his hands on his hips. "I think you better tell me this 'long story,' Jonathan."

So I did. I told Jesus all about the coke and my brother, and the woods, and Henry and Alistair's friends, and everything. Throughout the whole story, Jesus Jackson listened with what seemed to be rapt attention, having me stop often to clarify particulars, expand on assumptions, delve more deeply into details.

After I finished, he said, "Well that is certainly suspicious. Do you have a theory about what happened after you left?"

"Not really, no."

"But you're saying you think there was some, well…foul play involved?"

Honestly, up until that moment I hadn't actually let myself even consider such a thought—that Alistair really may have killed Ryan—and hearing Jesus say it, it kind of sounded a bit absurd. I mean, they were just kids, it was just an ordinary day after football practice. "No. I mean, I don't know. I don't think that's what I'm saying."

"So then what are you saying?"

"Just that it's strange," I said, now not sure why I had brought it up at all. "I don't know. It's probably nothing."

Jesus stared at me silently for few seconds. "Well, if you say so."

Just then, a bright red Jeep drove past us in the parking lot, with the words, "Rest with the Angels, Ryan Stiles," painted in multicolored wax on the windows.

I sneered. "You know what I really can't stand: all of this God crap."

This seemed to intrigue Jesus. He raised an eyebrow. "God *crap?*"

"Yeah, crap. Everywhere I go, there's a poster talking about how Ryan is in heaven, how he's with God now, or that he's some kind of a guardian angel, looking down over the school. People are packed into the chapel, praying and crying and lighting fucking candles—that they charge you a dime for, no less."

Jesus seemed amused. "So why does all that bother you so much?"

"Because it's all bullshit. It's fake. They don't know where Ryan is. They just choose a fairy tale and run with it. If they say he's watching over us in heaven with God and the angels, then they might as well say he's huffing glue at Burger King with Mickey Mouse and the Easter Bunny! He's just dead. Dead dead dead, and no one knows what the fuck that means except that his body is sitting in some freezer somewhere, waiting for some death doctor to cut apart his insides and replace his blood with chemicals, while some morons he never even liked recite bad poetry over a bunch of cheap-ass, ten-cent candles."

As these words left my mouth, I began to feel something very deep and strange and powerful mixing up inside me, like a volcano of nausea, fear, sorrow, and anger. It didn't erupt, though; it didn't blow over at all. It just stayed right beneath the surface: boiling and boiling and boiling until Jesus said, "But Ryan believed in all that, didn't he?"

"No, that's the worst part. He was the one who first told me that there was no such thing as God—or at least *their* god. He tried to make up his own damned religion when he was twelve. He didn't believe a word of that Catholic garbage."

Jesus raised an eyebrow. "Really? That's not what everyone else seems to think."

"Well they're wrong. Trust me, I know. We talked about it like a thousand times."

"People change, though, Jonathan. How do you know that he still didn't believe? Could he have found some sort of faith and just decided not to tell you? When was the last time you actually talked to him about it?"

"I don't know, it was probably—" but I had to stop myself. I knew exactly when Ryan and I had last talked about religion, God, and all of that other stuff. It was about a week before the first day of his freshman year at St. Soren's. And not once since. "It's been a while," I mumbled.

Jesus took a breath like he was going to say something, but then paused, as if he changed his mind. "But what about you? Do you have your own, made-up religion too?

I took a deep breath to keep it all at bay. "I don't have any religion anymore. I told you. I'm an atheist."

Jesus grimaced suspiciously. "Hmm."

"What?"

"Oh, nothing."

"Come on, what was that look?"

He shook his head. "It's really nothing. It's just that…" A pause. "Well, I hate to be the one to tell you this, but atheism doesn't really work for you."

"What are you talking about? It works perfectly for me!"

"I'm sure you *think* it does," he said. "Or at least *say* it does. But it doesn't."

"That's ridiculous." I pointed to a small group of students praying around the flagpole. "You think I'm one of them?"

"Walk with me," Jesus said, putting a hand on my shoulder. "I want to explain something to you."

"Okay...," I said, as we started a nice easy pace around the track.

"Now it might sound strange, but atheism—despite what anyone may have told you—requires a certain amount of faith if you want it to really *work*."

"Why the hell do I need faith to be an atheist?"

"It's really very simple," he said, grabbing my arm and pulling me to match his pace. "For atheism to really work—that is, if you want it to do its job of being for you what religion is for everyone else—you have to *believe* in *nothing*. You, however, just *don't believe* in *anything*."

"Well what's the damn difference?"

"The difference is faith," he continued, walking a bit faster, swinging his arms a little higher. "Look, I bet you are one-hundred percent confident that the world wasn't created in seven days by some old, white-bearded dude in a toga."

"Sure. One hundred percent."

"And more than that, you are one hundred percent sure that *all* religious beliefs, from Aztec mythology to Zoroastrian theology, are completely make-believe, utterly fictional, and totally pretend inventions, created by humans to make themselves feel better about the fact that no one has even the slightest idea what they're doing in their own lives, much less why they're hurtling through space on a tiny speck of rock in some random corner of the universe."

"Yes. Absolutely."

"But," he said, stopping and looking me right in the eyes. "Are you really that confident with the idea that your life has no metaphysical meaning *at all?* That there's no deeper purpose to your existence, no universal principles that influence your inner life, no unknowable significance to love or kindness or morality or consciousness? And when you die, when your brother died, are you really *one hundred percent certain* that everything just ends? That it's all darkness and nothing and that you'll never have another thought or feeling or see anyone you love ever again *forever?*"

"Umm…" He sort of had a point there. "I mean, I don't know. Maybe not one hundred percent…."

"Of course not. Because to have that kind of certainty, you need to have…"

"…faith."

"Precisely." Jesus smirked. "And you, my friend, just don't have any."

"I see."

"Lucky for you, though, you met me."

"Why so lucky?"

"Faith is my business. It's what I do. Like I said, I have a one hundred percent-faith-or-your-money-back guarantee."

"Oh, right. Your sales pitch."

"It's no pitch. Just a friendly, reliable offer."

We walked for a minute in silence, and I thought about this whole idea—faith, surety, *knowing* that there's nothing out there instead of just *thinking* that there's nothing out there—and it started to sound really comforting, really nice. "So you can give me one hundred percent faith in nothing?" I asked. "You can do that?"

And with that Jesus stopped short, causing me to nearly trip over my own feet. He stepped back and stared at me mysteriously. "Of course I *could*," he began. "Nothing is a rare kind of job, but I certainly have done it before. It's just that…"

"It's just that what?"

"I'm just not sure it suits you."

"It doesn't suit me?"

"I'm not sure. You might need something a bit more substantial than that."

"Wait." This was getting confusing. "You mean I don't get to pick what I have faith in? You pick it for me?"

"Yeah. It's part of the package."

"But what if I know what I want to have faith in? And that's nothing?"

"Sorry. I pick. It's the only way I can offer the one hundred percent faith guarantee."

"Why?"

"Because people never know what kind of faith is best for them. It's like when an overweight woman brings a picture of an anorexic movie star to her hairdresser and says, 'Make me look like this.' That's how most people are with belief. They bring in Buddha or a Muhammad or Jesus Christ, when what they really need is a Rastafari, or a high-pressure career, or socialism, or 1950s detective novels."

"Whoa. Those last three things aren't religions at all."

"Not to you," he said. "But to some people..."

"Okay, fine. But what good will faith do me—whatever it is—if it's fake? If you just make it up?"

"Does it matter that it's fake if you have complete faith in it? The point of a god is not to hear your prayers, but to have someone to pray to. You don't need a deity to *actually* create the universe." He swept his arms into the air. "The universe is already here, baby! You just need a little faith in how it *might* have been created to explain why the hell you're living in the middle of it."

I stopped walking and just stared at Jesus for a few moments, trying to decide if he was being serious, or if this whole Spiritual Contractor thing was some kind of a twisted joke. He stared back, betraying nothing more on his face than a look of hopeful expectation, just like the salesman he purported himself to be—holding his breath for the close.

"So," I said finally. "How much would all this cost me?"

"Oh, it's hard to say right up front. You see, in your case I could probably make some exceptions, a few allowances, maybe even some pro bono tertiary background work, et cetera, et cetera...but then of course I'd need to see your pay stubs, W-2 forms, investment statements, and other holdings to make sure you qualify for our reduced hourly schedule, and then the holidays are coming up, so we may be running some specials."

"Jesus," I broke in. "I'm fourteen. I don't have W-2 things or investment whatevers. The only money I have is what I make from mowing the lawns on my block, which is about to end because it's September."

"How much do you charge an hour?"

"Seven dollars."

Jesus squinted. "Can you rake leaves in the fall?"

"I guess."

He produced a small copper abacus from somewhere in his jogging suit, and began crazily flicking the beads back and forth. After a moment, he smiled. "Forty-eight dollars and seventy-five cents," he said. "But remember, that's only an estimate."

I reached into my pocket, and pulled out a tiny wad of crumpled bills. "I only have twelve bucks right now."

Jesus snatched the bills from my hand. "We'll call it a retainer," he said. "And I'll get on it right away."

And with that, Jesus Jackson took off running around the track, toward the gate that leads to the woods.

"Wait," I called after him. "Do I have to do anything?"

"Definitely," he yelled over his shoulder. "Go look into that Alistair thing. It all sounds pretty fishy to me."

And then he was gone.

Nine

It's hard to sleep without a god. Or anyway, it was hard for me, at nine years old, on my first night without one. It was like sleeping in the pitch dark, without a lock on the front door—blind and vulnerable. In the morning, I woke up exhausted, but with a purpose. I ate breakfast, told my mom I was going to a friend's house, and rode my bike straight to Saint Christopher's. No, I wasn't going to repent for my doubting, or pray for faith, or anything else so righteous.

Ryan had asked me to complete a task—to help figure out which god was the real one—and I wasn't about to let him down.

It was a Monday, and weekday mass began at nine. I got there at about five after, just as the opening hymn was coming to an end. I tiptoed into the last pew, neglecting to genuflect (which I had always hated doing, and decided instantly would not be a part of our religion), took out my little notebook and pencil, and wrote:

1. A real god would not make you kneel on the ground.
2. A real god would not make you sing stupid songs.

As the priest went into his opening prayers, I poked around the church, checking out the décor. I found it both fascinating and thrilling to be in the church not as a believer, but as an outside observer, a spy seeing it not as The House of The God, but simply as one possible idea of what the house of one possible god may look like. My eyes made their way over the stained-glass windows, the ornate woodwork, the iron light fixtures (which were all very pretty, but clearly impractical), before finally coming to rest on the gigantic crucifix hanging over the alter. As usual, Jesus was skinny, shaggy-haired, bleeding, and wearing only a loincloth. All of that I was used to, of course, but the thing I couldn't stop thinking about as I stared at him was the fact that he was dying. In that moment—the one being depicted by the sculpture—he was taking his last few breaths. Now, for all I knew, the sculptor may have meant for him to be already dead, but that's not the way I saw it. There was still some life left in him, a disturbing vitality present in his slightly flexed muscles, his unclotted blood. I wrote:

3. That scary, dying guy on the cross is definitely not God.

I shuddered and took my eyes away from the crucifix. By this time the mass had moved on to some kind of prayer where the priest talks for a few seconds, then the people all say something back to him, and then the priest talks again (and over and over again), but I didn't know what to say, so I just stayed quiet.

4. A real god would not make you memorize lots of stuff.

By the end of the mass I had come up with six more ideas, making a total of ten:

5. A real god would not make you just sit and be quiet and not do anything.

6. A real god would not write really really really long books.

59

7. A real god would not make you get up and sit down seventeen-hundred times.

8. A real god would not like gross crackers.

9. A real god would not be super super boring.

10. A real god would not make you fall asleep in church and be embarrassed.

Quite proud of my accomplishment, I hopped on my bike after the mass was over and rode straight home to show Ryan. I found him in his room, lying on his bed with his laptop on his chest and his head hanging off of the edge of the mattress, so he was looking at me upside down when I came in.

"Hey," I said, handing him my notebook. "Clues. Look. I just got them all at church."

He smiled, flipped over, and inspected my list. "This is good," he said, but with the hint of a frown. "Although, everything on this list is a negative."

"What do you mean?" I hopped up next to him on the bed, staring over his shoulder at what I had written.

"Look." He pointed from entry to entry. "Not, not, not, not, definitely not, not. They're all things that you don't believe or don't think God would do. There's nothing at all on the list that you actually think is true."

"Well, I know," I said. "That's because I went to a church with a *pretend* god."

He laughed. "Good point. But have you thought of anything at all about God, or whatever, that you actually don't think is pretend?"

I looked down at my feet. "No."

Sensing that I was starting to feel bad about the whole thing, Ryan sat up and grabbed his laptop. "So you want to hear what I've come up with?"

I nodded.

"Okay." He clicked on the keyboard and squinted at the screen. "Well, I've decided—or rather, discovered—that the whole hell thing is bogus."

"Really?" I was shocked. I thought that one had to be true.

"Yeah. Totally bogus. In fact, there are billions of people who believe that after you die you're just reborn into another person. Or even an animal, or a plant."

"A plant?" This was a bit much. "Like a fern?"

Ryan shrugged. "I guess."

"Well that doesn't sound very real."

"No," he agreed. "I didn't think so either."

"So what else did you find?

"Well, the problem is that there are just so many gods out there that people believe in, and they're all totally different."

I was intrigued. I don't think I'd ever considered the fact that there were people whose idea of "god" was different than my own. "Like what else?"

"Well, there's Buddha—"

"Isn't that the gold guy with the belly at China Garden?"

"Exactly."

"Hmm…"

"And there's also Shiva and Krishna and Allah and Mohammed—who is, like, as big as Jesus in some places—and Haile Sellassie and Vishnu and Zoroaster and Ganesh—who looks like an elephant but with four arms and a potbelly—not to mention all of the ancient gods who no one talks about anymore. There are like a million of those."

"Whoa."

"And people keep on making up new gods all the time. There's even this one called Xenu that some people believe in out in California. They get real excited about him, too, but as far as I can tell, the only thing he ever did was bring a bunch of aliens to Earth and then blow them up in a volcano."

This was just too much, and I couldn't stop myself from laughing. And soon as I started laughing, Ryan started too, until we were both in hysterics. Once we finally caught our breath, though, we both got real quiet, realizing that we were apparently no better off than when we started.

"So," I said at last. "Did you find anything that actually might be true?"

"No, he said, closing his laptop with a sigh. "I guess I didn't."

"Yeah, that's what I figured."

He jumped up and patted me on the back. "But don't worry, Jon Jon. We've barely scratched the surface. We just have to keep on digging. We'll find something eventually."

I nodded and said, "Okay." But I had my doubts. And to be perfectly honest, I think that Ryan had even more doubts than I did.

Ten

The thing about Jesus (Jackson, that is) is that once he's in your head, you just can't get him out. Every conversation we ever had would play over and over like a song blaring on repeat in my brain. His questions became deep existential dilemmas; his suggestions became obsessions. So it was no surprise that for the rest of that first day at St. Soren's, all I could think about was our meeting on the football field. Was he really going to build me a god? Was that even possible? Was I an idiot for giving him my twelve bucks? Did I even want a god? Was it just because of Ryan? And what about Ryan? And what about Alistair? And what the fuck really happened in those woods?

In the end, all of my questions faded but the last one, and its darkest manifestation: Did Alistair kill my brother?

Once I allowed myself to really consider that Ryan was murdered, the thought of it consumed me. A hundred different scenarios played out in my head—all beginning with Henry and me running for our lives, and ending with Alistair pushing Ryan into the ravine. The most plausible of them went something like this:

Once Henry and I were out of sight, the other three guys jumped in on the fight, taking Alistair's side, of course. They all began to beat on Ryan, circling around him, kicking him in the chest and stomach and kneecaps and face, while Ryan lay nearly helpless and curled up on the ground. When they finally stopped for a second, Ryan swung back into action, kicking Alistair into one of the other guys, giving Ryan just enough time to spring to his feet and make a break for it. Within seconds, though, they were all on his trail. Ryan sprinted straight into the woods, barreling through bushes and shrubs, scrambling over boulders and fallen trees, and stopping himself inches before toppling over the edge of the ravine. Before he even had the chance to catch his breath, Alistair came bursting out behind him, and without a pause, laid one right into Ryan's cheekbone. Ryan stumbled, swayed, and fell over the edge to his death.

I constantly rearranged the details in my mind, but the premise stayed the same: Alistair and Ryan fought; Ryan ran; Alistair pushed Ryan into the ravine.

The problem, though, was that I had absolutely no proof: not enough proof to bring to the police, not even enough proof to convince myself that I wasn't imagining the whole damn thing. I couldn't walk up to Alistair and ask him what happened, and the only other witnesses were the two dickhead friends who helped him out in the first place.

By the time I finally made it to lunch, I'd decided to focus on just getting through the day…which was turning out to be hard enough.

The cafeteria at St. Soren's, like the auditorium, was presided over by an enormous bronze crucifix, displaying an emaciated, tortured, and badly beaten Jesus. It struck me, as I stood holding my tray of pasty-looking pizza and soggy French fries, just how violent of an image this was to display over a sea of impressionable young minds. It transfixed me, for a moment, as I allowed my eyes to move from the oozing wound on his chest, to his caved esophagus, to his hollow eyes....

And then out of nowhere an image of Ryan, similarly beaten and bloodied, flashed over the one of Jesus. I could see it so clearly in my mind—the bruises on his face and arms, his eyes rolled back, a trickle of red streaking a line from his nose to his cheek.

I had to stop myself right there—take a deep breath, swallow hard, and shiver—just keep myself composed.

Somehow, thankfully, I managed to hold it together, and went off instantly in search of Henry. Within a few steps, though, I realized just how difficult a task this would be. Every time I approached a table to look for him, I was met with a barrage of smiling, sympathetic stares, and a general shifting of behinds to make a place for me to sit. Everyone knew who I was—everyone. Every eye at every table turned inevitably toward me as I passed, each obviously thinking the same awful thing: there goes the Dead Kid's Brother. Poor Dead Kid's Brother.

I found Henry sitting all the way in the far corner of the cafeteria, reading at a table all by himself.

"Finally," I said, setting down my tray across from his. "Why'd you have to hide all the way over here?"

Henry shrugged, placing down his book and staring thoughtfully at a tater tot. "You know," he said. "You don't have to sit over here." Apparently he had seen my walk across the cafeteria.

I turned, gazing back across the landscape of bustling tables. At almost every one a few heads were turned nonchalantly in our direction. I said, "Believe me, there's nowhere else I'd rather be."

This seemed to cheer Henry up. "So how was Biology?"

Before I had a chance to respond, I glanced down to see what Henry was reading, and lost my train of thought. It was called *Cop Hater* by Ed McBain, and on the back cover was a quote: "Perhaps the single greatest detective novel of the 1950s."

I stared suspiciously into his eyes. "I'm going to ask you a question," I said, "And it may seem a bit strange, but I just want you to answer it honestly, okay?"

This seemed to make him nervous. "Okay."

"Have you ever met Jesus?"

"Uh…what?"

"I mean, not the old Jesus. Not Jesus Christ. I'm talking about Jesus the contractor. The spiritual contractor, Jesus Jackson."

Henry's expression went from one of mild anxiety to one of sincere concern, with maybe even hint of terror. "What are you talking about?"

I decided right then and there not to mention Jesus again, at least not unless Henry brought it up first. "Nothing. Just, um…so what's that book all about?"

"Oh," he said, seeming pleased by the turn of the conversation. "It's amazing. It's about this detective, Steve Carella, and he's trying to catch this guy who's killing all of these cops, and it gets really into all of the methods and techniques that cops would really use to catch the guy, like in the real world, or like in those really real TV shows, and it's—"

"Hold on a second," I said. "Do you read a lot of these things?"

"Books?"

"Well, detective novels…"

"Oh, yes. Absolutely. I've read all of the Sherlock Holmes adventures and Philip Marlow and Sam Spade and Mike Hammer and—"

"Okay, okay. I get it. So, I've got a question for you. About, you know, detective stuff."

Henry's eyes opened wide. "Really?" he said. Then very seriously: "Shoot."

"If you think that someone may have committed a crime—say, murder—but you're not really sure, and you totally have no proof, how would you go about investigating it? Like, what would you actually do?"

"Well," he replied, dramatically stroking his chin, "that depends upon the circumstances of the murder in question."

"What about if you don't really know the circumstances?"

Henry leaned in close, gave a look around to make sure no one was near us, and whispered, "How did the victim... meet his demise?"

"A fall," I said. "Off a cliff."

And with those five words, the fun part of the game was over for Henry. "Oh," he said, staring down at his tater tots.

"Look," I said. "Just humor me. It's good for me to talk about things like this. It's, you know, processing things."

Henry let his eyes meet mine, but only for a second. "Okay, I guess. If it's just talking."

"Just talking."

"Well," he began, "I guess the first thing you'd want to do is investigate the crime scene."

Right. I hadn't even been to the ravine yet. "Yeah, yeah... Crime scene."

"Poke around, look for clues."

"Okay."

"And try to construct a narrative of what happened."

Of course. I had a hundred different stories floating around in my brain about how things might have gone down; what I needed was to come up with one plausible story. And who knows? Maybe it would just prove that the whole thing had been an accident, and I could leave it alone. "Great," I said. "So let's go right after school, okay? To investigate?"

Now Henry really looked scared. "Wait, you said we were just talking!"

"Yeah, just talking…and a little looking around."

"Oh, I don't know."

I reached over, put my hand on his shoulder. "It'll really help me process this whole thing."

"I'll miss my bus, though. And my parents…"

"We'll take the late bus, for the kids that play sports. It'll be fine."

"But shouldn't we just let the police—"

"Listen Henry, I wasn't going to tell you this, but Alistair said something really suspicious to me when we saw him earlier."

"Suspicious how?"

So I told Henry what Alistair had said to me, and then I filled him in on my whole theory about how things might have gone down after we left. He looked a bit uncomfortable about it all at first, but as I went on he clearly became more and more animated, more involved and more curious, as if allowing himself to sink into one of his novels.

Finally, he cut me off in the middle of one of my theories. "Well the crime scene itself is bound to be a disaster by now. Lots of cops and EMTs and everyone will have trampled through it, basically destroying any hard evidence that may have been left. But then again, if we go to the spot where we ran into Alistair, we might find something. I don't think the police would have snooped around over there, so far from the edge of the ravine."

"Alright, then. I'll see you at 2:05, behind the school."

"Okay," he said. "2:05."

Eleven

There have been few times in my life when I have felt more foreign, more incredibly *different* than I did every day after school at St. Soren's. Like every other school, the final bell heralded a great rush of students into the hallway, a great wave of relief and expectant freedom on their faces. But at St. Soren's I never shared in that relief, that freedom…and, if anything, I seemed to dampen it in everyone who laid eyes on me. I was a wandering freak show, a great big human-shaped sign that read "Pity me," "Feel sad for me," "Pray for me."

And I didn't even have the courtesy to force a brave smile, to thank them for their prayers.

So it was for more than mere convenience that I had Henry meet me behind the school, instead of at my locker or on the steps. And by the time he came bounding out of the doors, his tiny frame dwarfed by his gargantuan backpack, he seemed to have given up any reservations about our plan. He practically skipped up to greet me.

Dropping his bag on the ground at my feet, he reached into the outside pocket and pulled out a handful of plastic sandwich bags. "Here," he said, handing a few to me. "We'll need these to collect evidence."

"Where did you get all these?"

He raised an eyebrow, slyly. "I told the lunch lady I was diabetic, and needed to break up my Twinkie into a bunch of little portions."

"Good idea." I chuckled. "You know, a little weird, but good."

"Thanks," he said, clearly quite pleased with himself.

"So, what now?"

Henry took off his little wire-frame glasses, wiping them on his shirt. His eyes scanned the horizon. "First we should go to the scene of the crime. There probably won't be much there, but it's worth a shot."

"Alright then."

So we started off down the path toward the ravine. Maybe it was because I knew Ryan's last steps had gone through the woods, and not down the path, but it didn't hit me that I'd be standing in the exact spot where my brother actually died until we were right there, at the edge, where he fell.

And then the reality of it all hit me. There was no mistaking the exact point where Ryan went over—the path only opened directly onto the ravine for about three or four feet, which was now blocked by a makeshift wire fence and covered with police tape. The moment I saw it, all the blood rushed out of my head; my eyes welled. I sank to my knees.

Henry, who'd been almost giddy with anticipatory excitement, seemed to instantly realize, in a great avalanche of understanding, the unbelievable magnitude all of this had for me. He averted his eyes, and mumbled something like, "Uh, um…well. Do you need, I mean…is there anything, uh…are you alright?"

I was not all right. Not even close. All of my imaginings from the morning—all of my theories and visualizations about the fall—were now overwhelming me. I tried to breathe, failed, and whispered, "I'll be fine. It's just, you know, kind of a lot to take in."

Henry fidgeted for a second and then began to poke and prod around the foliage on either side of the path. I sat, silently watching him, until he first let me in on what he was doing.

"So, what we're looking for here is anything out of the ordinary. The problem is that almost everything is out of the ordinary, because you had so many cops and paramedics and everyone else in here poking around for so long." He made his way a little further down the path. "Maybe, though, if we can locate the exact spot that Ryan got onto the trail, we can trace his path back to the spot where we last saw him."

It was actually quite comforting, listening to Henry add a little logic to the situation. It gave a certain weight, grounding, to my flight-prone emotions. I struggled to my feet. "What do you mean, exactly?"

"I mean, the police assumed that Ryan had jogged down the path the same way that we came in, so they would have only looked for clues along the side of the path. But we, on the other hand, know for a fact that Ryan must have come straight through the woods, at some point breaking through the bushes along the side of the path, which would leave a noticeable amount of broken twigs, ruffled leaves, maybe even a few—"

Henry sank into a squat, poking his nose almost all the way into the dirt.

"A few what?" I asked.

He lifted a large, brownish oak leaf, revealing some seemingly random indentations in the dirt underneath. "Footprints."

"Oh."

Without a second's pause, Henry pulled out his phone, snapped a picture of the footprint, and began measuring angles in the mud with a green plastic protractor. He made a few complex algebraic calculations (about what, I have no idea) and then snapped his face toward mine and said, "Size 10 or 11 cleats. Nike, I think. Sound familiar?"

I felt the hairs rise along the back of my neck. "Those are Ryan's shoes. They're a ten and a half."

Henry did not look surprised. "Well, this is where he came through."

"So what do we look for now?"

"Now we trace it back to the clearing." And with that, Henry made a circle around the bush, and began to crawl on his hands and knees just past the edge of the path. I wanted to help him out, really, but I just couldn't take my eyes off the break in the brush where Ryan came through, and the line of police tape where he went over. I pictured a hundred different scenarios—each more horrid and violent than the last—and in each one, Ryan was fighting for his life, struggling against Alistair and his fuckwad friends, as they dragged him, kicking and screaming, to the precipice.

Finally, when Henry had made it most of the way to the clearing where the fight had happened, he cut off my awful thoughts. "Oh boy. You should come see this."

"What is it?" I asked, hesitating to catch up.

"Most of the ground back here is covered with pine needles and grass." He pointed around the woods. "So you're not going to find much in the way of footprints. But over here…" He walked a few paces deeper into the woods. "Over here there's a small patch of soft dirt, and look what I found in it."

Henry's discovery was pretty damn clear, even from where I was standing. In that little patch of dirt was a distinct set of footprints, obviously cleats, and perfectly formed down to the company logo.

And it was clearly from a different person than the one we had seen by the ravine.

"Holy shit."

Henry ignored my shock as he began circling the footprint, taking pictures of it with his phone, and scribbling down his measurements and calculations. A sudden uneasiness washed over me, and I had to turn away, take a walk. When I came back, Henry said, "Well, it's an Adidas, about an eleven or a twelve."

Henry seemed to be waiting for some kind of acknowledgement or encouragement to continue, but I couldn't quite bring myself to say anything at all. This whole idea, to investigate on our own, seemed brilliant a few hours ago, but now was bringing me far closer to Ryan's death than I was even slightly prepared to handle.

But I knew I couldn't give it up. After all, we'd made progress, probably even beyond what the police had. "Okay. Good," I said, struggling to get out the words. "So now all we need to do is match the footprints to their owners and take it to the police?"

Henry was too involved in his newfound cop role to notice my persistent desperation. He said, "Well, I'm afraid it's not that simple in this case. A few footprints alone probably won't convince anybody of anything. We need to trace these back to the ravine, hopefully find a few clues along the way, and then use whatever we come up with to create some kind of a narrative."

"A narrative. Right."

"When we do bring all of this to the cops, we need to have a story to tell them, backed-up with some actual hard evidence that reconstructs all of the events from the time we left until the moment that Ryan was pushed into the ravine."

A wave of dizziness and disorientation hit me, forcing me to stop and steady myself. "Sounds like a plan."

And so Henry began his unbelievably unhurried crawl through the woods. Seriously, the kid was moving at the breakneck pace of about three feet per minute. He'd move one arm, push up his glasses, press his face into the ground, peer at a patch of dirt or broken twig for a minute or more, take a picture of some invisible detail with his phone, and then move another limb to do it all again.

After about twenty minutes we still hadn't made it all the way back to the ravine, and I was about ready to scream. But right then Henry's hand darted at the ground. He brushed a few leaves and some dirt to the side, snapped his head around and said, "Look at this."

I hurried over. In his open palm was a large, dirt-covered, chunky silver ring, with the words, "St. Soren's '14" on one side, and an engraved picture of a football on the other.

"It's a ring," I said, stating the obvious.

Henry reached into his pocket, retrieving a plastic sandwich bag. "Not just any ring—a class ring."

"With a football on it…"

"Exactly. You get them junior year, customized with your favorite activity, class, or whatever."

We both stared at the find, while Henry turned it over in his fingers; there were no initials or inscriptions. "So we just need to find the football player without a ring on, and we've got them. Right?" I asked.

"It won't be that easy," Henry replied. "Not everyone buys a ring, and the people who do don't necessarily wear them all the time. Some people frame them, some give them to their girlfriends, some wear them on a chain, and some just leave them in the box."

"Ah."

There didn't seem to be anyplace else to look for clues, just a patch of pine needles between us and the clearing. I said, "So what do we do?"

Henry sat cross-legged on the ground, mindless of the mud and dirt. He placed his backpack in front of him and arranged three plastic bags in a straight line on top of it. He picked one up, put the ring inside, and said, "We need to find out who bought this particular ring. There have to be records, if not at the school then at the ring company. I'll look into it, but if I can't find anything, the police can always subpoena the ring company's records later."

This sounded reasonable. "Alright."

"Meanwhile, I also found this," he said, lifting a second plastic bag.

From where I was standing the bag just looked empty. "Is there even anything in there?"

Henry stood up and brought it closer, so I could see what was inside: a little triangle of rubbery, dimpled white fabric, maybe an inch across, with some strands of blue and orange thread stuck to the back of it. Two of the triangle's sides were straight and met at a perfect right angle, while the third side was jagged, as if it had been ripped from the corner of a larger shape.

"That linty stuff on the back looks like the school colors," I said.

"It *is* the school colors. I pulled it off of a prickle bush about twenty yards back." He examined it more closely. "But what's this rubbery stuff?"

"I'm not sure," I said, trying to view it from a better angle. Then it came to me. "It's a number! From a football jersey! Or at least it's a piece of a number."

Henry's eyes opened wide. "Yes! Yes, that's it exactly!"

"But what number is it?"

"Impossible to tell from this piece. But all we need to do is look at each of their jerseys, and find the one with the hole."

"Exactly. But how do we get close enough to do that? It's got to be a pretty small hole."

Henry put the plastic bags in his backpack. "I don't know. We'll have to give that some thought."

We began the slow trudge back up to the school. I was feeling such a crazy mix of emotions—triumph, sadness, excitement, nausea, fear—that I couldn't quite tell if I was about to burst out laughing, crying, vomiting, or all three.

I looked up at the huge stone crucifix towering above the school, and it came to me—a way we could get close enough to the football team.

"I've got it," I said.

"What?"

"Yeah, yeah…it could totally work."

"What is it?"

"We've got to go to that party."

Henry went white. Whiter than a cloud, whiter than a sheet, like a blank piece of paper painted white under a bright light. "That what?"

"That keg party. Friday night. The one Alistair *invited* us to. Every Friday night before a weekend game, the whole football team wears their jerseys to the keg party up by the radio tower. I saw Ryan leave for it a hundred times."

"Oh, I don't know."

"Yes you do," I said, putting my hand on his back as we came up to the parking lot, just outside the football field. "You're in high school now. You go to parties. Just don't forget to bring your little plastic bags."

Twelve

The first thing I had to do was get someone to take us to the party. The radio tower was about three miles north of town, at the top of a tall hill just off the side of the highway. Walking there was really not an option; skateboarding would be far too difficult (and I assumed impossible for Henry); and of course I couldn't ask either of my parents to take me. So for the whole bus ride home, I was trying to figure out how to scrounge up enough money for a cab, and wondering if it was really such a good idea to blow my last twelve dollars on Jesus Jackson.

Thankfully, though, the solution to my problem was waiting for me at home, right in my own kitchen: Tristan Mitchell, Ryan's three-year girlfriend and one of the only seniors at St. Soren's that I had ever actually spoken to before that day. As soon as I walked in the house and saw her standing at the counter, red-eyed and puffy-cheeked and drinking a cup of hot tea with my mother, I knew that I just had to ask, and she would oblige.

The hard part would be the timing. Tristan was right in the middle of what appeared to be an extremely emotional conversation with my mother, and I clearly couldn't just barge in and ask her for a ride to a keg party. On top of that, after seeing the looks of her—she was a mess: totally devastated—it seemed a bit doubtful that she would be planning on going to any kind of party for quite some time.

So I decided to wait it out. I took a seat on the living room couch in between the kitchen and the front door, where she'd have to pass before leaving, and pretended to read a magazine, waiting for them to be done. Unfortunately, this turned out to be quite a while.

I always hated our living room. That is, I always hated that particular living room—the new one, bought and decorated after my parents' divorce three years prior. Our old one, in our old house, was what a living room should be: a cozy, somewhat cramped hodgepodge of comfortable furniture, knickknacks, family photos, a coffee table covered in unread magazines and books and perhaps a solitary sock, all centered around a television that was on more than it was off. It had a greenish old carpet that you could spend a whole Saturday morning on, eating sugar cereal and watching cartoons in your pajamas, feeling just as comfortable as if you'd never gotten out of bed.

The new one couldn't possibly have been more different. Like the entire house, it looked as if it were copied inch for inch out of a home-decorating catalogue. Everything matched—the curtains with the sofa with the armchair with the painted trim around the outside of the fireplace—and nothing was comfortable. You couldn't sit anywhere without messing up some perfectly arranged pillow, you couldn't put anything on the coffee table without a coaster. The floors were hard and dark and smelled like pine, and besides, there was no more television, since it'd been relegated to an only slightly more comfortable "den."

The odd thing was that my mother had never been even remotely like that before the divorce. Sure, we had nice things and a nice house, but never in such a desperately "perfect" way. Never to be showy. Since the divorce, though, it was as if that house was the only thing my mom had left to cling to or to define herself with. Like losing a husband could be somehow negated by gaining a prime piece of real estate.

As I sat in that living room listening to my mother and Tristan cry in the kitchen, all I could of think was: What is she going to find to make up for losing a son?

Anyway, after about half an hour, my mom finally left the kitchen, walking right past the couch where I was sitting without noticing me at all.

"I'm home," I said.

She turned quickly, startled. Her eyes and face were red; her makeup smeared. But the moment she saw me she turned on her brightest, whitest, fakest smile. "Oh, Jonathan. I didn't hear you come in. How was school? Are you hungry? Would you like me to make you some dinner?"

"Mom," I said. "You don't have to be like this. You can—" But she didn't let me finish.

"I know…I'll make you beef stroganoff," she exclaimed, smiling even more brightly than before. "That's your favorite. Just give me a minute to freshen up." And with that, she turned on her heels and began to bounce up the steps.

"That's *Ryan's* favorite," I said quietly.

She stopped abruptly, turning halfway back toward me with a strained look of only half comprehension. "Oh. Was it? Well maybe just meatloaf in that case." And then she bounced the rest of the way up the steps.

I rose slowly off the couch and approached the kitchen door. Tristan was sitting on a stool at the counter, leaning over her cold cup of tea, wrapping her hands around the mug as if it were still warm. She didn't notice me there, so I coughed from the doorway. When she looked up, I said, "Hey, Tris."

"Jonathan," she said meekly. "Come here."

I walked over to her, and she stood up to greet me, wrapping me in a big hug and tousling my hair. "How are you doing?" she asked. "You hanging in there?"

For some reason this struck me as a very odd question, though clearly it shouldn't have. But the thing is, I felt sort of fine, at the moment. I wasn't depressed, or angry, or anything so severe. I was so consumed with thoughts about how Ryan died and what he believed about God and getting a ride to the party, that I don't think I could have made myself feel sad even if I wanted to.

I knew, however, that I had to play the part of the grieving brother if I wanted to get that ride, so I gave her my best puppy-dog eyes, looked at the floor, and said, "Not great."

"I know," she said. "Me neither." Then she hugged me again.

After a minute or so, she pulled away. "So I hear you went to school today."

"Yeah, I did. It was…weird."

"Well, it's kind of a weird place."

I nodded.

Her eyes were sad and swollen. "This is such a terrible way for you to start high school."

She had no idea. "Yeah well…" I said. "There's this huge memorial on the front steps. Did you see it?"

"Yeah, I've been over there a lot."

"Did Ryan even know all of those people?"

This made her laugh a bit, but only for a second. "Yeah," she said. "He was really popular."

"I never met any of them. The only friends of his I knew were you, the twins, and Jake."

Tristan sat back on her stool, staring down into her cup. "You know, he didn't really hang out with Jake or the twins much anymore."

I thought about it for a second, realizing that, in fact, I hadn't really seen them for a while. "Why not?"

Her eyes shifted around the room. "I don't know. They've been growing apart for years."

"Was it because of Alistair and those guys?"

Her eyes darted up at me. "What is that supposed to mean?" she asked, a slight quiver in her voice. She stared at me intently, seeming almost afraid of what my answer might be.

For a moment, I considered telling her everything, the whole story: what happened behind the school, Jesus Jackson, my investigation, Henry, everything.

But I didn't. I decided to play dumb for the time being. It seemed the safer way to go. "Um, nothing. I just heard him talking about hanging out with those guys. That's all."

Tristan still seemed wary. But I made my best attempt at a sadly innocent, slightly confused face, and she softened. She said, "Ryan kind of switched his whole group of friends, and Alistair and company were part of the new one."

"Oh. I didn't know."

"Yeah, well. It happens."

"What did you think of that? Do you trust those guys?"

"Trust them?"

"I mean, did you like them? Did you like hanging out with them?"

She looked off, over my shoulder. "They're fine. They were Ryan's friends, so you know…they became mine."

"I guess it just never occurred to me that he would have *so many* friends," I said, trying desperately to think of a way to broach the subject of the party. Luckily, Tristan did it for me.

"Well he did," she said, putting her hand on my shoulder. "But I'm sure you'll get to know them all, sooner or later. At least his real friends."

"Who are the real ones? Are they the people responsible for this God stuff all over the school?"

She laughed a bit. "Maybe some of them. It is a Catholic school, you know, Jonathan."

"Sure, but Ryan was no Catholic."

She looked confused. "What do you mean? What else would he be?"

"Well, he's…" But I stopped myself. She seemed honestly surprised that I would ever consider Ryan to be anything other than a perfectly normal, good Catholic kid. "Tristan, did you and Ryan ever really talk about, like, God and stuff?"

"No," she said, with a bit of a laugh, as if talking about God was an even crazier idea than not believing in him. "I mean, we had Theology together in tenth grade, I think. But we never just sat around chatting about Jesus."

I decided to drop the subject. Clearly, whatever Ryan truly thought about religion since he started at St. Soren's, he never felt the need to share it with Tristan. So I mumbled something about Ryan being a spiritual guy and then searched my mind for a good way to ask her for a ride to the party.

"About those real friends," I said. "Actually, I was wondering if you were going to the party Friday night. I mean, I know there's usually something going on at the radio tower before a big game, and I was figuring that lots of Ryan's friends would be there, and it might be nice just to be around people."

"Oh, I don't know, Jon. I wasn't really planning…"

I said nothing. I just gave a half-hearted nod and began to shuffle out of the room.

I barely made two feet toward the door. "Okay, okay. We can go up there, for a little bit. It'll probably be good for me. You know, to get out."

I turned my head, just slightly, over my shoulder. "Do you think we could bring my friend Henry along? Just, you know, for support?"

"Of course," she said, though now with a twinge of uneasiness in her voice. "Of course."

Thirteen

If you had told me three weeks before any of this started that I was going to be the most recognizable kid in the whole freshmen class, or worse, the whole high school, I would have laughed, probably scoffed, and said something like, "Let's hope not." But inside (I must admit) I would have probably been excited—or at least hopeful, assuming that such popularity would be due to my heretofore-overlooked wit and sarcastic charm. I think I would have enjoyed the high-fives in the hallways, the inside jokes with every clique in school, the love.

And of course, in a way, I did achieve a good degree of local celebrity, though for the worst of all possible reasons. Everywhere I went—every square foot of every hallway, every classroom, and every seat at every table in the cafeteria—people knew who I was. They knew my name, they knew my face, my life story, and they all just stared at me with the same nauseating look of sympathy and discomfort.

And really, I don't think it would have been nearly as bad if it weren't for all the goddamned God crap that seemed to multiply exponentially by the hour. At least if I were in a public school, the assistant principal wouldn't be able to add, at the end of every announcement, "And let us not forget to pray for the healing of Ryan Stiles' family, especially Jonathan Stiles, a new member of the St. Soren's family, who is particularly in need of our prayers and support."

It was all I could do to keep myself from running straight out of the school.

Then there was Mr. Finger. Clearly unsatisfied with our first meeting, he sent a pass to my homeroom on Wednesday requesting my presence immediately. I ignored the pass, along with the ones he sent to my third and fifth period classes as well. I made it all the way until Friday, actually, before Ms. LaRochelle finally showed up at Math to escort me there in person. I knew what she wanted the minute she came in the door and began whispering conspiratorially with Mr. McKenzie.

So I relented. I got up from my desk, left the class, and followed her silently through the halls, down the back staircase, and to the end of that awful basement corridor.

Mr. Finger was right where I left him, that blindingly idiotic smile still resting on his stupid face. And just like before, he said, "So, Jonathan. Would you like to start with prayer?"

"No," I replied. "No, I would not like to start with prayer. At all. Ever."

"I see. Uh…" He rifled through some papers on his desk. "Not everyone does…um…are you Jewish?"

"Excuse me?"

He stared at some hand-written notes on my file. "Is that why you don't want to pray? I don't remember reading that, but…"

"Jewish people pray too. You know that, don't you?"

"Of course," he said quickly, now looking seriously concerned, as if I were definitely Jewish and he had deeply offended me. "I didn't mean to say that you don't. Jewish prayers are…great! It's just that some Jewish students don't like to participate in…"

I sighed. "I'm not Jewish."

"Oh," he looked relieved.

"I'm an atheist."

"Excuse me?"

"An atheist."

"Oh no." He leaned back, away from me, curling his lips over his teeth. He looked shocked, uncomfortable, confused. I imagine he'd have had a similar reaction if I told him I was an arsonist, or had AIDS. "But why?"

His shock just annoyed me. Didn't this guy deal with kids all the time? I couldn't have been the only atheist in the school, or at least not the only one he'd met. "That's kind of a big question."

"Well being an atheist is a big decision."

"It's more of a realization than a decision. You just realize there's no God, and then you're an atheist."

He leaned forward in his chair. I noticed a speck of what looked like poppy seed bagel in his silky yellow beard. "You really believe that there is no God?"

I thought about what Jesus Jackson had said: how I didn't really have enough faith to be an atheist. How, rather than actually believing in nothing, I just didn't believe in anything. "Sure," I said. "I really don't believe in any god."

"Wow, that must be really hard for you."

"Not really," I said, feeling a little like a hypocrite or at least a liar. Because of course it was hard—it was worse than hard; it was impossible. I was paying a goddamned "spiritual contractor" to build me some faith because I could barely keep my shit together without any. And it was all so absurd, when you think about it. I mean, what the hell was I going to do?

Just shut my brain off and swallow whatever bullshit Jesus Jackson came up with for me? What if he tried to give me faith in this same old, tired-out Christian God? Or something equally absurd? But then again, wouldn't anything he gave me faith in be just as ludicrous as Christianity? Did I really think that there was one fairy tale out there that was magically going to ring "truer" than the rest, no matter how obviously false?

These questions kept swirling around in my brain, until I heard Mr. Finger whisper, his voice softening to its most affected, sympathetic-social-worker tone. "I would just think it would be especially difficult, you know, for someone in your position."

"And what position is that?"

His voice became even more saccharine than before. "Your brother, of course. If you don't believe in God, then what do you believe happened to him when he—"

I didn't bother to wait for him to finish the question. I hopped out of my seat, picked up my bag, and spent the rest of the period in the last stall of the first-floor bathroom, cursing Mr. Finger and Alistair and Jesus Jackson and everyone.

By the time I made it home after school I was exhausted—emotionally and physically. Each day that week there had been more religious posters, more sympathetic smiles, more strangers hugging me and crying and regaling me with their vast exaggerations of their deep connections with my brother. Honestly, the last thing in the world I wanted to do was to go to a party with all of those same goddamned people.

But then again, I couldn't bring myself to call it off. I just kept thinking about Alistair, and his smug face, thinking he'd gotten away with it. Thinking that I'd be too scared, or too stupid, to make him pay for what he did.

There was nothing about my house to suggest, even in the slightest of ways, that it was a place of such fresh death, of such ongoing mourning. There were no drawn curtains, no low lights, no lying around of the expected mess or disarray. There was no black. None. Well, except for my room, of course, but that had been black since long before Ryan's death.

No, my house, as always, had the gloss and sterile perfection of a model home in a real estate ad—everything impossibly aligned and dust-free. Every window thrown open, every light brightly burning, every color combined in a perfect tonal harmony, as if you were wearing some special glasses colored in pleasing blends of beige and powder blue. Not only that, but my mother had barely stopped cooking and cleaning long enough to sleep since Ryan's death, so everything smelled intensely of Pine-Sol and cookies. Add to this the Christmas music (yes, that's right: Christmas music…in September) blaring cheerily from the kitchen stereo, and you had a setting that would have seemed eerily festive under any circumstances… much less in the aftermath of a seventeen-year-old's death.

I think it absolutely floored Henry when he walked through the door.

And as if the house itself wasn't enough to overwhelm poor Henry, out came my mother, just as he arrived. She was dressed, as she had been all week, in head-to-toe pastel (all designer, all awful) with her up-coiffed brown hair and her flawless face, painfully gritting a too-bright smile. Personally, I thought she looked like a Ralph Lauren mannequin that had taken a bit too much Ritalin. I couldn't even imagine what Henry must have thought.

"You must be Henry," she said. "It's very nice to meet you."

Henry seemed to be staring at my mom's high-heeled feet. "Nice to meet you too," he mumbled.

"I'm just so glad my Jon as made a friend at his new *Catholic* school. He didn't make any real friends at his public middle school, which is no surprise, really, because of course his father made him go there."

She paused for some kind of a response from Henry, but his eyes never left her shoes. This was probably for the best. If he had responded, she just would've launched into all of the reasons why, had I gone to the public high school (as I had been begging her to for years) I would certainly wind up a criminal, a drug addict, or worse.

But she didn't. Instead, she just gave Henry a haughty turn of her disapproving chin and said, "Well, you boys have fun," and then click-clacked her heels straight back to the kitchen.

"Sorry about that," I said, as soon as she was out of earshot. "That's just kind of how she is."

Henry shrugged it off. "Mine's no better." Then he swung around his gigantic backpack and laid it on the ground. "So I've got all of the supplies we need for the night: plastic bags, rubber gloves, two magnifying glasses, headlamps, extra batteries, energy bars—"

I cringed. "Henry," I said, placing a hand on his shoulder. "We can't bring all this stuff."

"Why not?" He looked genuinely confused.

"We're going to a party. A keg party, in the woods."

"I know," he said after a moment. "That's why I brought bug spray."

I reached into his backpack and pulled out a handful of plastic bags. "Stuff these into your pocket, they may come in handy. If you bring any of this other stuff, we're going to look like we're on our way to a Sherlock Holmes convention."

"But how are we going to investigate without our magnifying—?"

"Think about this as an undercover job, Henry. Deep cover. You wouldn't bring a magnifying glass on an undercover job, would you?"

A great wave of realization seemed to wash over my little friend. He slapped his palm to his forehead. "Of course!" he said, breaking into fits of spastic laughter. "What was I thinking? We're going undercover with the suspects, we have to be incognito, we have to *blend in!*"

"Exactly."

Henry skipped over to the floor-to-ceiling mirror right by the entrance to the living room, and began to inspect himself carefully. "Well, my outfit won't really do at all, then. Will it?"

Now that was funny. He was right, of course—he actually didn't look that much different than he did in his school uniform. Instead of a navy blue button-down tucked into light khaki pants, he had on a light blue button-down tucked into dark khaki pants. "Well, you're right about that. Come on, I probably have some old clothes up in my room that will fit you."

So we went up to my room, where I managed to hook Henry up with a pair of acceptably worn jeans, an old vintage-looking t-shirt and a plain black hoodie. I stepped back to take a look at him. "Well, it's definitely an improvement."

He looked at himself in the mirror, and giggled. "I feel so emu."

I had to swallow back my laughter. "I think you mean emo, Henry. An emu is a large, flightless bird. Like an ostrich."

"Yeah, emo. I like it."

Just then I heard a car pull up to the house. I looked out my window; it was Tristan's Jeep, idling in the driveway.

"Our ride's here," I said. "Let's go."

Fourteen

Henry was visibly nervous as we descended the stairs, and went out into the night. I whispered, "Just relax. It's going to be fine," as I climbed into the front seat and he got in the back. "Hey Tris," I began, closing the door behind me. "This is Hen—" but I stopped short when I saw her. She looked up from the steering wheel, her eyes red and filled with tears, her face flush.

"I don't know if I can do this," she said, breaking down into a torrent of shivering sobs.

Now what was I supposed to do? I mean, this poor girl was obviously distraught—devastated, even—and all I could do was hope that she wouldn't totally lose it before we made it to the party. But I had to do *something*. So I reached over, touched her shoulder. I said, "It's okay, Tris. We don't have to go you don't want to."

She turned to me, then, with a sort of desperate heaviness in her eyes. She said, "You just sounded so much like your brother right then." She let out an abbreviated chuckle. "You're even starting to look a bit like him, too, as you get older."

I could feel myself blushing—to hear somebody (and, of course, not just somebody—Ryan's girlfriend) tell me that I was becoming more and more like him, well, let's just say it felt pretty huge. I said, "Thanks, Tris. But really, if you're not feeling up to this, we can get up there on our own."

This made her laugh. "Oh really, how? You're going to skateboard up a three-mile hill?" And with that she shifted the car into drive and pulled onto the street.

———

It wasn't until we pulled into the field next to the radio tower that I turned around to see how Henry was doing in the back. And he was not doing well.

To say the kid looked scared would be an understatement of enormous proportions. He looked horrified. Panic-stricken, even. He was pale, wide-eyed, and almost totally unresponsive. His little wire glasses were about to chatter off the end of his nose. Whether it was the car ride up with such a wreck of a girl, the apprehension of the party, or the fact that he was about to be face-to-face with Alistair, I can't honestly say. But whatever it was, it had Henry thoroughly spooked.

Lucky for us, Tristan needed a minute to compose herself, so I got a chance to shake some sense into Henry before we ventured into the wilds of the party. As soon as we were out of earshot, I grabbed him by the shoulders. "What's the matter with you? You look like you're about to have a heart attack."

Henry didn't move a muscle; he just stared at me.

"Okay, Henry. Take a few deep breaths, and tell me what's going on."

He did as he was told (reluctantly), breathing in deeply though his nose, and out through his mouth. Then, barely whispering, he said, "It's just that…at the party…I know that there'll be…"

"What, beer? It's a keg party, Henry."

He shook his head.

"Drugs? Are you worried about drugs. Because no one's going to make you do—"

"No," he whispered.

"Is it Alistair and those guys? You know they'd never do anything here, with all these people, right?"

Again, he shook his head, "No, there'll be…"

"What?'"

"Girls."

Okay, so I know that laughing hysterically was probably not the most sympathetic or kind response I could have had to Henry's statement. But it was the one that came to me first, so I went with it. Practically choking, I said, "Girls? You're this freaked out about *girls*?"

"That's what they have at parties," he shot back, almost angrily. "They have girls that will want to talk or flirt or make out or who knows what, and I don't know how to do any of it!"

I let out one final chuckle and then I started to feel bad for the kid. "Listen Henry," I said. "Yes, there will be girls up there, and yes, one or two may even attempt to talk to you. But I assure you, beyond the shadow of a doubt, with one-thousand percent confidence, that none of them will try to flirt or make out with you."

Now I know that sounds a bit harsh, but I think it was just what he wanted to hear. "Really?" he said with a smile. "Are you sure?"

"Absolutely. And besides, we're here to work. We're here as detectives, not pick-up artists. We need to get something on Alistair that we can bring to the police. Just one piece of evidence, or proof, or whatever. You have to keep your eye on the ball, okay? Can you do that?"

"Okay," Henry said, looking very serious. "I can do that."

Our plan was simple:

Step 1: Walk up the hill to the party, mingle (inconspicuously).

Step 2: Figure out if Alistair or any of his asshat friends were missing a piece of a number on any of their jerseys.

Step 3: Measure their feet (also, inconspicuously).

Step 4: Catalog which of them did (or did not) wear a class ring.

Just like everything else, though, it didn't quite work out how we planned.

First, let me set the scene of the party: you walk up a dark wooded hill smelling faintly of gasoline and garbage, and just at the halfway point you begin to hear a low roar coming from the top, but you're still too far away to see anything. So you climb and climb until you finally reach the crest and see, not the crowded gathering you'd expect, but nothing. Just trees and darkness and noise—lots of noise. It sounds like a thousand people screaming at once, but you can't see any of them, so you walk straight into the darkness until you find yourself in a clearing, roughly the size of a tennis court, with maybe a hundred teenagers packed shoulder-to-shoulder beside a hundred-foot tall steel tower, just standing around with their red keg cups, yelling and screaming at the top of their lungs.

But here's the thing—there is almost no light whatsoever. Really, it's practically pitch black, with just a faint red glare coming from the top of the tower, and the occasional flicker of a phone screen or a camera flash.

"Shit," I said to Henry. "This is going to be a lot harder than I thought."

Henry nodded his agreement. "I know. How are we going to see anything?"

Just then, as if in response to our complaint, a great beast of a pickup truck came roaring up the access road, shining its headlights over everything, and stopping a few feet from the edge of the crowd. A few kids shifted and whispered nervously, ready to make a break for it, but most just stood there, waiting.

The doors opened, and like a politician at a funeral, out popped Alistair St. Claire with a wave and a solemn nod, followed by one of his usual shitforbrains friends. The whole party turned to face him as he climbed on the hood of his truck, Budweiser tall boy in hand. He hushed the murmuring crowd with a sweep of his arm.

"I know it's fitting, on the night before the year's first game, for the captain to get up here and give a little speech." He paused for a practiced tear. "But our real captain couldn't make it."

Again Alistair paused, but this time for a bit longer. I looked around at the crowd and saw a few real tears shimmering in the headlights, which just made his little show all the more despicable to behold.

He continued, "Ryan was our leader. He was our inspiration. He was the best damn quarterback in this whole county." Again, more fake tears. "And he was my best friend."

Now this was just too fucking much. Was he kidding? There's no way Alistair was ever Ryan's best friend. I knew Ryan's best friends—Jake and the twins. I looked around for one of them to speak up and refute Alistair's bullshit claim, but then I remembered what Tristan told me, and of course they weren't there.

So Alistair went on with his speech, wiping his eyes for effect. "But the best way we can honor Ryan is keep him in our minds, keep him in our hearts, and beat the living hell out of Portsmouth!!"

And with that, a great roar of support rose from the crowd.

Alistair began to chant: "Go Soren! Go Soren! Go Soren!" My dinner began to rise in my throat.

"Go Soren!" the crowd chanted with him.

"Flip one for Ryan!" Alistair yelled, turning over his tall boy and spilling its contents to the soil.

"For Ryan!" the crowd yelled back, spilling their beers in an idiotic chorus.

Then, as if all of this wasn't disgusting enough, Alistair spotted me.

"Hold on a second," he said, waving his hand over the cheering, yelling, crying crowd; hushing them all. "There's someone here I want you to meet."

No, I thought. *No no no no no no no!*

"This is his first year at Soren, and though I know you've all heard his name by now, I think we should all welcome him with open arms."

Shit, I thought. *Shit shit shit shit shit!*

Alistair pointed over the heads of the crowd, directly at me and Henry. And like a sea of penguins, two hundred heads turned and stared at us with sad and curious eyes. "So much for incognito," I whispered.

Henry did not reply; He didn't even seem to be breathing.

"That there is little Jonathan Stiles. Ryan's younger brother." The crowd became instantly silent. "And I just want you all to welcome him, make him feel at home here and at school." Then he met my eyes. I looked straight through his drunkenness and his bullshit, and all I saw was a heart of the purest evil. "You're so brave, Jonny. To come up here. So soon…You're so brave."

I whispered to Henry, out of the corner of my mouth, "What the hell do you think he means by that?" But Henry, I think, was far too terrified to hear me.

Alistair raised his tall boy one more time. "To Jonny Stiles!" he yelled.

The crowd erupted into applause, and cheers, and whistles. Junior and senior guys raised their keg cups to me in reverence, as if I were some kind of celebrity, and more than one girl in the crowd had a tear in her eye and a shy smile on her lips. Honestly, I couldn't stand it. It was all bullshit; they didn't know me. Hell, they didn't even know Ryan…at least not the *real* Ryan. And what the hell did Alistair mean, anyway? What was so brave about me going up there? What kind of danger did he think I was facing?

After about a minute of applause (which, believe me, felt a lot longer) everyone turned their attention back to Alistair, who changed the subject of his speech (thankfully) back to how the Soren Seagulls were going to absolutely annihilate the Portsmouth Pirates (or whatever) in Saturday's big game.

Seeing that no one was staring at us anymore, I whispered to Henry, "I think now would be a good time to try to blend in a bit."

"Blend in?" he whispered fiercely. "Don't you think it's a bit late for that? We're now the most recognizable people at the party. The dead kid's brother and his little Asian sidekick!"

That stung a bit, and I shot Henry a look to let him know it.

He stared down at his shoes. "Sorry. I didn't mean it that way. I just—"

"It's alright. Anyway, you're only half right. Everyone's going to be looking at me, but I think you can still slip in under the radar."

"How?"

"We're going to have to split up."

Prior to speaking these words, I wouldn't have thought there was anything I could've said to make Henry more scared or uncomfortable than he already was. Clearly, I would have been wrong.

"What?" he screamed. "Split up?! No! I mean, that's not smart, or reasonable, or even really possible, when you think about it. What are we going to do, just wander around aimlessly? We'll look ridiculous, just walking around staring at football players' footprints and fingers. We'll stand out even more than we do now!"

I put my hand on Henry's shoulder. Again, I felt sort of bad for him. "No, Henry. You're going to have to mingle, a little."

"Mingle?" he questioned, as if it were some strange word in a foreign language.

"Yes, mingle. Talk to people. Get a beer and just hold it, if you don't want to drink. The point is that you need to blend in."

Henry paused for a moment, collecting himself. Finally, he nodded, slowly and carefully, as if he were a soldier who'd been ordered to throw himself on a grenade.

"Think of yourself like James Bond. Do you like James Bond?"

"No. His whole character is too implausible."

"Well, then…Whatever. Just imagine you're like a better James Bond, and you've snuck into some fancy party, and you have to be all suave and cool so that nobody will notice that you're planting the secret homing device, or whatever."

Henry swallowed hard. "Okay," he said at last, forcing a smile. Then he took one more breath, turned on his heels, and slunk—slumped shoulders and hung head—into the center of the party.

For my part, I did what seemed to be the most natural thing upon arriving at a keg party: I went to get myself a beer, and tried to attract as little attention as possible.

Fifteen

As soon as I walked into the crowd, though, it became very clear that "not attracting attention" was a task that I was destined to fail before I had begun. Everyone knew who I was. Everyone. And they were all staring at me. All of them.

At least, everyone except the guy guarding the keg.

Let me take a second to describe this guy for you. His name, according to the back of his jersey and the many whispers of frightened underclassmen, was Monster. And that was not a nickname, mind you—*that was his actual name*: Monster Michael Jones. He was about six-foot-seven, 300 pounds, had a big curly mop of black hair, and a straggly beard that appeared to start under his nose and continue all the way over his chin, down his neck, into his shirt, and straight out the bottom of his denim cut-off shorts.

Anyway, Monster didn't notice me at all until I picked up a red cup and reached for the keg. Then he saw me, all right. He promptly stopped talking to the comparatively minuscule linebacker beside him, reached his beefy hands to grab my shirt, and violently tugged me away from the beer. "Five dollars," he growled, "*freshman*."

"Oh." I reached into my pockets, hoping to find a few

crumpled bills. "Sorry. Just, um…hold on one second." Monster let out a self-satisfied snort, and stared at me menacingly. I pulled out my hand; I only had three bucks. "I don't think I—"

"Well if you don't think, then…" he began, when the linebacker tugged on his shirt and whispered something in his ear.

Instantly, Monster's entire demeanor changed. He looked at me with grief-stricken eyes, as his comically large and greasy lower lip stuck out like a circus clown. "Jonathan," he said. "I, I, I'm sorry. I didn't know…."

Still feeling a bit cautious, I decided it was probably best not to say anything. So I just tried to seem friendly, waiting to see what would happen next.

Monster grabbed a cup, knocked some kid to the ground who was headed for the tap, and poured me a beer. "You're money's no good here, anyway," he said.

And then he hugged me—a big, strange, awful-smelling hug. It was gross, and a little disturbing, but at least it got rid of any remaining fears that he was about to pummel me. I thanked him for the beer and began wandering around the party, desperately trying to find someone I knew enough to talk to.

I was, however, completely unsuccessful. Sure, everyone was quick to make eye contact, say hello, and tell me how sorry they were and how much they liked Ryan. But inevitably, within thirty seconds of my entering a group's conversation, everyone became so painfully uncomfortable that I just had to move on. And I don't know, maybe it was me; maybe I was putting out a sort of awkward, outcast-vibe (that's certainly how I felt). But whatever it was, it happened again and again until I finally found myself standing beyond the very edge of the party, right beside the radio tower, alone. I decided to climb up a little and sit on an overhanging rail, to look out over the town and the crowd. The view was phenomenal from up there. You could see out for miles. I figured I should be able to see all the way to the high school, but I couldn't quite make it out in the distance.

I sat there for maybe ten minutes, all alone. Squinting into the dusty night. All I ever did make out were the lights of the interstate, a few neon-lit shop signs, and the great black ocean behind everything, stretching out toward the invisible horizon.

I was just about to give up looking for the school when I was startled by a girl's voice, calling out from directly beneath my feet, "Hey, kid."

From where I was sitting, her face was almost completely obscured in shadow. I squinted to see if I could recognize her, but it didn't help. "Um. Yeah?"

"What are you looking at up there?"

"I'm trying to find the school."

"Well you're looking the wrong way." She pointed back toward the party. "School's that way."

I turned to look where she was pointing. I still couldn't make anything out. "Where?"

"It's over by the highway, near the—just hold on a second." And with that she grabbed the first bar, hopped deftly onto the tower, and climbed up to my perch. As soon as she hoisted herself beside me, her face came into the moonlight, and I had to grasp the rail a bit tighter to steady myself.

Okay, so she was pretty. Not glossy-magazine make-believe gorgeous, or even perfect-blond-cheerleader-hot like Tristan. But in her own, sort-of-nerdy-sort-of-punk way, she was striking. And besides, she had a hot pink streak in her bright red hair and she was wearing a tight-fitting Sonic Youth t-shirt… which was all I needed to see.

And, for the record, she just happened to graze my knee with her breast—just barely, just enough—as she pulled herself up over the last bar.

Anyway, neither of us spoke for a few seconds—me, because I was too dumbstruck to say anything. And she, well, I think she was just enjoying my gawking.

Finally, she twirled herself toward me. "I'm Cassie."

"Oh, okay. Hi. I'm—"

"Jonathan," she said with chuckle. "I know who you are."

"Right. I guess everyone does."

"You're kind of the most popular kid in school now. Everyone's talking about you down there."

I guess it shouldn't have, but this surprised me. "Really? Why?"

She flipped her hair, and I caught a whiff of her shampoo. "I don't know. I think everyone just thinks it's really cool that you came here tonight. Freshmen usually don't come to parties at all until the end of the year, so for you to come tonight, you know, when everyone's really missing your brother..."

I looked out over the crowd, wondering how many of these kids had ever even spoken to Ryan. "Did you know him? My brother?"

"A little. He was two years older than me, but—"

"Oh, so you're a sophomore?"

"Yeah," she said, turning to meet my eyes again, and again severely disturbing my stability. "What did you think I was?"

"I, uh...I didn't really think anything. But sophomore is... good."

Cassie smiled. There was flirtation in her eyes, but just a little, and under the surface. She said, "Yeah. Sophomore is good."

Oh, how I wanted to freeze that look in her eyes, right in that moment, and just soak it up for hours and hours. But as it usually goes in my life, it was right then—at that very instant—that my evening collapsed. It started with a few distant murmurs, then some shouts, which came closer and closer, until I noticed some kind of commotion weaving its way through crowd. It was almost like a tiny animal was wandering around the party, biting at people's ankles, and all you could see was a snaking trail of agitation, spilled beers, and cursing.

"Oh no," I said.

"What's wrong?" asked Cassie.

"Henry."

"Who's Henry?"

As if on cue, Henry, crawling on all fours, came tumbling out of the edge of the crowd, flashlight in one hand, a fistful of plastic baggies in the other.

"That's Henry," I replied. Then I shouted for him. "Henry! Over here!"

Henry, however, did not hear me. Finally free of the jungle of legs, he took off running toward the path down the hill. "Now why would he go running—" I began, but my question was answered before I had the chance to finish it.

Alistair and two of his shitfaced friends came barreling through the crowd, looking more than a little pissed off. As soon as they were in the clearing they looked all around, pointing and mumbling angrily about why that "weird little Asian kid" was messing with their shoes. I even heard Alistair say, as he strutted back into the party, that he was pretty sure the damn kid was taking pictures of his ass.

I turned to Cassie. "I'm, uh…sorry. I have to go…that was my friend."

"No," Cassie said, as I began to climb down the tower. "I'm the one that should be apologizing. He can be such an asshole sometimes."

I stopped climbing, confused. "Who, Alistair?"

"Yeah, I'm sorry. He's always been like that."

"How do you know Alistair?"

Cassie looked at me as if I just asked her how she knew that water was wet. "He's my brother. You didn't know? He and Ryan were so close."

It was so depressing it was almost funny. "No," I said miserably. "I guess I didn't know." Then I climbed down the rest of the tower and looked back up to Cassie one more time. "Well, bye."

"Wait," she said. "Will I see you in school on Monday?"

"I don't think so. The funeral is on Monday."

Cassie dipped her eyes, out of sympathy, or discomfort, or maybe both. "Well, I'll see you there, then," she said. "The whole school will see you there. You be strong, Jonathan."

Now I'd be lying if I told you that I didn't—at that moment—consider (for the barest of a second, perhaps, but, yes—consider) just letting Henry find his own way home (or not find his way home, as would probably be the case), but I just couldn't do it. I had to find him. So I mumbled a half-hearted thank you, too deep in self-pity to offer up a real one, and took off running down the trail.

As it turned out, Henry found me. I was roughly half-way down the hill, the first twinges of regret starting to itch beneath my skin, when I spotted a blinking flashlight about fifty yards into the woods. "Henry," I called. "Is that you?"

"Jonathan?" he squeaked.

"Henry, get out of there. No one's following you."

"How can you be sure?" he whispered, clearly panicked.

"I saw the whole thing from the tower, where I happened to be sitting with Alistair's sister, and they all just turned around and went back into the party."

Henry emerged from the brush, dirt and leaves caking his cool new clothes. "You were talking to a girl?" he asked.

"Yeah. Cassie St. Claire, as it turns out. Why are you so filthy? Those are nice clothes."

"What did you talk about?" he asked, paying no attention to my question.

"Nothing much," I replied. "Seriously, though. What happened in there?"

"Was she, like…into you?"

"Henry!" I yelled, grabbing both of his shoulders. "What happened with Alistair? What about the investigation?"

"Well, I didn't get everything I had hoped for, but I did get a few things…maybe even enough to go to the police."

"Really? That's great news! What did you get? Were any of them missing their ring?"

Henry squatted on the ground, hunched over his backpack. All triumphant-looking and covered in dirt and sweat, he looked like some prehistoric hunter examining his fresh kill. He unzipped the bag. "Yeah," he said. "All of them."

"Oh."

"But I did confirm that Alistair wears roughly a size eleven sneaker and that one of his friends wears about a thirteen."

"That's good…close enough, I guess. What about the brands?"

"The footprints were football cleats, so no one was wearing the same shoes."

"Right."

"Anyway, the last piece of news is that all of their jerseys have pieces of the numbers missing.

"That's not good," I said. "Is it?"

"No, not really. But this might be…" He took out his phone and started scrolling pictures. They were all a bit out of focus (and taken from knee-height), but they did seem to capture each of our suspects' jerseys. "I managed to get a picture of everyone's number. If we can blow them up big enough, we might be able to match one of the torn numbers to the piece we found in the woods. It's kind of a long shot, but it's worth a look."

I was impressed. Really impressed. To be honest, I figured that Henry would come back with a few blurry pictures of someone's sneakers, but this stuff looked like actual evidence. "How did you pull all of this off, Henry?"

He gave me a hangdog look. "It was a lot of crawling around," he said. "Basically I just ducked down at one point and crawled on my hands and knees, measuring feet, staring at fingers, and taking pictures of people's backs. Everyone was standing so close together and taking pictures of each other already, that hardly anyone noticed. It was weird."

"So why was Alistair chasing you?"

"Someone kicked me into his leg right as I was trying to get my last picture of his jersey. I wound up just getting a picture of his big butt."

I found the idea of this absolutely hysterical, and couldn't stop myself from laughing. "Well, save the picture," I said. "You never know what those detectives might find useful."

Henry was not amused. He ignored my laughter, and bent down to arrange all of the evidence in his backpack. When he was done, we started down the trail toward the parking lot.

"Hey," I said. "When you were crawling around the party, did you notice Tristan anywhere?"

"No," said Henry thoughtfully. "I don't think I did."

"Strange."

"Strange."

But when we made it down to the parking lot, we saw quite quickly that the situation was not just strange. It was downright awful. Tristan's Jeep was gone, and we were three miles from home.

I looked at Henry. "I guess we better start walking."

Henry looked at me. "I guess you're right."

Sixteen

And then there was Monday (there always is), and this Monday was the worst. It was the day of Ryan's funeral, the day they put him in the ground.

My parents, in their wisdom, decided to hold the service at the St. Soren's chapel so that all of his so-called friends could come pay their respects without disrupting their school day. There have probably been worse ideas in the history of humanity, but on that morning I couldn't think of any.

I can't really describe the service itself: it was all a blur of crying kids and consoling parents and empathetic counselors and a whole pile of crap about God. My uncle Frank gave the eulogy, which I couldn't focus on enough to explain except to say that it was mostly about football. My mother cried; my father looked shell-shocked. For my part, I'm not sure I really *felt* much of anything. I just listened to the priest and the parents and the counselors and my uncle Frank talk about what a darn good Christian Ryan was, while I wondered, bitterly, if it would be rude for me to vomit under the pew.

For the record, I decided that, though justified, it would.

The thing that really got to me, though—the thing that really pissed me off—was just how *comforted* everyone else seemed to be by all this bullshit. By this idea that Ryan was just floating around all happy and content in their make-believe-fairy-cloud-fucking-castle in the sky, while I (and seemingly only I) had to sit there with the knowledge, the truth, that he was just fucking dead. He was just lying in that damned box with his wounds barely stitched and covered in makeup, his veins filled with chemicals, his skin and his brain and his eyes and his organs just waiting for the opportunity to decay into the dirt just like everything else.

It wasn't fair. Why did they get to feel their way, while I had to feel like this? It almost made me wonder if something was biologically wrong with me. But beneath all of that, I just knew—in my gut, my heart, or whatever—I just knew that if anyone was screwed up, it was all of them, and not me.

Not surprisingly, I never found any resolution to any of this, and at the end of the service, I wandered off toward St. Soren's, unable to deal with all the heartfelt condolences and sincere offers of sympathy. Eventually, I made my way inside the school and up to the roof, where I took a seat right beside the giant concrete cross and looked down on the town below.

Even after I saw everybody file into their cars, I just stayed there, watching the hearse weave my brother through the parking lot, around the tennis courts, across the highway, and to his grave. Of course, I should have been down there, too— somewhere along the great processional that was following him—grieving with my family. But from my perch up beside the cross, the cars just seemed to be moving so slowly, and winding such an absurdly circuitous route from the chapel to the churchyard…I don't know, it just felt more logical to stay up there—at a safe distance, from a better vantage point, at a higher altitude.

So I waited. I knew they wouldn't begin until the last car was parked in the last spot beside the graveyard, and not until that very moment did I climb back into the steeple to begin my long descent.

But I never quite made it to the gravesite. It wasn't the grief, though, that kept me away. Oh no. And it wasn't my nerves or my discomfort or my disdain for everything that was being said around that gravestone. No, it was just Jesus (what else?); it was only Jesus Jackson.

This time, he was decked out in a velvety white, gold-pinstriped tracksuit, jogging around the perimeter of the football field. He was barefoot, which I thought was odd (I mean, who jogs barefoot?), but Jackson or no Jackson, he was still Jesus, so I let it go.

"Jonny-boy," he called out across the field. "What's shakin'?" He veered off his course, jogging straight in my direction.

I gave him a little half-wave and waited for him to reach me. "Hi, Jesus."

He put his palms on his knees, bending over to catch his breath. "We're friends now. You can just call me G. Pretty much everybody does."

"But your name starts with a J."

"No. Jeeee," he said. "Like half of Jesus."

"Um…okay, Jee."

"So what's up? No school today?"

"Ryan's funeral is today." I nodded toward the graveyard across the highway. "They're going to bury him right now."

"Ahh." He followed my gaze. "Well, I'll let you get over there, then."

"They'll get by without me."

Jesus took a step back; he gave me a suspicious once over.

"Well, if that's how you want do it...So, any word on the Alistair situation?"

"Actually, Henry and I did a little research on Friday night."

"And?"

"And we think we've got some real evidence. Or at least, some clues that kind of point to Alistair and his buddies having something to do with Ryan falling into the ravine."

A look that almost hinted at pride came into Jesus' eyes just then, though I'm not really sure why. He said, "Well, lay it on me, brother. What'd you find?"

So I told him everything: about the footprints and the jersey number and the rings, and about how Henry managed to make connections, at least partially, with two out of our three clues. I also told him about how Alistair made a big speech at the party, singling me out to everyone and ruining what little anonymity I still had at that school. Then, when I started to tell him about Cassie, he stopped me after only a sentence or two.

With a very concerned, almost calculating expression furrowing his brow, Jesus asked, "So, do you like this girl?"

"Yeah, I mean, she was really nice and everything, but she—"

"No," Jesus interrupted me. "I mean, do you *like* like this girl?"

He was worse than Henry. I said, "I, uh...I don't know. Maybe I could, but there's kind of a problem."

"What's the problem?"

"She's Alistair's sister."

At this, Jesus laughed openly, and loud. "Wow," he said. "You're not going to let this get boring for me, are you?"

Again, Jesus confused me. "What do you mean, boring for *you?*"

"Never mind. Tell me what your plan is. First for Alistair, and then for his sister."

"I don't have a plan for Cassie."

"That's okay. You're young. You probably don't need one. So what about Alistair?"

I didn't know what Jesus was getting at about Cassie, but I decided to let it go. "Well, I guess we're going to go talk to the cops."

"Yeah, that's one option."

"What do you mean, that's 'one' option? That's the *only* option. Why wouldn't we tell the cops?"

"Well, for one thing, you still don't know how Ryan wound up at the bottom of that ravine."

"Sure we do: Alistair pushed him."

"And you have proof of that?"

"I just told you about the proof! The Jerseys, the shoes, the—"

Jesus shook his head dismissively. "That's not proof. Maybe that will show that Alistair was in the area, but it still doesn't tell you what actually happened to Ryan."

Well, I hated to admit it, but Jesus did have a point. If I was going to do it, I might as well do it right. "Okay," I said. "Fine. But what kind of proof would that even be?"

"Well, I'm no cop," Jesus said. "But I think you need some hard evidence, some *real*, unquestionable physical evidence that links Alistair to the scene of the crime and tells you exactly what happened, why it happened, and how Ryan wound up going over that edge. Like a video. Or better yet, something where he admits it in writing, like a text message or an email."

This was almost too much. "How am I supposed to get that kind of stuff? Videos and emails? They probably don't even exist!"

Jesus shrugged. "Well, I can't argue with you there. In all likelihood, that kind of proof doesn't exist at all. But that doesn't change the fact that if you want to know the truth—if you *really want to know*—then that's the kind of proof you're going to have to find."

"Well if that's the case, then I might as well just give up!"

"Now, I wouldn't say that. There's no reason to stop searching just because the answers might not be out there."

"Might not? More like definitely are not."

Jesus shrugged. "Well, you won't know that unless you keep on searching."

I was so angry, I could barely even respond to him at all. "Fine," I said. "Whatever."

"And while you're searching, you might want to try getting to know Cassie a bit better. That certainly can't hurt, no matter how this whole thing turns out."

And with that Jesus gave me a wink and a pat on the back, and began to jog off. Before he made it to the gate, though, I called out after him: "Hey, Jee, how're you doing with the whole giving-me-faith-in-nothing project?"

Without even turning around or slowing his stride, he replied, "Doing pretty well with it, I think. Starting to put together all of the pieces to the puzzle."

And then he jogged on off, around the school and out of sight.

I sat out there on the bleachers for quite a while after he left. Just thinking. Just staring. I couldn't bring myself to get up and walk over to that graveyard. I kept on trying, but I just couldn't. Every time I rose to my feet I just sank right back down again. Failure after failure. So I gave in. I sat back down for good and I tried to distract myself. I tried my damnedest to think about anything but where Ryan and my family and the whole goddamned universe were at that very moment.

But there was only one real distraction, only one that could work for me: Cassie St. Claire.

Sure, I had every intention of getting to know her better (how could I not? How could I not at least *think* about it?), but Jesus seemed to be suggesting a whole lot more than that. He wanted me to use her, to manipulate her, to "play" her to get to Alistair. And I just didn't know if I could pull that kind of thing off—emotionally, ethically, or logistically. And what would be the point of it all, anyway? What would I prove if I did succeed? What would I solve? Ryan was dead. They were putting him in the ground as I sat there and he was never coming back and no matter what everyone else said, I just couldn't bring myself to believe that he had "gone to a better place" or that he was "watching over us all" or "finally at peace" or any of the other bullshit clichés and platitudes I heard over and over since he died. He was dead. Just fucking dead—and whether he fell into that ravine or Alistair pushed him—that one simple fact was going to remain.

It took me almost an hour, but I finally dragged myself down off those bleachers, walking back to my house in an almost desperate state of apathy.

Seventeen

So I need to give you some context, a little history about those first few months after Ryan told me the truth about God, and we began our quest to find his replacement. Although our original plan was to find a "real" god to replace the imaginary one, after five long months of looking, we still weren't even close. Dozens of secret meetings, hundreds of Internet searches, and countless hours at the library (not to mention my visits to every house of worship within bicycling distance), and we had not come up with a solitary deity that seemed any less pretend than the one we started out with.

By the end of the summer, Ryan decided that our best bet would be to use the process of elimination, and he began to write The List: a complete accounting of every faith, god, religion, and theology that we determined to be absolutely, totally, and unequivocally *not* true. It started with just the big ones (Christianity, Judaism, Hinduism, Islam), but before long there were dozens of them, with more being added at each of our secret meetings. By Christmas, The List had grown to include more than 250 entries, and filled nearly every page of a college-ruled, marble notebook.

Anyway, it was right about then (January or February, I think) that all of this stuff went down:

I was sitting in the living room, playing the new Batman game on my Xbox, when I felt an icy draft blowing in from the back door (which had been mysteriously left ajar), followed immediately by the pungent odor of lighter fluid and smoke. It didn't quite seem worth pausing my game to investigate, so I just shrugged it off and continued battling the Joker and his minions of thugs…until, that is, my mom started screaming Ryan's name from the backyard.

Ryan appeared at the top of steps. He whispered to me, "What is she doing out there?"

I had not yet actually taken my eyes off the game. "I think she's burning something."

"Well pause that stupid thing and take a look."

"Fine." I did as I was told. When I peeked out the window, there she was, wearing a puffy coat and two scarves, looking livid and disheveled beside a billowing inferno bursting out of the barbecue. She was staring at the flames as she poured on lighter fluid, adding fire onto the fire. "Wow," I said. "She's going to town with that fire. She looks really mad."

Ryan's face turned stony. He seemed to know exactly what was happening. "Okay. I see."

"What is it? Do you know?"

He walked down the stairs solemnly, as if heading for a funeral. He stared at the back door. "I knew this would happen sooner or later."

"You knew it would happen? What are you talking about?"

He forced a brave smile, but I didn't believe it. "It's The List. She must have found it."

"Oh, shit."

"Don't worry," he said. "There's nothing in your handwriting. You just pretend you know nothing and let me handle this."

I nodded my assent.

From the backyard, my mother screamed Ryan's name a few more times, with venom in every syllable. Ryan told me not to worry, took a deep breath, and headed out to accept his fate.

I ran to the window, pressing my face against the glass to see what would happen. But my mother must have seen me there because as soon as Ryan reached her, she quieted to a whisper. She grabbed him by the ear and dragged him to the other side of the yard, setting the stage for a more effective interrogation.

The suspense was almost too much to stand. I knew Ryan wouldn't give me up—not on purpose, anyway—but our mother had an uncanny sense about such things, and some powerful means of persuasion. I cupped my hands around my ears, straining to hear, to get a sense of what they were saying. But I got nothing.

When Ryan was finally dismissed, I knew that things hadn't gone well. My mother remained where she stood, her head low, her fingers at her temples. I thought I caught a sob or two, but I couldn't quite be sure. And Ryan...well, Ryan looked haggard, to say the least. With slumped shoulders and his chin at his chest he made his way back to the house, shuffling into the living room like an animated corpse.

"Well I was right," he said. "She found the list."

Oh, crap, I thought. "But how?"

"I don't know...I was up late last night doing research in den, and I must have just left it on the couch."

"And what did she say?"

"It was kind of a blur," he said, sitting down with a heavy-sounding *thud* on the couch. "But it was pretty clear that she never made it past the parts about Catholicism and Jesus. She seemed to think the whole blasphemous notebook was just about her precious faith."

"Oh man…"

"I told her you had nothing to do with it, but I'm not sure that she believed me. I doubt she suspects you helped with any of it, though. If anything, she probably thinks that I tried to indoctrinate you, or something."

That was a relief, but only a small one. "So am I in trouble? Are we getting punished?" I glanced tentatively at my Xbox, wondering when I would next get to play it.

He shook his head. "You're fine. I'm grounded. She wants to talk to Dad before she decides on how long to ground me for, but I have a feeling it's going to be a long one."

"Well talking to Dad is a good thing, right? He's definitely not as crazy as mom when it comes to things like—" But before I could finish the thought, I was cut off by my mother's appearance at the door. I froze.

Her left hand was splayed over her forehead, still rubbing her temples. "Jonathan," she said, with barely a whisper. "Can you come here, please?"

Ryan averted his eyes. I swallowed hard and did as I was told.

My mother took me by the hand and led me to dining room. She sat me down at the table and sat herself right beside me. When she looked at me, it was not with anger, but with an intense and surprising look of sadness.

"Jonathan," she began, "what exactly did Ryan tell you about these …these…ideas that he has? These ideas about God."

I was on the very edge of panic—leaning against it, feeling the terror pull me toward its abyss. I had been so busy worrying that she'd take away my video games that I never got my story straight with Ryan. I thought hard. Did he tell her that I've known about Ryan's beliefs since the beginning? Does she think that I stopped believing in God too? Does she know about the meetings?

I decided to play it dumb. I shrugged. I made circles on the floor with my foot. "I dunno. Not a lot."

"But he did tell you something, right? He has talked to you about God?"

"Yeah. A couple times."

"A couple times? Really?" She sounded angry, but gratified. "I knew it…."

Crap, I thought.

"And last summer, when you asked me if God was fictional or real—was that because of something Ryan told you?"

"I don't know. Maybe. I don't really remember."

She put her hand under my chin, gently. She lifted my face so that my eyes had no choice but to meet hers. "Well he is real, okay? It's Ryan's ideas that are made up. It's what he told you that's fiction."

There was a silence then, as she seemed to calculate whether more explanation was necessary. Finally, seeming unable to make up her mind, she said, "Well at any rate, if Ryan tries to talk to you about anything like this again, you just turn around and walk away. You come right to me, okay?"

"Okay," I mumbled.

Again, there was silence. While my mom seemed pleased, in her own condescending sort of way, that I didn't argue with her like Ryan, I'm sure she would have liked me to be a bit more penitent about the whole thing—maybe even ask her if Jesus still loved me, or something absurd like that.

In truth, though, I wasn't penitent at all. I was relieved that she had taken it so easy on me. I was a bit worried about how badly she was going to punish my brother, and about what she would do to me if she found out that I had lied to her about what Ryan had told me. But more than anything, as I walked back to take my place in front of the TV, I was annoyed—annoyed that my mother felt it so damned important that we believe the same stupid thing as her; annoyed that her religion didn't allow for any different ideas about the universe, or about life or death or faith or God. And most of all, I was annoyed about The List. We had worked so hard on it, put so much time into distilling our ideas into clear, definitive, and irrefutable facts. And now all that work was gone.

When I got back to the living room I walked right up to the Xbox, hit the power button, and then went upstairs to find Ryan. He was sitting on his bed, his head in his hands, looking sad and defeated. I closed the door behind me.

"We have to start a new list," I said. "Right now."

He shook his head. "Jon-Jon, look…no one is more upset about this than me, but that list took us almost a year to write. Even if we did start a new one, it would be months before—"

"Then we'll make a shorter one," I said, determined not to let our mother win this. "Just the basic ideas. Just the clip notes."

The hint of a smile came to his face. "You mean *Cliff's Notes*," he said. "But we can't do it. If Mom finds out that you had anything to do with this, there's no telling what she might do."

"Let her find out! It's not fair. She can't tell us what to think." I grabbed a piece of paper from the desk and handed it to Ryan. "Come on. We're making a *Cliff's Notes* of The List, and we're doing it right now."

Ryan stood up and walked over to me, placing a hand on my shoulder. He looked more proud of me at that moment than anyone had ever been of me in my life. "Sure, Jonathan" he said. "Take a seat. I'll get a pen."

It took us most of the morning, but by lunchtime, we had succeeded in writing an acceptable abbreviation. It was nowhere near as exhaustive as the version we had lost, but it got the basic points across. And more importantly, it strengthened our resolve to continue the search for a god that we could actually believe in.

This is what that the abbreviated list said:

The List (Cliff's Notes): Religions that have been categorically ruled out and determined as 100% false.
By Ryan AND Jonathan Stiles

Section 1: The Big Ones

1. *Christianity: Obvious reasons: Virgin Mary, resurrection, angels, gay marriage, water-into-wine, communion wafers, etc.*

2. *Judaism: Also obvious: basis for Christianity, world created in six days, Adam and Eve, pretty much all of Genesis...*

3. *Hinduism: Caste system, too many strange (and silly) deities, Karma, the whole "cow" thing...*

4. *Islam: Too similar to Christianity, Sharia, too much praying, waaaaay too strict about everything, fasting, hijab, etc.*

Section 2: Religions that are basically the same as the big ones:

Sikhism, Baha'i, Shintoism, Christian Science, Eckankar, Hare Krishna, Jehovah's Witnesses, Mormonism, Rastafari, Seventh-day Adventist, Shinto, Zoroastrianism, Bábism, Samaritanism, Meivazhi, Manichaeism, Sufism, Martinism, Hermeticism...

Section 3: Religions that seem very nice, but don't even have the slightest bit of evidence to back them up at all:

Buddhism, Unitarian Universalist, Jainism, Taoism, Wicca...

Section 4: Religions that are just totally ridiculous:

Scientology

Eighteen

If there's one thing I learned from this whole ordeal with Ryan and Alistair and Jesus, it's that nothing cures depression quite like anger. When you go to a doctor and tell him you're depressed, he'll always try to cheer you up, tell you to look on the bright side, give you some drugs to make you smile like an idiot all day. But that stuff never lasts. Drugs wear off, bullshit fades, smiles fall. What the doctor should do is make you angry—really angry—piss you off to the extent that your sadness is a distant and pathetic memory. Because anger is lasting; anger is deep and abiding and real.

That's how I got past Ryan's funeral. It took me two full days, two full turns of the clock, until right before school on Wednesday morning. I was walking up the front steps when I saw Alistair, flanked by friends, girls, and well-wishers, pretending desperately to cry right in the middle of Ryan's burgeoning makeshift memorial. Since leaving the football field, I had spent every minute alone with my thoughts, mostly locked in my room, and throughout all of that sadness and misery there was this anger, this hatred and spite for Alistair just boiling and boiling and boiling under the surface.

So to see him there, playing the sad friend, the pitiful

teammate, the broken-hearted pal…well, it was all I could do to keep myself from running up and (surely with very little success) tackling him to the ground. I could barely even bring myself to think about Ryan at all—every pleasant or mournful or sad or funny remembrance I would begin would be interrupted by an image of Alistair, with that same rage he had in his eyes in the moments before Ryan saved me, pushing my only older brother off a cliff.

But then Alistair saw me. He raised an arm from the middle of a group hug, inviting me to join. I turned away, and stormed into the school.

I got lucky, though. Henry was right there, waiting by my locker, sitting cross-legged on the floor with his face buried in some math textbook. He looked up when I walked over to him, contorting his face into something resembling a smile, but just barely. I dropped my bag and sank down to the squeaky-tiled floor beside him. "I didn't see you yesterday," he stuttered. "At the service…and, um…I just wanted to express my…you know, condol—"

"Yeah, thanks," I said. "Listen Henry, we've got to kick this whole thing up a notch, okay?"

"What whole thing?"

"The Alistair thing. You know, all the detective work."

"Oh," said Henry. Then he stopped to study my face. He looked confused, suspicious, maybe even a little scared. "Yes, of course, the investigation. Did you want to bring the evidence to the police later?"

"No. I don't think we have enough yet, and I don't want to risk hurting Ryan's good name unless we're one hundred percent positive we can make this stick."

Henry looked relieved. Clearly, he wanted nothing to do

with the actual authorities. "Good," he said. "But, you know, one hundred percent may be hard to accomplish."

"I know, I know" I looked around to see if anyone was within earshot, then whispered, "But I have a plan."

Henry swallowed. "Oh yeah?"

"It involves Cassie. And it's going to take a joint effort."

"Alistair's sister?"

"That's right."

"Why would she help us?"

"That's the thing," I said. "She can't know that she's helping us."

"Oh."

"I'll explain everything after school." I stood, swinging my bag over my shoulder. "Meet me behind the bleachers."

"But why can't you just explain it to me at lunch?"

"I'll be busy."

So, the first part of my plan (which, to be honest, I was sort of making up as I went along) was set into action on that very afternoon, under the bright fluorescence of the St. Soren's cafeteria. As usual, I bought myself a turkey sandwich from the lunch ladies, and ventured out into the staring hordes of classmates. Walking across the cafeteria floor was like dragging a cinderblock through a still pond—I left a wake behind me of stolen glances, head-turns, and everyone trying to catch their daily glimpse of the Dead Kid's Brother. So many of them were still wearing RIPRS (Rest In Peace Ryan Stiles) bracelets and "45 in Our Hearts" t-shirts (45 was Ryan's football number), or at least the simple RS pins they were selling for a dollar at the bookstore (supposedly to help "Ryan's family," but I never saw a penny of it). On that day, though, instead of making a beeline for Henry, I tried a different approach: I spotted

Cassie, sitting with her friends, and then found a seat all by myself about two tables away, directly in her field of vision.

I sat down and opened my little carton of milk. I ate slowly, stared sadly, and waited for her to notice me.

Within thirty seconds—I kid you not—she had picked up her lunch and walked over to my table, one big sweet smile under bright red hair. Clearly bent on cheering me up, she pretended not to notice my melodramatic play at misery. "Hey, stranger. I was wondering when I was going to run into you again."

I took a slow, conscious breath before looking up from my sandwich. I was trying hard not to show even a little of my excitement. "Oh," I said. "Hi."

"Mind if I sit down?"

"No. Of course not. Have a seat."

As she took her seat, I forced myself, once again, into a visage of the sincerest sadness I could muster. I chewed my sandwich at a glacial pace. I let my eyes hang on my milk carton and sighed after every bite. She watched my play at melancholy just long enough for me to get bored with it. Finally, she said, perky as can be: "So, how are your classes going?"

I had to stop myself from laughing. I don't think I'd heard, read, or written one word of schoolwork since the year began. "Honestly, I have no idea."

My amusement must have been obvious, despite my efforts at hiding it. Cassie let a smile slide onto her face. "Well that sounds hopeful."

"Yeah, I guess I'm a bit preoccupied."

"Understandably." She placed her hand on my forearm. I could feel each crease of her palm; I almost closed my eyes, but thought better of it. "No one's going to expect you to be paying much attention to school right now."

"Yeah, I guess."

"Have you spoken with your guidance counselor? They're not good for much, but they can usually help you get out of schoolwork for personal problems."

"Not really," I said. "I've kind of been avoiding him. I just don't want to talk about it."

"Well then you don't have to. You can always just get some extra help and make up the work later. Your teachers will understand."

This was it: my opportunity. "Hmm. I wonder if you would…oh, never mind."

She cocked her head. "If I would what?"

"Nothing," I said. I was trying to appear shy (not, of course, that this was any great challenge), in an attempt to gain her sympathy.

"Really, what? If you need anything…" She gave my fore-arm a little squeeze. "…anything at all, just ask."

She was so sweet, so damn good. I could feel the guilt crawling up my back, like ants under my clothes. But then she said, "You know, Alistair and Ryan were such good friends, I feel like you and me already know each other. Like there's already a closeness there, you know?"

That was all I needed to strengthen my resolve. I gave her my most pitifully sad eyes. "Actually, I could use a little help with something. You know, if it wouldn't be too much to ask."

Well, with that she cracked right open: all grins and jitters and suppressed little giggles. "Of course. Of course. Anything. Of course."

That twinge of guilt struggled to resurface, to come up and punch me in the face. But I swallowed it down. "I know it's only the second week of school, and my teachers are all being really great about everything, but I haven't gotten one piece of work done yet, and the make-up assignments keep on piling and piling and I was just wondering if—"

She gave my hand and squeeze. "Of course I'll help you with your work. I think I still have some of my notes from last year, and I can totally bring them over to your house later…"

"Oh," I interrupted. "My house isn't such a great place these days. What with my mom, still so upset, and everything."

"Right, right. What was I thinking? You come over to my house. Bring all of your assignments and we'll work through them piece by piece, okay?"

I smiled, though for far different reasons than Cassie could have ever imagined. She smiled back, our eyes meeting in a false complicity as we finished our turkey sandwiches and our tiny cartons of milk.

———

Here's my theory about Henry:

When I met him, the kid had barely been out of his bedroom since birth. He was way too close with his parents, he did everything he was ever told, and the thought of punishment—of any kind, from anybody—scared him the way that most people are scared of mass murderers or cancer. But here's the thing: unlike most shut-in, smothered, slavishly obedient kids, Henry dreamed. He dreamed big and he dreamed dark. He read his seedy old noir novels about sex, violence, and the underworld, and he dreamed that somehow, someday, if he could just cross over into that universe, he could be a real hero. He could be exactly the opposite of what he was. And when I came along, I gave him an opportunity to do that…albeit, in a pretty small-town, amateur sort of way.

But the second I told him about my plans for that evening, and how he'd have to sneak into Alistair's room to search his computer for evidence…well, I think it all just got a little too real for him.

"No way," he said. "No."

"It'll be simple," I assured him. "Every Wednesday, there's a scrimmage at the end of practice, so there's no way Alistair will be home before seven. We'll be long gone by then."

This did not seem to comfort him much. "But what about his parents?"

"Well, that could get a bit tricky. It's just their mom—I think their dad lives a few towns over, or something—but we have to assume that she'll be home."

Henry sat on the ground, pressing his forehead into his knees. "I don't know, Jonathan…."

"Don't worry," I said. "Really, I have a good feeling about this."

"Sure, *you* have a good feeling. You're going to be 'studying' with the pretty girl while I'm risking my life."

"Come on now, Henry, it's—" I paused. "You really think she's pretty?"

"Uh, yeah. You don't?"

"Oh, I do. Completely. Totally… I was wondering if it was just me, though, you know? She's sort of unique…quirky, but beautiful…like in a way that you wouldn't necessarily think of right away."

"Hold on." Henry jumped to his feet. "Do you like this girl?"

"Whoa there. What do you mean? This is about Ryan… this is about getting Alistair."

"Just answer the question, Jon. Do you like her?"

I honestly didn't know. Or at least, I hadn't let myself think about it in such black and white terms. I mean, really: I was fourteen years old and I met a pretty, older girl at a party who actually paid attention to me. Did that constitute *liking* her? Could it possibly have constituted anything else?

At any rate, I didn't want to admit it if I did like her. "I can't...I just can't answer that question," I said. "Not yet, anyway."

"But you might like her."

"I might, sure. But this is about Ryan. You know that."

Henry paused, shook his head. He looked like he wanted to punch me in the face...which I admit, was a bit comical. "Just make sure it doesn't start being about Cassie while I'm stealing Alistair's computer files, okay?"

"Okay."

Nineteen

Before I could put the plan into action, I first had to deal with my mother. For obvious reasons, her moods had become a bit unpredictable, and I just couldn't risk the chance that she'd say no (or worse, decide that she wanted to help me with my schoolwork herself). And besides, if I told her that I was going to a girl's house, she would have a whole bunch more questions that I really didn't want to get in to.

The point is that I needed a suitable reason for leaving that night that would not arouse suspicion, and would be impossible for her to turn down. This was not an easy task. And by the time I got home I still hadn't come up with anything. I decided to head straight to my room, avoiding my mother, so I could work out my plan in private.

As I headed down the second-floor hallway, I noticed a light on in Ryan's room. I stopped before walking past the open door: What should I do? If my mom was in there, and I turned around, she'd wonder why I didn't pass. She'd yell after me, make me come back, talk, eat, stay; if I walked past, she'd probably just strike up a conversation…but then again, maybe not. I listened for a second. I thought I heard some quiet crying, and I decided to try for a clean pass across the doorway.

I tiptoed right up to the edge of the door. I readied myself, held my breath, and began my quietest quick-step past the opening. But then, glancing just slightly out of the corner of my eye, I saw that it wasn't my mother in there at all. It was Tristan, lying curled on Ryan's bed. Sobbing into her knees.

I couldn't just pass; it was too heartbreaking. I'd never seen such display of grief—so sincere, so all-encompassing, so *real*. I stood there for a moment watching her, when the strangest feeling came over me—a kind of angry discomfort, making me want to yell at her, or run away, or both. It was so out of place, so wrong for the moment, that it took me a second to figure out what it was. And it was jealousy. I was actually jealous of Tristan's grief.

But I had to ask myself: Why? Why did I want to feel that way? Why did I want to be so overwhelmed with angst and pain that I couldn't even move? I'd been sad, of course; constantly sad. And I'd been angry and confused and everything else you're supposed to feel when someone dies. So why did I want—why did I need—to feel it all more?

I thought about this for a while, as I stood watching her from the hallway, but I never came up with any answers. So I tried to just detach myself from this strange emotional state. I wrote it off as some "stage of grief" the school counselor would try to tell me about—some brief pain to grit my teeth through—and I walked over to sit down beside Tristan on the bed.

Her sobs shuddered to a halt and she peeked one bloodshot eye out from behind her knee.

"It's pretty bad, huh?" I said.

"It just doesn't make any sense." She was clearly holding back hysteria by a thread. "I mean, he could have gone on with his life…even if I had nothing to do with him, he would have had a *good life*...I know that." Then she started sobbing, miserably, again.

I would've tried to console her, but I just didn't know how. Not then. Not in the state I was in. All I came up with was this: "That's just not how life works out, I think." And as soon as that sentence left my mouth, it sounded like the coldest thing in the world.

"Yeah, I know," she spat back at me. "I get it. *God* has a bigger plan. *God* has a purpose. Ryan is with *God* now, so we should all be so fucking happy for him and *God* and the wonderful time they're having together."

"That's not what I meant."

She didn't say anything, not for a while. She just stared at me. And I couldn't tell whether she was mad at me, mad at God, mad at Ryan, or mad at herself, but she was damn sure mad at someone. I started to think about how stuck we all are—every one of us—no matter what we believe about God. If you think that he really is up there in the sky somewhere, controlling you, controlling everyone, controlling everything, then you have to deal with him killing your boyfriend, or your brother, or your son. You have to deal with him letting babies get addicted to drugs, allowing child abuse and murder, permitting genocide and war. And if you don't believe it... well, then you have to deal with there not being a reason for anything at all. You could have never been born, and it wouldn't matter. If someone hurts you, it doesn't matter. If someone dies, it doesn't matter. If they could've not died, or if you could have saved them, then it wouldn't make a damn bit of difference to the universe at all, except that you wouldn't have to feel this way.

So, knowing that there were no words that could make her feel better, I just sat there, letting Tristan glare at me, soaking up her anger until she softened, and softened, and softened, and again began to cry.

She had a few hard sobs—they looked deep; they looked like they shook her through her insides—but then she got herself under control. She sat up against the headboard. She drew her knees into her chest. "I'm sorry, Jonathan," she squeaked. "I know this is probably harder on you than on anyone, even me, and that you just have your own way of showing it. I'm not mad at you. I'm just…I'm just…" Then she fell back into the tears, but this time even harder, like she had collapsed completely inside herself. Like she was choking.

So then I wasn't quite sure what to do, what to say, how to handle the situation. I mean, do I comfort her? Do I just scoot right on over and put a hand on her back and tell her that it's all right and say something wholesome or optimistic or whatever, just to get her to calm down, or at least to stop crying?

I waited for a pause, but she just kept going. And going. Finally, I patted her on the knee, cautiously, and said something lame, like, "I'm sure Ryan wouldn't want you to be so upset."

Her sobs slowed to a halt. She looked up at me, wiping her eyes. "What makes you so sure about that?"

"I don't know. It's just something to say, you know, to—"

"I know. I'm sorry. Never mind." And then she seemed to drift off again, staring at the wall like if I wasn't even there.

I looked at Ryan's alarm clock, and saw that I had better get moving if I wanted to make it to Cassie's house in time. "Well, I've got to, um…change. So…I'll see you around."

Tristan's gaze wandered over to me. She blinked, shivered. "Bye, Jonathan."

I took in the room, for the millionth time and for the first. It was all still there, like it always had been: Ryan's trophies and posters, the pictures of him in his uniforms, and one with Tristan at a formal dance the year before. And it seemed foreign for those few seconds. In truth, I hadn't spent much time in there over the previous years…I almost felt like I was trespassing.

"Okay, bye," I said. And I was about to leave, when it occurred to me that Tristan just might be able to help me with my mission. I swung back around. "Hey Tris?"

"Yeah?"

I felt sheepish, shy, timid. "Before you leave, can you just happen to mention to my mom that there's…I don't know… like a student prayer service or something at the school later?"

"A prayer service? *You* want to go to a prayer service?"

"No. Of course not. I don't even think there is one. I was just wondering if you could maybe mention to my mom that there is."

It took her a second, but she got it. "Ooooh." Then she chuckled. "Well, you are in high school now, I guess you have to start sneaking out sometime."

"Right."

"So what is it? A party? You better not be drinking on a school night."

"No, of course not. No party, no drinking."

"So?"

And here's the problem: I couldn't possibly tell her what it really was (how could I, I mean, really?), so I tried get close to the truth, as close as I could, anyway. I said, "It's…it's a girl."

"Really? A girl?"

"Yup. A girl."

"Who is she?" Tristan asked. "Do I know her?"

"Oh, I doubt it," I mumbled. "She's just some girl…anyway, I've got to go…finish up my homework. You won't forget to tell my mom about the prayer service?"

"No," she said, but she must have been distracted by some thought. "I won't forget."

I tried to look sincere. "Thanks, Tris." Then I made a dash for my room before she could ask any more questions.

Twenty

As agreed, Henry was waiting behind a tree at the edge of my lawn at precisely five o'clock. Getting past my mom was easy (Tristan must have done her job well) so I was feeling pretty good as I walked up and patted Henry on the back. "So you ready, Detective H-Bomb?"

Henry looked up at me, anxiety painted all over his face. "I don't know about this, Jonathan."

I reached down, helping him up. "What's not to know? It'll be fine."

"But what about Alistair?"

"Alistair won't be anywhere near that house."

"But what if he is? What if he shows up unexpectedly?"

"Then we run away. He's not going to do anything to us at his own house."

"Fine," he said, stuffing his hands in his pockets. "Let's get this over with."

So we began the thirty-minute walk to the St. Claire house, and I filled Henry in on the details of the plan. It was really very simple: I go in, and start working with Cassie until I have the lay of the land, then excuse myself to use the bathroom. On the way to the bathroom I stop in Alistair's room and open the window (making sure to close his door on my way back out). Then Henry climbs in, makes a copy of the hard drive on Alistair's computer, and climbs back out when he's done.

Also (as I assured Henry a hundred times during the walk) if for any reason things seemed too dangerous, we'd just abandon the whole thing, I'd finish my homework with Cassie and we'd come up with another idea for another day.

"Just remember," I told Henry. "We need real, solid, irrefutable evidence this time, so make sure to get as much as you can from his computer. Videos, email, phone records, whatever. Did you bring something we can use to copy files from his computer?"

He nodded and pulled a tiny portable hard drive from his pocket. "It's 512 gigabytes," he said. "Should suffice."

"Good," I said. "Perfect. But don't lose sight of the other evidence either. If you see a football jersey or a dirty pair of cleats, you grab those too."

"He's at football practice now, Jonathan. He will be wearing his jersey and cleats."

"Right," I said. "Good point. But still, you know, keep an eye out."

Henry rolled his eyes. "Sure."

All in all, it seemed like a solid plan: conservative, uncomplicated, well-thought-out, and with plenty of opportunities to adapt, adjust, alter, or abort. And at the beginning, at least, everything looked quite positive.

First of all, we couldn't have asked for a better house—it turned out to be a sprawling ranch, all one-story, with plenty of tall shrubs around the yard, easily capable of concealing little Henry. So I was feeling optimistic when I stepped up to the front patio and rang the doorbell, finally setting our plan into action.

Cassie's mom came to the door. This, I must admit, was a little disconcerting. I expected her to be home, of course, but in my imaginings I somehow figured that she would be permanently out of sight, holed up in the den or the kitchen like my own mother always was.

"Hi," she said, elongating the "iiiiiii" in the same sappy, sympathetic way every adult did with me since Ryan had died. "You must be Jonathan."

I decided that the best idea would be to play up the brokenhearted-brother angle to gain her trust, so I put my saddest, brave-little-man-smile on and said, "It's nice to meet you, Mrs. St. Claire."

"It's Miss Morrison now, or again, rather, but anyway it's nice to meet you too. Come on in. Cassie's in the kitchen, having a snack. Are you hungry?"

Well, this was good news and bad news: good that Mrs. St. Claire was now Miss Morrison (so I was right about the dad not being around), but bad that Cassie was having a snack in the kitchen, where surely Miss Morrison would want to linger and ask all sorts of questions about how I, and my family, were doing. "Sure," I said, trying my best to imitate a wounded puppy being offered a bone. "I'd love a snack. Thank you."

"Of course," she said. "Right this way."

She led me back through the house toward the kitchen, and instantly I began inspecting and cataloguing everything I saw. It was a nice house—warm and cozy, decorated in a haphazard country sort of style with lots of wallpaper and curtains, pictures of family on every wall, trinkets and vases and bowls of candy on every surface—in other words, it was the exact opposite of the magazine showroom that my own house was. I also noticed, more importantly, that I was right in my initial assessment of the layout. The bedrooms all seemed to be bunched up at the far end of the house, right where Henry was waiting.

As we turned into the kitchen, Miss Morrison was saying, "Cassie, your friend is…" but I lost the rest of sentence as soon as I saw her. I guess it was because when we first met it was dark, and the next time she was in her school uniform, but this felt like the first time I'd ever *really* seen her. Now, as I said before, Cassie wasn't "classically" pretty the way your typical leading-lady-movie star or fashion magazine cover girl is pretty—her features were somehow sharper, more angular than that, and her eyes, my God, her long almond eyes, pale blue with strawberry eyebrows—one always cocked just a little higher than the other; like she was trying to figure out your secret, or else tease you with her own.

"Hey Jon," said Cassie in a singsong sort of voice. "Take a seat. Have a brownie."

Peeling my eyes away from her, I found the next most appealing thing to settle them on: a tray of steaming straight-from-the-mix brownies sitting right beside a frosty bottle of milk. It struck me as so strange (my mother was incapable of making anything so normal). It almost made me laugh, looking so perfect and simple and wholesomely American.

"Thanks," I said, taking a seat and picking up a brownie.

The brownies were delicious, of course, and I was just about to complement Ms. Morrison, when she picked her purse up off the counter, swung it over her shoulder and said, "Okay, I've got to run up to the school for the parents' association meeting. I'll be back in about an hour and a half. You guys need anything before I go?"

Cassie shook her head as I began to calculate this new turn of events: one and a half hours without having to worry about anyone but Cassie getting in my way. This was well within the time frame I originally had in mind.

"Well, alright," Miss Morrison called from the front hallway. "See you in a bit."

"Bye Mom," yelled back Cassie.

"Thanks for the brownies," I said.

Cassie looked down the front hall as her mother's steps sounded toward the door, and finally through it. When the screen door slammed, she said. "Thank God she's gone. I was afraid she wouldn't leave us alone if she stayed here."

"Yeah, thank God."

She stared straight at me, her face all business. "Okay. So what's your whole deal?"

"My whole...deal?" I said, confused. "I, um...I don't know. I'm just a regular sort of kid, I guess. I like punk music, and skateboarding...but I'm not sure what you're..."

"No," she giggled. "What's your deal with school? What are you falling behind in?"

I paused for a second, even more confused than before. Then I remembered: Ah, yes. This was my reason for coming over. "Right," I said. "Sorry. I'm a little flustered these days."

"Don't worry about it."

"Math, mostly. And Biology, a little. We haven't really done anything in my other classes yet, as far as I can tell."

"Well I'm sure you have, but you're right to be most concerned with Math and Bio. If you fall behind in those, it's really hard to catch up."

"Right."

"So let's go, then," she said, snatching one more brownie and popping up from her chair. "Grab your backpack."

"Okay." I grabbed another brownie for myself and followed after her. "Where are we going?"

"My room. We can look through my old assignments."

"Old assignments?"

"Yeah, I'm a packrat. I have pretty much everything I've ever done since kindergarten in my room. We'll just find the assignments you're missing, you can copy them into your handwriting, and we'll be done with the whole homework thing in no time."

"Wow." I was impressed.

She paused for moment just before opening her bedroom door. "Then we can pick back up with your whole skateboarding and punk deal…"

I shuffled in, sitting myself down on her thick yellow carpet that was covered in clothes and magazines and schoolbooks. Just from the look of her room, I could tell this girl was unusual—in the best possible of ways. Her walls were a collage of hastily painted patches of black and neon green, surrounded by rock posters and drawings and pixelated meme print-outs and at least a million tiny stickers (mostly pink and purple unicorns, with the occasional My Little Pony thrown in).

I just sat there, taking it all in as she searched through her train-wreck of a closet for the homework. Not surprisingly, it took a few minutes before I realized that, as entranced as I was, I had completely forgotten to look around the hallway for Alistair's room, an open window, or much of anything that had to do with my actual purpose for being there.

From inside the closet, I heard Cassie's muffled voice saying, "Okay, I found Bio. Now where the heck is my math work?"

So I was faced with a major dilemma: I could only really "go to the bathroom" once. If I went right away, then I risked not finding Alistair's room at all (it could have, after all, been on the other end of the house, or even in the basement, for all I knew). If I waited, then I might not have an opportunity to leave Cassie's room until after her mom (or worse, Alistair) returned home.

What I needed was another reason to wander back out into the house, preferably alone. But before I could come up with one, Cassie emerged from the closet with a big stack of papers, sat down Indian-style in front of me, and plopped them all onto the ground. "There," she said. "Math and Bio, ninth grade. Now let's see your planner."

"My what?"

"Your school planner. That thing with the school crest on the front that they give you to write all of your homework in."

"Oh," I said. "Right"

"You really haven't paid any attention at all in school yet, have you?"

I unzipped my backpack and began fumbling through its contents. "No," I replied quietly. "Not really."

She watched me search in vain for a little while. Then out of nowhere, she asked, "Do you think about Ryan a lot?"

Her question froze me. It was the first time someone had asked me about Ryan when I couldn't just shrug and walk away. When I didn't want to just walk away. So I decided to tell her the truth: "Constantly," I said.

"Really?" She sounded almost surprised.

"Is that hard to believe?"

"No," she shot back. "You just don't seem so…I don't know…"

"Sad?"

"Yeah. Why is that?"

"I don't know. I *am* sad. But, it's…"

"It's what?"

"It's like I have to concentrate to feel it. And even then, it's far away."

She slid a little closer to me on the carpet. "I don't think that's so weird. I felt the same way when my grandmother died. And you…this is so much bigger."

"But shouldn't that just make me sadder?"

She looked off thoughtfully, staring out the window, where a few raindrops were beginning to splash onto the glass. "I think it works the other way around. The bigger something is, the harder it is to feel. The longer it takes to sink in…"

"Yeah."

"I guess that's why people believe in God. To make sense of it all in the meantime."

I turned to her, suspicious. "Don't you believe in God?"

"Sometimes I do. And then sometimes I don't. And most of the time I just don't know." She shrugged. "What about you?"

Figuring, well, as long as I was going with honesty, I said, "No, actually. Not at all. Not even a little bit."

She looked surprised, and a little curious, as if I'd just revealed that I was really a secret agent. "Not at all? That's pretty bold. Why not?"

"That's a big question."

"But you must have a reason."

A million different reasons came barreling into mind, but I couldn't quite organize my thoughts into a coherent or concrete *why*. Before, when I'd been asked this question (like with Mr. Finger) I just brushed it off. Usually, people didn't really want to know why, they just wanted to look for some kind of flaw in your psyche, a trauma from your childhood, or some other "problem" you have that makes you different from everyone else so they could paint you into a corner and not have to worry that they might ever be like you. But I didn't want to do that with Cassie. I wanted to tell her—to try to tell her—why I just couldn't believe. But those days, ever since Ryan and Alistair and Jesus Jackson and the rest of it, my reasons were even more confused and conflicted than ever before. So I just started talking, hoping something coherent would come out eventually.

This is what I said:

"It just doesn't make sense. And it's a little absurd, when you think about it—the whole concept of some white-bearded guy up in the clouds, making every little decision about every little thing in every little person's life. Listening to your thoughts, giving a crap about whether you tell a little lie, or curse, or copy someone's homework." I gestured down at the stacks of paper, and Cassie giggled, charmingly. "It's all so damned convenient, you know? Life is too complex, too random, and too fucking sad for it all to wind up in some kind of marsh-mallow wonderland in the sky, where everything that ever happened, happened for a reason. I don't know, it just feels like some cheesy ending to a crappy movie."

Cassie didn't meet my eyes for a few seconds. She stared at her fluffy yellow carpet, seeming unsure of what she was about to say next. I was afraid that I'd offended her, so I said, "Look, I'm sorry. I didn't mean to insult you—"

But she cut me off. And she asked the one question that I'd been avoiding since last Saturday: "So, where's Ryan, then?"

"That's a good question."

"But don't you want to believe he's in heaven…or whatever, don't you believe that he's *somewhere*? I mean, I don't believe all the stuff about fluffy clouds and angels and whatever, but I do believe that we go somewhere after we die. That there's something more than this. Don't you?"

"I would love to," I whispered, thinking about Jesus Jackson out there constructing my faith in….something (or nothing, as the case may be). "If I could just snap my fingers and have faith, I'd like to believe a lot of things. I'd like to believe that I'm not going to feel like this forever. I'd like to believe that nothing bad will ever happen to anyone I know again, and that there won't be any more war, or famine, or AIDS in Africa, and that I'll grow up to be a millionaire rock star living in a huge mansion with a girl like you."

This last part just kind of slipped out. I got nervous for a second, but then Cassie smiled—this big, proud, awesome smile—and reached her hand behind my head, pulled my face to hers, and kissed me.

I should mention that this was not, technically, my first kiss. But from that point on I would consider it as much. After all, this was no mere middle school swirling of saliva, no awkward summer-camp smacking of lips and groping of unknown and underappreciated parts. She tore into me, Cassie did. This was deep, and furious. This was bordering on obscene. This was *awesome*.

At any rate, we kissed for a little while (I really don't know how long), and, of course, during the whole time I did not think once about Henry or Alistair or Ryan or Jesus-goddamned-Jackson. In fact, I didn't think about a thing until about a minute after we stopped, when Cassie looked at the clock and said, "Wow, my mom will be home in like fifteen minutes and we haven't even done anything yet."

Then it all came crashing down on me—my purpose, Alistair, Henry outside in the bushes. I jumped up from our still-curled position on the floor. "I have to go to the bathroom," I blurted.

She looked at me strangely. "Okay...it's down the hall, on your right, just after Alistair's door."

I smiled awkwardly and darted into the hall, thankful, at least, that I got lucky about Alistair's room. I paused in the hallway, listening for any sign that Cassie would peek out her door. I heard her turn on some music, so I figured I was safe, and darted into Alistair's room. I unlocked the window, threw open the screen, and found myself face to face with a sopping wet and very angry Henry.

I looked past him, to the deluge that had begun at some point while I wasn't paying attention. "When did it start to rain?"

"An hour ago," he hissed. "Where were you?"

"I got held up. Long story. Listen, you're going to have to hurry."

"Obviously."

"Hold on," I said, looking back over my shoulder. "Give me two minutes to go flush the toilet and get back to Cassie's room. Then you come in, but be quick about it."

Henry glared at me, fuming. I attempted a reassuring smile, but I don't think it did much good.

"Just make sure no one comes in here," Henry whispered, as I closed the door behind me.

When I got back into Cassie's room, I found her pacing back-and-forth, chewing on her fingernails, and clearly distressed. I was about to ask her what was wrong, when she turned to me and blurted out, "I'm sorry. Okay? I'm just... really sorry."

I stopped, one hand still on the doorknob. "What for?"

"I just...I shouldn't have done that, you know? I shouldn't have kissed you." She continued pacing, but even faster than before. "You were opening up to me in a very real and honest and vulnerable way and, you know, I had just thought you were really cute at the party the other night, but even then I told myself, I said, "Cassie you know you really should just let this guy be, let him heal, the last thing he needs in his life right now is you,' and I was totally and truly planning on leaving you alone, but then you—" She stopped, pointing at me almost accusatorially. "You came up to me in the cafeteria and you were still just as cute—maybe even cuter, all asking me for help, and then still, as I was eating my brownie and waiting for you to get here I was saying, `Just don't kiss him, Cassie. Just don't kiss him, Cassie. Just don't kiss him, Cassie' and what do I do the minute you say just one thing nice about me—which, of course, was in a hypothetical scenario anyway so doesn't even really count—but what do I do? I kiss you." She turned, pressing her head into her dresser. "So STUPID!"

What could I say? I was stunned. Completely speechless. Of course, the kiss itself was a surprise, but this subsequent meltdown was just completely out of left field.

Seeing that I was not about to respond too quickly, she said, "Anyway, sorry. I'll understand if you just want to leave."

Once again, without anything sensible to say, I resorted to honesty. "What are you talking about? That was great."

Cassie walked over to me, a sadly patronizing look on her face. "You're sweet," she said, gently touching my chin. "I know it was great. But it was still a terrible, terrible idea."

"Why?"

She flopped back onto the floor, pulling her knees into her face. "Because I'm a mess! I'm a train-wreck and a disaster of a girlfriend even for regular boys, for perfectly healthy, didn't-just-lose-their-brother boys. It would be awful for you. Awful."

Truth be told, my mind ceased to clearly recognize anything she said past that one word: girlfriend. Yes, I caught that she was saying that it was a bad idea—that much I understood—but just the fact that she was saying it was *any* kind of an idea, just saying that it was on the table as a possibility blew away every other thought of why I was in that house, what had just happened in my life, or anything other than that one word: girlfriend.

I was about to say something about it, too—at least, to gain some clarity on the matter—but right at that moment I heard a door slam somewhere on the other side of the house, and a loud, deep, masculine voice, yelling, "Cassie! Where the hell is mom?" And then a pause. And then, "Cool. Fucking brownies."

All the blood rushed right out of my head; I nearly passed out. How long had it been since I saw Henry? Five minutes? Two minutes? Thirty seconds? Damn this redheaded vixen! She'd messed up my entire sense of time and organization. However long it'd been, I was sure Henry was still in Alistair's room.

Cassie must have noticed the worried look on my face. She peered out the window and rolled her eyes. "Practice must have been rained out. Don't sweat it, he won't bother us…too much."

"Right, yeah, no problem." I was just hoping that Henry heard Alistair as clearly as we had. But what if he hadn't? What if he was behind Alistair's desk, or in his closet, or under his bed, and couldn't hear a thing? I had to think of a way to get myself out of Cassie's room again, if only for a moment.

Before I could think of anything, though, Cassie walked over to me and took both of my hands in hers. She said, "Maybe someday we can do this. Maybe this summer, or next year…once you've healed."

I didn't know what to say. I had this incredible urge to scream—in protest, in fear—but then all I could focus on was the sound of those footsteps approaching from the other side of the house. So I froze. Half of me was trying desperately to pull away and go running out to save Henry, while the other half wanted nothing more than to stay right where I was and convince Cassie that she was wrong—terribly, terribly wrong.

In the hallway, just outside Cassie's room, a door slammed. And then Alistair's voice, loud, yelled: "What the *hell* is going on here?!"

The bottom dropped out from under me. My knees wobbled and sank. I whispered, "I'm sorry."

Cassie cocked her head a bit, seeming confused by my barely audible apology. She opened her lips to speak.

BANG BANG BANG. It was Cassie's door. She let go of my hands, yelled, "What?!"

Alistair threw open the door, yelling, "Why the hell—" but cut himself off when he saw me. His whole demeanor changed, and he looked—I swear—a little scared. "What are you doing here, Stiles?" he asked.

"I'm helping him make up his class work," Cassie said. "What do you want?"

Alistair's eyes darted from me to Cassie and back a few times. He said, almost in whine, "Someone left my window open. My carpet is all wet."

"You probably did it yourself. Now leave us alone, okay?"

Alistair glared at us both, whispered, "Whatever," and shuffled out of the room.

———

Two minutes later, after having given Cassie some phenomenally lame excuse about forgetting a dentist appointment, or something, I was bursting out of the St. Claire's front door, running headlong into the pouring rain.

I made it about twenty feet through the front yard when I heard Alistair's voice calling, "Wait!" from somewhere behind me.

I stopped in a puddle of mud. I could feel the muck seeping in through the mesh in my sneakers. I turned, and there he was:

standing on the front stoop, staring me down while the rain drenched his hair and his clothes. "Oh," I said. "Hey, Alistair."

He didn't move; he didn't even seem to notice the rain. "What's this all about, Stiles?"

"What do you mean? I'm just—like Cassie said—getting some help with my class work."

"Since when do you know Cassie?"

"We met at that party. You know, the one you invited us to?"

He wiped some of the water from his eyes. "Yeah?"

"And then she offered to help me out."

Alistair drew a deep, slow breath. Then another. "So how'd it go then? The class work?"

"Good," I lied. "We got a lot done."

"So then you won't need to come back here?" he said, taking a single step in my direction. "Right?"

I got the hint. "Right."

Alistair's shoulders seemed to relax a little. He stood there for another few seconds, then turned without a word, and walked back into the house.

Twenty-one

It took me almost ten minutes of searching behind shrubs and trees and mailboxes and cars, before I finally found Henry. He was all curled up in a little ball, cowering beneath a rose bush in a yard across the street.

"I thought you were a dead man," I said.

"I almost was," he replied, shuffling over to me like a little boy who just got his lunch money stolen, his clothes and face covered in grass stains and dirt. "I had to dive out the window at the last minute. I think I sprained my face."

I laughed. "So how did it go?"

"Bad," he said, his eyes remaining glued to his feet. "Really bad."

Shit, I thought. "So you didn't find anything?"

"Nothing," he replied. "But that's not the bad part…"

Now I was confused. "What do you mean? What could be worse than not finding anything?"

Henry looked apologetic, even embarrassed. "I left the hard drive in there."

"You did what?"

"I was in the middle of copying files when he came back, and I didn't even think about it. I just jumped out the window…"

"So we've probably been figured out already? Is that what you're telling me?"

"No," he said. "Probably not. It was an older desktop computer, so I had to plug the hard drive into the back. Unless he happens to look on the floor behind his desk, he'll never know it's there."

"Jesus, Henry," I said, shaking my head.

"Don't get mad at me!" he snapped. "What took you so long in there anyway?"

"Well, she kind of…kissed me."

"She what?!"

"It wasn't my fault."

"I was in there risking my life and you were making out?!"

"Well I couldn't just *stop*. She would have been suspicious!"

Henry threw his arms up in exasperation. "Right. Of course you couldn't. I'm in there, on the verge of a brain-damaging beating, all for *your* brother, and you couldn't possibly think of a way to NOT be hooking up!"

I stared at my shoes. He was right, of course. I had forgotten all about Henry and my brother and our whole plan while I was in there. "Sorry," I muttered.

"You know what?" he said. "I'm done. This whole thing is absurd, anyway. You want to play detective, play it by yourself." And with that, Henry turned and stormed off toward his house.

I didn't know what the hell to do. Maybe he was right. Maybe this whole thing was stupid. How was a kid like me going to prove anything to anybody? I still had no hard evidence, no real idea what happened to Ryan after I left, and no hope of figuring any of it out at all. As far as I could see, there was pretty much no good reason for me to continue with any of it. I might as well just give up, and get on with my life. What difference would any of it make in the end, anyway?

There was just one thing holding me back: the look on Alistair's face when he first saw me in Cassie's room, and then again in the yard. It wasn't just confused, or concerned, or even worried. There was fear in his face. Real *fear*. I was sure of it.

No, I decided, I couldn't just give up. There was no turning back now. No wussing out of anything. Alistair was hiding something, something about Ryan…and if I didn't figure out what it was, no one ever would. And that just wasn't acceptable.

So I started off back home, thinking about what my next step should be, when I heard an all too familiar voice calling my name. "Jonathan. Hey, Jonathan. Over here!"

I wheeled around, already knowing exactly who I'd find, in full view of the streetlight, the house, yard—everything. It was Tristan.

I tried to play it cool. "Hey, Tris. What are you doing over here? I was just getting some homework—"

"Get in."

I swallowed hard, walked over, and climbed into her jeep. My first priority was not to give up anything until I was sure she already knew it. I looked over at the house, and sure enough, both Alistair and Cassie's windows were visible, though at least partially obscured by some bushes. She very well may not have seen Henry sneaking in. I'd just have to feel it out.

But as soon as I closed the door behind me, Tristan said, "Why are you here? And what the hell did you and your little friend steal from Al's house?"

"Nothing," I said. "We didn't steal anything. And I was just doing some homework with Cassie. Why are you here?"

"I gave Alistair a ride home," she snapped. "I was just about to leave when I saw some kid jumping out of Al's window and then you come running like a crazy person out of their front door."

Okay, so playing this safe was no longer an option. "Look, it's not what you think."

"I don't know what to think. I don't think anything. I just want to know what the hell you guys are up to."

"Just…just don't worry about it, okay?"

"Don't worry about it?" she said, with kind of a nervous, manic laugh at the edge of her voice. "Are you kidding me?"

"No," I said. "It's nothing."

She put a hand on my shoulder, gently. "Is this about Ryan? Because if this is about Ryan, then…then you *have* to tell me what's going on."

For the first time since I got in the car, I looked Tristan in the eyes. Far from the angry woman I was expecting, what I saw looking back at me was just a broken, shattered little girl, on the edge of falling into tears. It occurred to me that, whatever it was in me that needed to find out about Alistair and Ryan and what happened behind the school, Tristan probably had it too.

I gave in. "So, how well do you know Alistair?"

"What do you mean?" she asked. "I know him fine…."

"Well," I said, taking a long pause. "I have reason to believe that he may be at least partially responsible for Ryan's death."

Out of all of the responses I'd have thought such an accusation would have elicited—surprise, laughter, suspicion, skepticism, concern—the one I got was the last one I ever would have expected.

A halted, choked-back cry of emotion tried to escape from her throat, but she swallowed it back to a barely audible squeak. Her voice shaking, almost on the verge of collapse, she whispered, "I figured that's why you were over here. So what have you come up with? Anything we can use?"

Instantly, my entire view of Tristan changed. Where I had been thinking of her as an obstacle, here she had revealed herself, with a few short words, to be a possible ally in all of this.

And sure, maybe I should have been a bit more skeptical. Maybe there was something a little too easy about how quickly she revealed her suspicions; something, perhaps, even calculating about the way she inserted herself into the middle of my plan. But what can I say? At the moment, I had nothing—or almost nothing—and my one ally just left me standing in the rain on a street corner.

So, what else could I do? I said, "Are you willing to help?"

"Of course," she said, wiping a tear from her cheek. "I've already started. Look." And with that she pointed over at the St. Claire house, toward Alistair's window. Inside, Alistair was rummaging around, appearing as if he lost something rather important. "That's a little suspicious, don't you think?"

"It sure is."

"So what did you find?"

I shrugged. "Unfortunately, not much. Today was a total failure."

"So you have nothing? No proof, evidence, anything?"

"No," I said. "I mean, not *nothing*…" and then I began to tell Tristan the abbreviated version of the story (leaving out, among other things, my make-out session with Cassie), while she drove back to my house. It took the whole ride for me to get through just the shortened version, so we were pulling into the driveway when I finally said, "…and then you came out of nowhere and scared the hell out of me."

Tristan nodded, deep in thought. "Well, we're going to have to do better," she said. "And we're going to have to get that hard drive back."

"Yeah, I know." Honestly, I was hoping for a little more insight from her than that. "Any ideas?"

Tristan stared out at my house, in the direction of my brother's window. His light was on, which means my mother was in there somewhere, probably dusting, or refolding already clean clothes, or just standing at his closet door, holding onto a sleeve of his favorite jacket. "Why don't you tell it all to me again?" she said, her voice cracking slightly. "But this time don't leave out anything. Not a detail."

And so I proceeded to tell Tristan everything, in the utmost detail…or at least, almost everything. I left out Jesus Jackson, of course, and the fact that I had just kissed Cassie so long and so wonderfully. But everything else, I laid out in its entirety: what happened in the woods, what Henry and I had found, the party, jersey numbers, the footprints, the plan with Cassie—everything. After all of it, though, Tristan didn't come up with any new ideas. She just listened intently, seeming to lose her concentration every so often, glazing over as she stared up at that window.

After I said good-bye and went inside, I found my mother right where I thought she would be, in Ryan's room, sitting in the center of the floor. But she didn't notice me. Her eyes were closed, and she looked as if she'd been crying. I saw that her lips were parted, and barely moving, as if repeating some silent prayer. I hurried past, not wanting to disturb her.

A few minutes later I looked out my window to find Tristan's car still right where I had left it in the driveway. She, like my mother, was just sitting there: her eyes closed, her cheeks wet, silently speaking words I could never know, or understand.

Twenty-two

My mother was never the type of woman to admit defeat easily. By the spring of 2009, when she finally kicked my father out for good, it was only after chasing off no less than four of his varied and voluptuous mistresses—the last one right across our own front lawn, in front of me and Ryan (we had been told to "wait in the car"), holding a carving knife in one hand and a few inches of the woman's black hair in the other.

And yet she had no choice but to admit defeat when it came to the salvation of her sons. After all, in the wake of our response to the "burning of the list," what other choice did she have? Instead of scaring us back toward the path of righteousness, her strategy had just strengthened our resolve to find a path of our own. And by the end of that school year—a year in which she lost not only her sons' souls, but her marriage and her house as well—she had finally had enough.

You see, the first thing Ryan did after we wrote our new list was to march out into the hall and tape it to his bedroom door. When my mom ripped it down in a fit of rage he just wrote a new one and taped it up the following day…until she ripped that one down, too…and the next, and the next. It wasn't until that June, when he made a hundred photocopies and pasted them around his room with wallpaper glue, that she finally relented in a storm of tears.

The next day she informed us that Ryan would be starting at St. Soren's in the fall, and that if I didn't shape up, I would be joining him there too. Even worse, she told us that we would both be going to a "counseling session" with Father Kevin just as soon as she could schedule one.

The threat of a meeting with Father Kevin made us back off for a little while, and things settled down for the better part of the summer. Then, about a week before Ryan was supposed to start at St. Soren's, he decided (without consulting me, by the way) to tape another copy of the list to his door.

Within twenty-four hours, our mother had scheduled a meeting with Father Kevin.

At first, I didn't think too much of it (except for being annoyed about the counseling session), but then I noticed one day that there was an asterisk next to the first item on the list: the one that listed the reasons why Christianity was false. I looked to bottom of the page and found the following footnote, scribbled in tiny handwriting in the margins of the page:

Also Mom—no way she's right about all of this.

A few days later there was another footnote—this one scrawled across three or for Post-it notes under the original.

**More important than any of these reasons, however, is the fact that Christianity is fundamentally immoral. Any god that would create a living being, and then allow that living being to spend eternity in Hell just for not bowing down and worshipping him, is clearly lacking in any sense of morality, and must therefore be considered both evil and corrupt.*

Even this, however, didn't concern me that much (after all, we had discussed ideas like that plenty of times before). And I didn't really start to question Ryan until the night before our meeting with the priest.

As usual, we were in Ryan's room, sitting at his desk, with me at the computer and Ryan taking notes. At the moment, I was searching through Wikipedia trying to figure out if any of the more antiquated religions (Manichaeism, Tengriism, Ashurism, etc.) were supported by any kind of actual evidence (spoiler: they weren't), when I noticed that Ryan was scribbling down notes at feverish pace, despite the fact that I hadn't given him anything to write about.

"What's all that?" I asked.

"What's all what?" he asked, not even looking up from the page.

"That stuff you're writing."

"Oh," he said, looking up. "This…right. Well, I'm working out an argument comparing the basic principles of Catholic Theology to the speeches that Adolf Hitler gave in the years before World War II."

"But…why? We already have a like million reasons why *all* denominations of Christianity are fake."

"I know, I know. I just think we need a slightly more sophisticated set of arguments against a religion as corrupt and self-righteous as Catholicism."

"But Ryan, you were the one who said that we're not supposed to be focusing on things we *don't believe*. We're supposed to be trying to find something that's *actually real*."

"Of course," he said quickly. "You're right. I mean…we are looking for things that we *can* believe in, it's just that… It's just…"

"It's just what?"

He dropped his pen and put his head in his hands. After a long while of silence, he whispered, "It's just that I don't think I can take it there, Jonathan."

Instantly, I knew he was talking about St. Soren's. Up until that point he hadn't spoken about starting school there much at all (except in the usual ways: he would miss his old friends, he wanted to try out for the football team, he heard the food there was awful…), but I knew it must have been freaking him out.

"I figured you were dreading it. But all you've talked about is joining the football team and making friends and stuff."

He ran his palm up and down the back of his head, staring at his socks. "All that will be fine, I guess. But I've been talking to people. People who go there. They have these masses… and assemblies…and prayers, God, prayers before every goddamned class. The Our Father, and Hail Mary, and whatever, and you have to say them over and over and over, like it's some kind of a brainwashing technique, and even that wouldn't be so bad, except that everyone I've talked to just accepts it all. All of it. They just eat that god shit up like they've never thought about what it all means for one second in their whole lives."

Ryan seemed genuinely pained. I tried to think of something to say, but nothing came to me. After a while, he continued: "I don't know, Jonathan. Maybe you're right. Maybe it does go against the basic idea of what we're doing here, and maybe we do already have more than enough reasons to not believe in this one god…but I just feel like I need more. Like if I'm going to spend the next four years surrounded by this one religion—if we're going to sit down for an hour with a priest tomorrow—that I need every reason I can find for why this god isn't the right one. Does that make any sense to you?"

I thought about it, trying to put myself in his shoes. I was just facing down one meeting with Father Kevin, but Ryan was facing four years at St. Soren's—four years of sitting in that school all day, four years of listening to those prayers, of forced confessions and communions. Four years of being an outcast—different from everyone else at the core of his personality.

Finally, I said, "Of course, it makes perfect sense. Whatever you want to do, Ryan, I'm right behind you."

Now, in retrospect, I wonder what would have happened if I hadn't added those last four words; if I hadn't promised him my complete and utter allegiance. Surely having me behind him must have bolstered his confidence, must have been a large part of egging him on to the things that he would say that next day to Father Kevin. Perhaps if I hadn't gone along with it, things would have been different. His actions, and his philosophies, wouldn't have descended so quickly. Perhaps everything would be different. Maybe he'd still be alive

Twenty-three

By my estimation, I had learned exactly three things in my first six days at St. Soren's Academy.

One: If I entered the school through the cafeteria loading dock exactly thirty seconds before the start of first period, I could make it all the way to my class without having to make eye contact with anyone.

Two: Jesus Christ (or God, or the Holy Spirit, or whatever) really fucking loved my brother but decided that he should totally die anyway.

Three: People generally seemed more comfortable the further away I was from them.

So, considering all of that (and the fact that I really didn't want to face Cassie), I decided not to bother with school at all on the morning after my night of espionage at the St. Claire house. It turned out to be fairly easy to get out of, luckily—no faking of nausea or headaches or fever required. I just wandered down to the kitchen in the morning and told my mom that I wasn't quite up for it. She started beaming like it was fucking Christmas, and launched right into the preparation of yet another elaborate breakfast. I wasn't actually hungry, but I figured it was a small price to pay for a free day off school.

She was so excited that she forgot to call my father to tell him not to pick me up for school. So about twenty minutes later I heard a knock on my bedroom door, and his voice calling, "You ready, champ?"

I shuffled over and cracked the door. "Champ of what?"

He looked uncomfortable and confused, but only for a moment. "I don't know...whatever you want. Why are you still in your pajamas?" He gave me a little pretend punch in the arm. "Let's get this show on the road, little buddy!" This was just like my father. It was as if he picked up all of these catch phrases and behaviors from watching fake fathers on TV, but could never quite get the timing right.

"I'm not going to school today," I said, shuffling back to bed. "Didn't you notice Mom making breakfast?"

He shook his head, taking a few steps into the room. "No, I didn't notice."

"Didn't she tell you anything?"

"She mumbled something...about something...but I didn't really catch it." He wandered over to my desk and began inspecting the piles of junk, books, and magazines, as if he actually knew, or cared to know, anything about them at all. "So are you not feeling well?"

"I just don't think I can deal today."

"Oh. Okay."

There was a long pause.

"So...," I said, waiting for him to take the hint, and leave. "You don't have to, you know, drive me anywhere."

"Were you aware," my father said, clearly pretending not to have heard me, "that the Buddhists believe that when someone close to you dies you should do good works? That is, you should work hard—or a lot, rather—to, I guess, help them along."

"What are you talking about?"

"I'm just saying…that's what the Buddhists believe. That you should work, hard…or good…I think they're the same thing."

"Since when do you care what Buddhists think?" My father had never once uttered a word about religion that didn't fall somewhere between sarcasm and disdain. That's not to say that he'd ever professed himself an atheist, exactly. He just seemed to think the whole subject was a pointless waste of time…like video games or celebrity gossip. So frankly, it was a bit worrying that he'd chosen this particular moment to start preaching to me about Buddhism.

"I just find it interesting," he said, looking even more uncomfortable than usual. "And helpful. That's all. I think they have some good points, especially about death."

"You? Think the Buddhists have good points? About death?" This was too much to comprehend at such an hour of the morning. "What's next, are you going to start saying the Pope has some good theories on birth control?"

He shot me a slightly annoyed, sidelong glance. He looked as if he was about to reprimand me, but thought better of it. Instead, he walked over and sat at the foot of my bed, giving the mattress a tap (which was a major sign of affection, for him). "Do you think Ryan believed in God? I mean, really believed?"

"No," I replied, although of course I had been obsessing about this question for the entire past week. "Why, do you?"

"I don't know. He seemed to. He told me he did."

I propped myself up on my elbows. "He did? Really? When?"

"About a year ago, after a game. They had been down by twelve for most of the first three quarters, and pulled off a win with just a few minutes to go. He told me the coach prayed with them during halftime, and that's why they won. At first, I thought he was joking."

"He wasn't?"

"He said he wasn't, and acted sort of annoyed when I thought he was. It's just that…"

"What?"

"I don't know…it was probably nothing."

"What was it? What happened?"

My father paused, seeming unsure how to put his thoughts into words. "I just didn't believe him. It just felt like he was giving me a line."

I lay back down and stared up at the ceiling, unsure what to make of any of this. Ryan never said anything like that to me, and I just couldn't picture him saying it to my father. And if he had, what did it mean? I could understand why he'd lie to Mom about believing in God, and even Tristan. But our father? The only sense I could possibly make of it was that Ryan was lying to himself as much as he was lying to our dad. But why? Is that faith? Just lying to yourself without questioning anything? Is that what Jesus Jackson was trying to "build" for me?

"But anyway," my father continued, interrupting my train of thought. "Forget about all that. Do you want to go get some breakfast or something?"

"Mom's making me some already," I pulled the comforter up tight around my neck. "I already told you that."

He stood, nodded. "Well, I'll see you tomorrow then, okay?"

"Yup."

And then he walked out the door, leaving me reeling, lost. So my father's a Buddhist? Is this really what's happening? And my brother—the person who first told me that God doesn't even exist, who taught me how to doubt and question and deny every religion on Earth, especially Christianity—*my brother* believed that God had won his fucking football game?

I couldn't take it anymore. It was one thing for a bunch of relative strangers at school to make assumptions about Ryan's faith, but for our own father to do it? That was just too much.

It seemed pretty clear that I needed to talk to Jesus Jackson.

Twenty-four

The obvious problem, however, was that having stayed home from school, I couldn't just go waltzing past St. Soren's front door and onto the football field. For a few minutes I considered waiting until three, but then, of course, there would be people all around, with practice until six…and this just couldn't wait an entire day.

I decided to take the stealth route. After sneaking out the back door, I skateboarded up to the school, stopping just at the edge of the far fields. The main drive up to the front steps was too obvious, so I looked around for a slightly more hidden entrance. Unfortunately, the only thing I could find was a narrow pathway between the chain-link fence and some large, prickly bushes. I'd clearly have to crawl for a long way if I took it, but from where I stood it seemed that it would lead me right to the gate of the football field unseen.

So I went for it, crawling and squeezing and scratching my way along. By the time I emerged out by the bleachers, my shirt was ripped, my jeans were muddy, my hair was a mess, and I had tiny scratches all over my forearms.

But, at last, I walked out onto that empty field to find… nothing. No Jesus. Not even Nino.

I took a moment to consider what was happening. After all, thus far, every time I'd come to the football field to look for Jesus, he'd been there, so it never occurred to me that maybe I had just been fortunate in my timing. I mean, he probably had other clients, a home, or maybe even another job to go to

But then again, maybe not. Maybe he just waltzed into town, snagged as much deposit money as he could, and waltzed right out when he had his fill.

I walked out onto the field, staring out toward the woods and all around, but I didn't see anything. Eventually, I wound up lying down flat in the end zone, staring at the lazy autumn clouds. *Well,* I thought, *I guess this is what's become of my big plan.* I had nothing on Alistair, Henry hated me, I made a fool of myself with Cassie, and to top it all, I got ripped off by Jesus.

Oh yeah, and my brother was still dead. I didn't want to forget about that one.

I closed my eyes, letting myself sink into the damp grass, feeling the wind blow right over me. And just as I was really getting comfortable with my self-pity, I heard a rustling just beyond the edge of the track. I peeked one eye open, strained my head up a bit to see, and there was Jesus Jackson, walking straight at me from the other side of the field.

I realized right away, though, that something was wrong. Jesus was limping. At first, I assumed he was just walking funny, like he was almost dancing, with a little beat in his step, but as he came closer I realized he was dragging his left foot behind him. Then when he got closer, I began to see that there were rips and scuffmarks and grass stains on his suit, and that his right hand was dangling as limply as his left foot.

I hopped to my feet and ran across the field to help him walk. And as I approached I saw that his face was haggard and beaten: his right eye swollen and black, his cheekbones bruised and puffy, and there was dried blood around the outside of his mouth and in his beard.

"Jesus," I yelled as I ran up and put my arm around his shoulder, supporting some of his weight. "What the hell happened to you?"

"Some…," he began, struggling for breath. "…hooligans… in the woods…I was just walking…jumped me.…"

"Who were they? What did they look like? Was it Alistair?"

Jesus stopped walking, shaking his head as he bent over and put his palms on his knees. "No…they were…older, I think… definitely not high school…kids."

"What did they want? Did they steal anything?"

"I don't…have anything."

"Well we need to get you the emergency room. You could have internal bleeding or something."

Jesus stood upright, or as upright as he could. "No," he said sternly. "I'll be fine. Just…help me over to the bleachers."

So we walked the last few yards across the football field, and up into the stands. Jesus sat down, very slowly, clutching his right knee and wincing as he lowered himself onto the bleachers. He wiped some sweat off his brow and some blood off his lip with the sleeve of his tattered suit, and he said, "So, Jonathan. What's up?"

I still wanted to hear more about this mysterious assault, but since Jesus didn't seem very open to talking, I sat down and filled him in on my own depressing circumstances, starting with Cassie in the cafeteria, and going all the way through Tristan outside the St. Claires' house. It's funny, but as I recalled it all for Jesus, it seemed so improbable (and even impressive) that I'd actually done all of that stuff. For my whole life, I'd been the guy standing on the edge of everything, never diving in with more than a sarcastic comment or joke. And now I was right in the center of the action. Hell, I was the action. Of course, my self-satisfaction only lasted until I finished telling the story…when I had to admit that, of course, I was no better off than when I started.

After I finished, Jesus looked at me, nodded sincerely, then struggled to his feet, holding on to my shoulder for support.

"Good," he said. "So things are going well. Keep it up." Then he began to limp back toward the field, as if he was just going to walk off and leave me there.

I jumped up and took off after him. "What are you talking about? Things are going horribly. I've made no progress, I've alienated Henry, and I've ruined my chances with Cassie!"

Jesus stopped and snapped his head around. "Chances for what?"

"For…well, you know…the investigation. To get any information."

"Ah," he said, clearly suppressing a smile. "Well, you have two options, the way I see it." He wiped a fresh drop of blood from under his nose onto his soiled white sleeve. "Your first option is to give up. Consider yourself beaten, and just go on with your life. Finish high school, go to college, get married, have babies, and die without ever resolving anything, and try your best to ignore that nagging doubt that you did the wrong thing, or that persistent feeling that you'll never know the truth."

I chuckled. "That's about what I was thinking I would do."

"Or you could take plan B."

"Which is?"

"Seize the opportunity."

"Excuse me?"

"Pick yourself up and *make something happen!* Take charge of the situation, use your resources, *find the truth!*"

"And how do I do that, exactly?"

Jesus began to pace, growing excited. His injuries seemed to be fading right in front of me. "First of all, I doubt you've ruined anything with anyone. I would bet cash money that it won't take anything more than a simple apology to get Henry back on your side."

I kicked at the grass. "I guess."

"And what about Tristan?"

"What about her?"

"She seems to be pretty sympathetic to your plan. Why don't you put her to work? Use her as a distraction for Alistair, or something?"

"Maybe."

"What do you mean, maybe? Now is not the time for maybes. Now is the time to act!"

"Sure." I said. "Fine. But how exactly do you propose I do all of that?"

Jesus stopped pacing. "I haven't the slightest idea. You'll have to figure out that one for yourself."

I put my head in my hands. Figures. This Jesus was turning out to be about as much help as the other one. "Well what are you going to do, then?" I asked him.

"About what?"

"Getting all beat up. I guess you've got the same two options as I do, right?"

A sneaky little smile crept onto his face. "Oh, I'm choosing plan B."

"And what is that?"

His smile turned into a frown—chilling, terrifying, dangerous. "Oh, I'm going back into those woods," he said. "But don't you worry about me. You've got your own plan to worry about, young man." And with that he turned and walked back across the field—not even the hint of a limp in his stride—until he disappeared into the trees.

Twenty-five

Surely, if there were a god, then Friday never would have come, and I never would have had to go back to that awful place. But there wasn't, there isn't, and I did.

The awkwardness and misery that descended on me from the very second I entered the front doors of St. Soren's was truly astounding: the stares, the half-nods of half-condolence, the rippling quiet that followed me like some cartoon rain cloud, dropping discomfort on everyone in my immediate vicinity, the ever-expanding array of saintly Ryan posters, each one more hokey and ridiculous than the last: "Our Guardian Angel" or "Soren's Hero" and worst of all, "Ryan Stiles: Class of '95 Valedictorian in the Sky."

Really, I almost considered turning right around and leaving after seeing that one.

Anyway, I was rushing to my locker with my eyes firmly glued to the floor, when I felt a hand grab my backpack and pull me through an open doorway into a darkened classroom. My heart instantly started racing, my first thought being that it was Alistair, and somehow he knew that I had let Henry into his room and had thus come to kill me.

But it wasn't. It was just Tristan, squinting conspiratorially, and whispering, "Alistair asked me to go out with him tonight."

"What?"

"He asked me to go out tonight. Alistair did."

"Like, on a date?"

"No way," she said, then paused. "I mean, I guess it's possible, but I don't think he would sink that low."

I did not have nearly the faith in him that Tristan did. "Why not?"

"Well, I don't know. That would just be so…cruel."

I shrugged. "So you said no, right?"

She looked at me like I was crazy. "Of course not. I said yes."

"Why the hell did you do that?"

"Because," she said, lowering her voice to a whisper, "that way I can press him for information, try to find out what really happened that day."

"Right," I said. "Of course." I should have seen that this was where she was going, but I guess I was blindsided by the fact that Alistair had asked her out in the first place.

"And who knows? Maybe he'll even let something slip. Maybe after a few beers…"

"Wait," I said, suddenly remembering Jesus Jackson's advice about using Tristan as a distraction. "Can you, maybe, keep him away from his house tonight? Like, far away?"

"Sure, I guess. But why?"

"Maybe I can get back into the house. Get back that hard drive. See if there's anything incriminating on it."

"Oh…"

But then, of course, I remembered something else: Cassie, and how I hadn't exactly left things on solid ground with her. "Crap," I whispered back. "But it might not be that simple."

"Why not?"

"Well, it might be kind of hard for me get invited back over there."

"Why?" She looked at me suspiciously. "What happened?"

I didn't really wanted to tell Tristan about the kiss, and my subsequent freak out, but it was beginning to look like I had no other choice. "Cassie and I sort of made out."

Tristan took a step back as a deep furrow worked its way across her brow, like she was trying to figure me out. "But why would that be a problem?"

"Well it wouldn't be, except that Alistair got home in the middle of it and I kind of ran out of the house, totally without doing any of the homework and barely even saying good-bye. And I haven't called her or anything since."

"Oh. Well that could be bad. Maybe it would be better if I just went out with—"

"But," I said, cutting her off, "maybe you could help me. You know, tell me how to smooth things over."

"Hmm," said Tristan, and then paused, thinking—working out, I assumed, whether or not I actually had a chance at success. Finally, she relented "Well, did you kiss her or did she kiss you?"

I thought back, and to be honest, it was still sort of a blur. "I think she kissed me."

"Are you sure?"

The memory of it came back to me more clearly, making me blush. "Yeah. I'm sure."

"Then there's no problem," she said with a sigh.

"Really?"

"Look," she said, putting her hand on my shoulder, trying to smile. "Your brother just died, you're falling behind at school, and you went over to her house for help with your homework, in no way expecting any kind of romance, right?"

"Yeah."

"So when you ran out of there after kissing her, she's not going to think you're just some asshole who got a little action and then left. She's going to think you were uncomfortable, sad, mourning, whatever, and that she made it all worse by insensitively kissing you."

"Okay," I said, growing a little less skeptical. This seemed to make some sense, and Cassie had been quite apologetic, after all. "So what do I do?"

Tristan thought for a second. "Just go up to her today, tell her that you're sorry you ran out of there, that your emotions were just overwhelming you, and that you'd like to try again, but this time without the homework."

"Hmm…And you think that will work?"

"Absolutely. Just suggest renting a movie, or something, and you're golden."

Right at that moment the first bell rang, signaling four minutes until class. Tristan rolled her eyes and opened the door to the hallway, pausing only to whisper "Good luck" in my ear. Then she turned with a snap, and strode briskly out into the crowd.

———

My first class was Algebra, and as usual Henry was sitting right in front of me. I caught his eye as he came in the door, but he quickly turned his gaze to the floor, refusing even to look at me. When I attempted to pass him note after note about the new plan for that night, he just let them all fall, unopened, onto the floor.

I decided that I'd try to catch up with him after class, but just before the bell rang, Ms. LaRochelle—looking hideous and as hatchet-faced as ever—came slithering in the door,

staring straight into my terrified eyes. She whispered something to Mr. Carnegie, who asked me to join our faithful
principal in the hallway.

Once outside the classroom, she stared at me for what
seemed like a decade, her cakey, wrinkled, overly made-up
eyes wide with something between suspicion and sympathy.
Finally, she said, "So you haven't been seeing Mr. Finger, I
understand?"

She made it sound like a question, but I wasn't quite sure
how to answer.

"Well," she went on, "it's very important that you do. Not
only is he your guidance counselor, he's also the only certified
grief counselor we have."

"Mm-hm."

"And he's a very good psychologist."

"Well, not really," I said, before I could think better of it.

Her eyebrows rose, sending the wrinkles in her face spiraling into a pattern of menace. "Excuse me?"

"I mean…he only has a B.A. He's not even a doctor."

"The nerve…" she huffed. "He was right to schedule this
meeting. You come right along with me."

This meeting? What meeting? What the hell was she
talking about?

She marched down the hallway, and I shuffled dutifully
after her, more annoyed than ever. When we finally made it
down the steps and through the dark hallway to Mr. Finger's
door, I could tell that whatever I was about to step into, it was
going to be bad—there were clearly a few people in that tiny
room with him.

As I suspected (or perhaps intuitively knew), there, squished
into the fading gray, metallic chairs of Mr. Finger's tiny office,
were my parents—both of them. They looked up and stared at

me when the door opened. My mother seemed a bit confused, although I'm pretty sure this was just an act (*I don't understand. Mr. Finger...Jonathan seems just perfect at home....*), while my father pursed his lips, offering a halfhearted shrug.

"Oh crap," I mumbled, just loud enough for everyone to hear.

"Jonathan!" said my mother, with a what's-gotten-into-kids-these-days look from Mr. Finger to Ms. LaRochelle.

Mr. Finger smiled warmly. "Take a seat, Jonathan." Then, to Mrs. LaRochelle, "Thanks for bringing him, Lucy. I think we'll be okay now."

Mrs. LaRochelle turned on her heels and clickety-clacked herself down the long hallway and back up the steps. I took the only available seat—a little stool, clearly meant for a third-grader, squished into a corner opposite the three adults.

"Well now," said Mr. Finger. "Now that it's just the three of us, Jonathan, why do you think I brought you all here to my office today?"

I was in no mood for this. At all. "I don't know. To justify your paycheck?"

Mr. Finger and my mom exchanged a frustrated glance. My dad smirked, though I could tell he felt guilty just for being there. Mr. Finger said, "Really now, this is about healing, not sarcasm. Why do you think we're here?"

I decided to lay it on the line for him. "Look," I said. "You seem like a nice guy, Mr. Finger. I don't want to waste your time. So why don't you just go ahead and tell my parents what's wrong with me, so they can blame it on each other, ignore the issue completely, and we can all get on with our day? Does that sound like a plan?"

"Jonathan!" said my mother.

"Aw, Christ," muttered my father.

Mr. Finger shifted uncomfortably in his seat. "Okay, then, Jonathan. Now I've been speaking with your mother, and we agree—and I'm sure your father does as well—that you've been having a difficult time these last few weeks—"

"Oh, no shit," I broke in. "You must be some psychologist. Did you go to undergrad for that?"

He swallowed hard and tried to ignore me. "And, Jonathan, we think that you may be having a crisis of faith, as a result."

"A what?" I let out an audible gasp. Had he been talking to Jesus Jackson? No, it couldn't be...

"A crisis of faith," Mr. Finger repeated. "It's when, during a difficult or traumatic period in your life, you begin to doubt your faith in God...usually when you need it the most."

Now this was too much. It was one thing to take this crap from Jesus Jackson (who I was, after all, paying for it); I wasn't about to listen to it from this loser. I looked to my father (who should have known better) for support, but he was studying his palms, refusing to make eye contact. "Mr. Finger, I haven't believed in your god, or any other fairy tales, since I was nine years old. So whatever kind of crisis I'm having, it's not one of faith."

He looked questioningly at my mother, as if she had assured him the exact opposite were true. Which, in all likelihood, she had. She probably told him that I was saying grace before every goddamned bowl of Cheerios the week before Ryan died. But my dad? First the Buddhism, and now this?

"Well, whenever it began," said Mr. Finger, shuffling through some papers on his desk, "we're going to help it come to an end. We've arranged for you to have daily prayer meetings with the school chaplain, starting tomorrow, and—"

I stared at my father. "Are you really just going to sit there?" I asked him. "Are you *really*?"

He blinked his eyes up at me, sheepishly. "Look, son…I mean, what can it possibly hurt? Believing in something? What do you have to lose?"

So that's how this was going to go. My mother deceiving the school counselor into thinking I was a good Christian; my father, the proud heretic, supporting daily prayer meetings.

I put my head in my hands, trying to work it all out. "So," I said finally, "is there, like, any way you can physically force me to attend these meetings? I mean, will I be expelled or arrested or held in chains if I refuse to go?"

"Of course not," said Mr. Finger. "These meetings are supposed to help you, Jonathan."

"And what about coming here? Can I be expelled or whatever for not going to see my counselor?"

Mr. Finger looked a little hurt. "Well, no."

"Good." I stood up, throwing my backpack over my shoulder. "Then it was nice to know you, Mr. Finger, but our relationship is officially over. And you people?" I turned to my parents, both looking defeated, pathetic. "I just don't even know what to say to you people." Then, to my father: "Especially you. I expected more from you."

Then I turned, walked through the door, and went back to class.

Twenty-six

I was quickly coming to the conclusion that this whole school thing just wasn't for me. Sure, I had tolerated it, more or less, in elementary school; I had gritted my teeth and put up with it through middle school. But this high school thing (and especially *this* high school)—this was just not happening for me. I had pretty much succumbed to doing nothing more than sitting with my head in my hands through all of my classes, and I probably would have skipped out after lunch, had I not happened to step into the cafeteria line right behind Ms. Cassie St. Claire.

She was talking to some girl in front of her, so she didn't notice me right away, which was fine with me, as I was more than a bit nervous after what happened at her house. For a moment, I considered sneaking away. But before I could try it, Cassie turned her head, and caught sight of me out of the corner of her eye.

She snapped her head around, meeting my eyes. "Jonathan. Hi!"

The girl in front of her peeked to see who Cassie was talking to. Then, realizing it was me (a.k.a. the Dead Kid's Brother), she quickly began inspecting the boneless rib sandwiches.

"H...h...hey," I stuttered.

She looked down, fidgeting with the hem of her plaid skirt. "Hey, Jon," she said, then paused: a very awkward, seemingly endless pause. "Look, I'm really sorry about the other night. I really don't know what got into me. We were just in my room and I was feeling really comfortable and then I just remember thinking that you looked really cute as you were saying something, and now I can't even remember what you were saying, but anyway I must have liked it because I kissed you even though I know I shouldn't have and that it was totally inappropriate so I'm sorry. Okay?"

The girl behind Cassie turned slightly away from the rib sandwiches, clearly eavesdropping.

"Umm. Wow." I had expected Cassie to be at least a little angry about my abrupt departure, so this caught me off guard. For a few seconds, I was speechless.

"Say something."

"Well, actually I was going to apologize to you, so now I'm sort of at a loss for words."

"Why were you going to apologize to me?"

"For taking off like I did."

"Oh, no," she said emphatically, touching her hand to my arm. "Don't apologize. You have so much going on, and then I do that...it was probably just overwhelming. You have nothing to be sorry about."

Well, I guess Tristan was right after all, I thought. And now that Cassie had taken care of about ninety percent of what I wanted to say to her, there was just one thing left. "So, would you have any interest in trying it again...except this time without the homework? I mean, I still have to do all that homework eventually, so it would be nice if you could help, but I mean, some other time...we could just, maybe—"

"Sure." She leaned in close. "That would be great."

"Um, is tonight okay?"

"Oh no," she said. "Tonight won't work. I've got Meghan Beauregard's sweet sixteen tonight. Tomorrow, though."

Dammit, I thought. Tristan was getting Alistair out of the house tonight. I had no idea if she could make it work for the next day. "Oh…"

"But, wait…why don't you come?" she asked.

"Oh, I don't know about that." I could feel my face getting redder by the second. I was going down in flames. "I mean, I wasn't even invited."

"That doesn't matter. Meghan thinks you're awesome. She told me so. And besides, you'd be my date."

"Um…"

"Do you own a suit?"

"A suit?" This was getting out of hand.

"Or at least a sports jacket?" She was clearly growing more excited by the second. "It's a formal, but most of the guys will just be semi-formal, so you can be either."

"Oh, Jesus," I said.

She frowned.

"I mean, yes," I said. "I do. Lots of them. It…um…it sounds great."

By this point we'd reached the cashier, and I realized that I hadn't actually taken any food. So I grabbed one of the infamous "Rib-B-Q" sandwiches just so as to not draw attention to myself. Cassie paid for her salad, I paid for my sandwich, and then she spun around, grabbing my elbow and widening her eyes as soon as we were both past the lunch lady. "Oh, I forgot," she said. "Meghan has a limo for all her close friends. It's supposed to be huge, so I'm sure she won't mind one more. We'll pick you up around seven, okay?"

"Super."

"Great," she said. "Try to wear some blue. That way, you'll match my dress." And then she strode off to her table full of gaggling girls, who all, within a second of her sitting, turned in unison to look at me with painfully assuming smiles and miserable giggles floating about their eyes.

I threw my rib sandwich on the table directly across from Henry. He looked up at me. "I'm sorry," I said. "And just to show you how sorry I am, I'm going to eat that rib sandwich."

Henry cracked a tiny smile, then quickly suppressed it. "Whatever."

I sat down and began talking anyway. "I've got a problem."

But Henry just pretended not to hear me.

"I said I've got a problem."

Finally, he relented, but only slightly: a glance at my face, a curt nod.

"Alistair's going to be out all night tonight—Tristan's making sure of it—and I'm stuck going to a sweet sixteen party with Cassie."

"Sounds awful," he muttered.

"Funny. The point is I don't know when I'm going to get another opportunity like this to find some actual evidence on Alistair. I really don't want to waste it."

Henry nervously glanced around, as if looking for an escape from the conversation. But he didn't go anywhere, of course, perhaps realizing that I was the only person he'd ever spoken to in the whole cafeteria. "Okay," he said. "Fine. Give me the details."

So I filled him in on the conversations with Tristan and Cassie. He sat focusing and frowning very seriously, the way he always did, and it made me happy to have him back. It's funny, I'd been considering Henry more of a project partner, or a business associate, than a friend, but as I looked around that cafeteria I had to admit that we were really in the same boat; he was the only friend I had in that room, too.

Anyway, when I was done relating the events of the morning, Henry shook his head and stared straight into my eyes. "You do realize that you only have one option, don't you?"

"What?"

"You have to get her to invite you back to her house, and into her room…after the party."

"That's insane. It'll be late, her mom will never let her have somebody over, especially a boy."

"Well, if her parents won't let her, then you'll have to get her to sneak you in."

"Oh," I said, finally taking a bite of my rubberized rib sandwich. "And how the hell am I supposed to do that?"

Henry's cheeks reddened a bit. "I think you're asking the wrong guy."

"Right," I said. "Sorry."

And so we sat there in silence until the bell rang, forced by a mystery into wondering what most guys our age spend most of their time thinking about for no reason at all: how does a guy like me convince a girl like that to take me back to her room?

Not surprisingly, we didn't come up with much. Henry suggested I buy a corsage, which I thought was a pretty good idea, but that's about as far as we got. All I came up with was that I should probably consult Tristan, which was exactly what I did as soon as the last bell rang at 2:15.

I found her in the senior hallway. I pulled her aside, and quickly told her about Cassie and the sweet sixteen. She seemed a bit apprehensive, though, glancing left and right and over my shoulder. I asked her, "Is something wrong?"

"No," she said, putting on a sunny smile and looking me right in the eyes. "Hey, why don't I just come by tonight? I can, um…help you get ready. We can talk then."

It seemed a bit odd, but probably helpful. "Sure. Okay."

"Great," she said, turning quickly into the flow of the hallway. "See you then."

When she did arrive that night, Tristan was quite a bit calmer, and I was already mostly dressed.

She appeared at the door of my room, took one look at me and said, "Oh you can't wear that."

I checked myself out in the mirror. I'd done what I thought was a decent job of not looking overly dressed up, while still maintaining the requirements of formal attire: khaki pants, white button-down, casual brown shoes. "What's the matter with me?"

"Where do I begin?" she said, clearly having to hold back her laughter. "First of all, that shirt is three sizes too big. It makes you look like a cotton garbage bag. Secondly, you're wearing khaki pants, and thirdly, they're pleated. And are those really the nicest shoes you have?"

"Umm…"

"Where's your closet?"

"Over there." I pointed toward the back wall of my room, and proceeded to look again, though now with a bit more disgust, in the mirror.

She rummaged around for a minute, and then said, as I thought she might, "There's nothing in here."

"Yeah, I know."

"Come here, and stand up straight."

"Okay." I did as I was told.

She put her hands on my shoulders, my waist, turning me around, seeming to mentally measure me. Finally, she said, "No, it won't work."

"What?"

"Ryan's clothes."

"No." I sighed. "I'm a little too short."

"But your mom bought him so much nice stuff…designer jeans, beautiful suits, expensive shirts. Didn't she ever get anything like that for you?"

"Um, sure, but I never wear any of it."

"Well, where is it all?"

"You can try the hall closet, where we keep the towels and stuff."

She ran out into the hall, and after a few seconds started to "ooh" and "ahh" like a little girl at a parade. She burst back into my room, carrying three or four shopping bags overflowing with clothes. "Jonathan! How can you just let all this stuff sit in shopping bags? These are some really nice—and expensive—clothes!"

I glanced over at the ripped jeans and old t-shirt I had been wearing all day. Honestly it had always been a sort of battle-of-the-wills between me and my mom. She'd buy me these clothes, I'd tell her that she was wasting her money, and then she'd grit her teeth and swear that I would wear them someday. "I don't know…they're not really my style," I told Tristan.

"Well, they are tonight," she said.

What happened then was nothing less than torture for me, though I'm quite sure it was some of the most fun Tristan had had in a while. She'd hand me an outfit, I'd go put it on, come back, and she'd say something like. "Fabulous, but not quite fabulous *enough*," and then send me back with more clothes to do it all over again. When she was finally satisfied, she finished it off by spiking my hair with some mousse from my mother's bathroom, and then stood me up in front of the mirror, clearly quite proud of her accomplishment.

I looked at myself, thoroughly uncomfortable with the outfit: a tight-fitting, blue button-down shirt, designer jeans, and a pinstriped blazer. I grimaced. "Everyone's going to think I'm gay."

"Everyone's going to think you're hot."

This, I had to admit, was a novel concept. Sure, I'd occasionally been referred to as "cute" by the girls in my middle school (or at least the ones who recognized my existence at all), but *hot*…well, that was a new level for me entirely.

"Whatever," I said.

"I'm serious," she said, messing up my hair a bit more. "You look really, really hot."

"You're just biased because I look like Ryan."

The second these words left my lips I knew they were a mistake. Tristan was being so jovial, so carefree, so normal, but it all ended abruptly with the mention of my brother's name. You could literally see the smile sour on her face, until she swallowed it like a pill.

Tristan turned away from the mirror. "It's almost seven," she said. "I should be getting out of here. You wouldn't want your hot date seeing an older woman in your window."

"Right," I said, as she grabbed her purse and made for the door. "Hey. Any last words of advice on how I can seal the deal tonight?"

She paused in my doorway, and looked at me with an expression that I can only describe as somewhere between affection and fear. "Yeah, just find a quiet moment and stare at her with those big blue eyes until she kisses you." She let out a quiet chuckle. "It always worked for your brother."

Twenty-seven

The limo arrived at a few minutes past seven, and I walked out to greet it with no small amount of apprehension. After all, Tristan was biased, no matter what she might have said. And clothing aside, I was getting into a limo with a bunch of relative strangers, with the mission of getting a girl to take me back to her parents' house at God-only-knows what hour of the night, in what may prove to be the last attempt to find proof that my brother was murdered.

Needless to say, the pressure was on...

As it turned out, the limo ride wasn't so bad at all. I didn't know if it was the clothes, or the spiky hair, or my lame attempt at self-confidence, or the simple fact of the social resurrection of the Dead Kid's Brother (in truth, it was probably the combination of all these), but for the first time in years (or maybe more) I didn't feel like all of the other kids were looking at me like I was some kind of freak. And after a few minutes, I was finding myself feeling more and more comfortable, more and more at ease—probably what most people call normal. Sure, there was a part of me that felt a little fake, a little put-on, especially when I laughed at some joke that clearly wasn't funny, or agreed with some ridiculous opinion on pop music or

TV that, underneath, made me simultaneously want to laugh and choke myself on a corsage. But it didn't really bother me; not the way it usually did. I didn't let it get under my skin.

And then we arrived at the party.

As soon as the limo pulled off the main road, we found ourselves on a long straight driveway, lined on either side by these gargantuan oak trees, forming a kind of arch over the road. We passed a sign that read, "Goldcliff: a Rutherford Estate," and within seconds the limo swung around and we found ourselves face-to-face with the façade of this mansion that made the nicest house in my neighborhood seem like a doublewide trailer. The whole thing looked as if made of white marble and gold, with intricate seraphim-covered porticos, cherubs eating grapes and figs over the doorways, and ironwork gargoyles guarding the roof, and huge arched windows that let you see clear through the house out to the ocean beyond.

We were the first to arrive, of course, and the girls all ran in, yelling and laughing, to check out the ballroom. But I hung back a bit, taking my time. I watched Cassie through the giant front windows—she looked amazing in her little blue dress, curled hair falling over bare white shoulders—and I strolled up slowly to the front entrance, giving myself a chance to really take it all in. I didn't know if it was a psychic premonition or gut instinct or just some kind of nervous nausea, but I felt, right at that moment, like I was on the verge of something big—some kind of monumental change in myself or in my life. What I couldn't figure out about it, though, is whether I should jump right in, or run screaming for the exit.

Perhaps I should preface all of this, though, by giving an example of how every other party or dance or other such social gathering I'd ever been to had gone down. It always happened sort of like this:

I would get the invitation or announcement or whatever and promptly announce to anyone who could possibly care (a.k.a. my mom and Ryan) that I would not be attending. My mom, understanding as she always was, would send in the RSVP or buy the ticket or whatever, and then announce that I had no choice but to go or face some sort of dire consequence. Ryan would plead my case, to no avail. I would inevitably give in, and go on to arrive at the party/dance/whatever hideously over- or under- or just plain badly dressed, bearing a gift when one was not necessary, or forgetting a gift when one was. After three minutes I'd run out of fingers and toes on which to count the number of people trying (unsuccessfully) not to laugh at me, and proceed to spend the rest of the time hiding in the bathroom and/or lobby and/or bushes, until Ryan (and since he got his license, it was—thank God—always Ryan) picked me up, consoled me, and somehow managed to get me to tell my mother that I had a great time.

So anyway, I thought this night could not possibly be any worse than all of my previous experiences.

And things were looking up, in a nice, tame sort of way… that is, until all of the people arrived. Now, while I would've liked to have believed that it was my attitude, my phony confidence, or at least the fact that I had the beautiful Cassie on my arm, I knew quite well that the reaction of the crowd was neither more nor less than the inestimable repercussions of the Dead-Kid's-Brother effect. Because as soon as that ballroom filled up, it became very clear that I had become something of a minor celebrity.

I couldn't walk to get a glass of punch without thirteen people patting me on the back, smiling, shaking my hand, or introducing themselves. Almost every time I found myself within earshot of an unaware couple, they'd say something, at some point, like "Can you believe Jonathan Stiles is here?" or "I know, he's so brave" or "He looks so much like his brother. Just…littler."

It was only after getting over the initial shock of my presence that people started to approach me in earnest, and in large numbers. Usually a group of four or five would kind of sidle up to me at once, and a spokesman for the group would say something like, "Hey. You're Jonathan Stiles. It's really cool that you're here." And then everyone would nod in agreement and I'd nod, too, and say, "Thanks. It's, uh…a cool party." And then the spokesman would say, "Totally. Meghan's the best. Hey do you swim (or play golf, or lacrosse, or act, or write poetry, or whatever) 'cause at Soren, we have this awesome team (or club, or choir, or whatever) and you should totally join." And then I'd look around at all of the other people in the group, who'd all nod enthusiastically, echoing their spokesman with "Yeah" and "Definitely" or "You really should" and "That would be really cool."

Of course, I never had one iota of interest in joining any club, or team, or other extra-curricular activity, so I would just smile and nod, tell them it sounded like fun, and then excuse myself to use the bathroom.

The strangest thing about the night, though, was just how revolting I *didn't* find it all. I should have, clearly; after all, nearly every syllable of every word of acceptance and praise I received was fake, or contrived, or based solely on the fact that, amazingly, I had both (can you believe it?) really nice clothes *and* a dead brother.

But I've got to be honest: I just didn't care that much.

It was just too much fun, too much of a fantasy, twisted as it was. No matter what anyone tells you, even the darkest, Gothest, freakiest loner-outcast wants, on some level, to be the life of the party, the most popular kid in the room. Maybe not permanently, maybe not as a lifestyle or an identity, but for a night. Yes—every one of us. Absolutely.

It did all start to get a bit overwhelming after a while. And after a few hours of such incessant mingling I had to step outside to get some air. I'd been dancing (surprisingly without embarrassing myself...I think) and I could feel the sweat beading under my collar. So I took off my jacket and leaned over the railing to catch a bit of the ocean breeze. I didn't even notice that Cassie had come outside until she was just a few feet behind me "Well, you certainly have a way of blowing away a girl's expectations," she said.

I turned quickly, startled. "Oh, hey. What do you mean?"

She sauntered over and leaned against the railing beside me. "First it was the clothes," she said, smiling a little as she glanced at me through the corners of her eyes. "That was a huge shock."

I laughed. "Right."

"And then there was the fact that you actually smiled and talked and joked with everyone in the limo, which was also a pleasant surprise."

"Thanks."

"And then we get here to the party, I go to get one glass of punch, and when I turn around you're practically the guest of honor. You've got a new group surrounding you every five minutes, everyone here is talking about how cool you were when they talked to you, you're tearing it up on the dance floor...and don't think I haven't noticed the way those girls in there are all looking at you. Even the seniors!"

At this, I had to laugh. "I really don't know what you're talking about."

"Sure," she said, sliding down the rail a few inches, leaning her body into mine. "So what happened to that brooding, anti-social atheist kid I asked out at lunch today?"

Taking the cue, I put my arm around her shoulders and looked back into the party. "Don't get too excited. He's just playing along. He'll be back."

"What if I want him back now?"

"I don't think he'd survive very well at a shindig like this."

"So then let's get out of here."

I leaned my head back and turned, looking her in the eye. "And go where?"

"My mom is out. Let's go back to my house. The limo can get us there and be back long before Meghan needs it."

I have to pause here for second to explain something. Since we had arrived at the party, I had barely once thought about why I was really there in the first place. Not only that, but once I was quite abruptly reminded of the reason, and by its success, no less…I wasn't sure how to feel about it. After having dreaded the party all day, I actually felt sad to leave—and (I have to admit this) sort of guilty that it had all been a big lie.

But this only lasted a second; a moment's hesitation. The thought of really finding some solid evidence on that hard drive—something real, something I could use—not to mention being in a limo alone with Cassie…well, it was clearly worth passing up a few more hours of my Cinderella story.

"But how do we get through the party without calling attention to ourselves?"

"Simple," she said, pulling away from me and hoisting her right leg over the railing of the verandah. "We don't. Follow me."

A few steps through the grass, a shuffle through some bramble bushes, and we were safely in the limo. The driver, God bless him, had the good sense to put up the divider without even having to be asked.

Twenty-eight

Okay, so I won't go into too much detail about what actually happened in the back of that limo, but I will just say that for the whole ride back to Cassie's house, I didn't spend too much time thinking about Alistair or Ryan or Henry or Jesus Jackson.

It all came back pretty quickly, though, when Cassie said, as the limo drove away, "So my mom went to some party and shouldn't be home until after one."

I looked at my watch. It wasn't even ten yet. "All right, then."

This was obviously good news on a lot of different levels, and I felt instantly at ease about the whole plan. After all, Alistair was being taken care of by Tristan, their mom was hours away from becoming an issue, and Cassie and I had the house to ourselves. So when Cassie excused herself to the bathroom, I laughed a self-satisfied sort of chuckle, and began confidently strolling around the house.

I soon made my way into the living room, where I found dozens upon dozens of the St. Claire family pictures, all framed on the walls and the coffee table and the TV stand and on windowsills: the St. Claires on vacation somewhere tropical, Alistair and Cassie as children on Santa's lap, Cassie's mom with some old woman (presumably her grandmother)—the usual type of stuff. As I was looking at these pictures, though, I started to become more and more aware of a potentially serious dilemma. Every time I looked at Alistair, I started to feel viscerally angered, almost to the point of violence (which I guess was natural), but every time I looked at Cassie, I smiled, felt lightheaded, and had this sudden urge to sigh.

Now, although I guess it should have been pretty obvious, this was the first time that this very disturbing fact actually surfaced in my mind: I was falling for, not just Cassie, but Alistair St. Claire's sister.

I know, I know: Duh. But you've got to understand that before this very moment I considered her more of a pleasant obstacle in my plan, a surprisingly enjoyable way to get through to Alistair. I looked up, catching my reflection in the window of the living room, when I felt Cassie's hand on my shoulder. I turned, now looking at her a bit more wearily, which she didn't seem to notice as she kissed me, hard, and then pushed me back onto the sofa.

Of course, as soon as I was on my back, looking up as Cassie took off her shirt and unclasped her bra, all of my thoughts about a conflict of interest came to an abrupt and immediate end. I tried to bring them back, thinking, *No, no no.... Focus... The plan...The plan...* But it was no use.

What followed was something like forty-five of the best seconds of my life, followed immediately by twenty of the worst possible minutes.

This is what happened:

There I was, lying on the sofa, my tongue exploring the reaches of Cassie's mouth while my anxious hands explored her body, when what did I hear, just on the other side of a thin plaster wall, but the opening of the front door, followed by the unmistakable sound of Tristan's voice, and then a far lower voice, surely belonging to none other than Alistair himself.

"Oh shit," said Cassie. "Al." And then she rolled off onto the floor, hiding between the couch and the coffee table as she struggled back into her shirt. From the front hall we could hear the footsteps and the voices clearly moving toward the living room, and on top of that, there were more voices and footsteps—quite a few more—steadily making their way in through the door. I grabbed Cassie's bra and stuffed it under the rug just as she hoisted herself back on the couch (disheveled, but presentable) just a second before Tristan and Alistair turned the corner and saw us.

They stopped for a moment, staring at us. Alistair, holding a case of beer, appeared surprised, and then angry; Tristan met my eyes for a moment—pleading, apologetic, embarrassed— and then turned away.

"What are you doing here?" asked Cassie, with a nervous giggle.

Alistair didn't even acknowledge her. He just glared straight at me. "Mom called earlier. She's staying over at Aunt Kim's. What happened to the party?"

I avoided meeting Al's gaze, as Cassie said, "Oh, I wasn't really feeling that great. So we were just—"

"Yeah, I know what you *were just*," he broke in, as the rest of the guests filed in around the corner. Of course, it was both of the other stupidfucks who had been there when Ryan died, each clearly wobbling and obviously confused by my presence.

Phil, the tall one, looked as if someone had just asked him the square root of pi. "Al," he said. "I don't get it. What's going on?"

Alistair looked from me, to Cassie, and back several times. I tried to get a read on things from Tristan, but she just avoided my eyes. Finally, Alistair said, "Nothing's going on. We're just having a few beers." Then he strutted across the living room, sat down between Cassie and me on the couch, cracked open a can of beer, and handed it to me. "Relax," he said.

The two meatheads clearly didn't need any convincing, and started right in on drinking, laughing, and speaking in some dialect of dumbfuck that seemed to resemble English, but just barely. Tristan found a seat at the end of the couch, clearly placing herself on the other side of Alistair and Cassie so I'd have no chance of making eye contact with her at all. When I did catch a glimpse of her, she was hunched over, head resting heavily in her hands, staring painfully at Alistair.

After a few minutes of hanging out with Al and the boys, I felt like scratching my eyeballs out, so I mumbled something about not feeling well, and speed-walked to the bathroom. Once safely locked in, I splashed some cold water in my face, stared at my bloodshot eyes in the mirror, and realized that my whole plan was officially screwed. So I tried to come up with an exit strategy. The first thought that came to me was the bathroom window, but I decided that would be a bit rash, and might ruin my chances of ever getting back into the house with Cassie. I then considered a few more options, all equally as useless: faking a seizure, chugging five beers and then stumbling out mumbling, passing a note to Cassie telling her to meet me outside so we can run away together to Mexico.

In the end, I decided that the best course of action would be to put up with it until an appropriate lull in the conversation, and then make up some excuse about a curfew and take off. I felt good about this decision, too. It seemed reasonable, doable, and perfectly sane…of course, it lasted all of about thirty seconds.

As soon as I stepped out of the bathroom, without even seeing it happen, I felt a hand grab my arm and pull me into a dark room. For a moment I thought (wishfully) that it was Cassie with a plan to get out of there. But it wasn't. It was Alistair.

He pushed me further past the door and turned on the light, revealing that it was his room we were in. "What's this…" I began.

"Shut it," he said, closing the door.

"Sorry."

Alistair came closer, leaning in mere inches from my face. "This has to stop," he growled. "Now."

"What has to—"

"No. Shut the fuck up. You know what I'm talking about."

I began to say, "I really don't know…" and then SMACK. He whipped his arm around and slapped his palm into the back of my head. "Ow! Jesus!" I screamed.

"I'm sorry. I'm sorry," he said, now pacing back and forth as I rubbed my scalp. "I didn't mean to…well, I did. I just—" He stopped pacing, and got real close again. "Look, I get it. I see what you're doing."

He paused, as if waiting for me to say something, to confirm his suspicions. I remained quiet, and pissed off.

He continued, hushed and frustrated: "The snooping, the following, the spying, your little Chinese friend just lingering somewhere every time I turn my head, and now this crap with my sister. I get it. And it ends tonight."

"Actually, he's Korean. But I don't know what you're—"

SMACK! He hit me again. Same spot, but a lot harder. My vision went purple for a second, and I dropped to my knees.

When my vision came back into focus, I realized that I was staring right at the tower for Alistair's computer. I peeked to the right a bit and, sure enough, there was the hard drive, right on the floor next the power chord. I snuck a look back at Alistair, who had now started pacing, and (I almost couldn't believe my eyes) he actually seemed to be crying. I saw my opportunity, and I took it: quickly grabbing the hard drive and stuffing it in my shirt.

"Whatever you're trying to get, whatever you're trying to find, just forget it." His voice was cracking now. "There's nothing there. Just give it up and leave Cassie alone!"

It occurred to me at that moment that Alistair wasn't just some bully who might slap me in the head a few times. He was a murderer. Clearly not a rational or a cold-blooded one, but a killer, nonetheless. There was something honestly crazy and uncontrollable in his eyes right then. Something sad and tortured and undeniably dangerous.

"Okay, man," I said. "Fine. It's over."

He nodded, somewhat spastically. "Good," he said, wiping his eyes and nose on his sleeve. "Good." And then he walked out of the room.

I stayed there for a few seconds, trying to decide what to do next. Clearly, my suspicions about Alistair were correct, but if he knew I was on to him, and he'd already gotten rid of the evidence…what would I wind up with but a concussion, or maybe worse?

But then I saw it: his phone. *Alistair's actual phone*, lying right there on the floor by the bed. He must have dropped it while he was smacking me around.

This was so much better than a copy of his hard drive (which probably didn't contain anything other than plagiarized papers and porn, anyway). I picked it up, and began scrolling through his messages, going back to the day that Ryan died. And then I saw it: two lines of text—one sent to Ryan, and one received back.

Sent: We got it. Meet in usual spot in woods?
Received: Great. We'll be there.

So, what else was I to do? I thought about Cassie, back there in the living room, sitting miserably with Alistair and Tristan and the boys. And I sighed, resolving myself to my fate. When I heard what sounded like Alistair being greeted by his friends in the living room, I put the phone in my pocket, opened the window, and ran out into the night.

Twenty-nine

I began speed-walking through the darkness as I scrolled through every text message, app, and voicemail on the phone. As far as I could tell, there was nothing else even remotely tied to Ryan's death, but I was sure that those two messages would be enough. They had to be...

I was about halfway home when I noticed a car following me, barely crawling along the side of the road, about fifty yards back. At first I just noticed the headlights hitting the bushes beside me, creeping at the exact pace I was walking. I began to panic a little, picking out lawns on either side of the street that I could sprint through to get away. After about twenty seconds I ventured a sideways glance, trying to make out if the general size and shape of the headlights matched the ones on Alistair's pickup. But I couldn't quite see enough to tell much of anything.

I took a right onto a side street to see if the car would follow, and when it did, I broke for it—sprinting into the nearest backyard, hopping three fences, crawling through a prickle-bush, and finally taking refuge in a little girl's plastic playhouse in some backyard about a half-block away from where I started.

I tried to sit on the pink plastic chair, but it kept falling over, so I finally just let myself flop down on the dirt covered floor. There was a thin layer of grime covering the floral printed walls and the fake little stove and the tiny plastic sink. But I didn't care. I was clutching the phone, just happy to be safe.

I stayed there for what felt like hours (though was surely only minutes) before I began to hear the yells. They were muffled at first, only recognizable as a voice in the distance—I couldn't make out anything of the content or the speaker. But then it began to grow clearer. It sounded like a girl, trying hard not to wake up the neighborhood, trying to whisper and yell at the same time. A breathy call that finally materialized as: "Jonathan. Jonathaaaaaan! It's Tristan, Jonathaaaaan."

My heart rate slowed to a more human pace. It was only Tristan. Not Alistair, his boys, or even Cassie (which might have been the most frightening of all, at that point). I opened the little plastic shutters and called out, "Over here."

There was some rustling in a nearby shrub, and then Tristan's voice again, only a few feet away. "Jonathan?"

"In here."

"The playhouse?" she said, walking closer.

"Yeah."

"Well get out of there, come on."

"No," I said. I kind of liked it in there. It felt safe, comforting…I don't know, maybe it was the plastic tray of plastic cookies on top of the plastic oven. I found it oddly soothing.

She opened the door, crouching down to see inside. "I'm sorry," she said.

I shrugged.

"Do you want to talk?"

I shrugged again.

Tristan glanced around the yard to make sure no one was coming, and then crawled inside and sat down beside me. "Alistair didn't tell me we were going back to his house."

"I figured."

She paused. "What did he say to you?"

"Same as before, but with a little more violence."

"Are you okay? Did he hurt you? Did he threaten anything bad?"

"I'm fine. It was nothing." Then I took a deep breath, not sure if I wanted to know the answer to my next question. "Did Cassie say anything after I left?"

Tristan winced. "She was pretty upset."

"Shit."

"I mean, you just left her there. Alistair walked back in the room like everything was peachy, and you were just gone."

"Shit, shit, shit."

"Oh, don't sweat it too much." She put her hand on my back, rubbing my shoulder. "She'll get over it, eventually."

I didn't say anything. All I could do was picture Cassie, sitting on that couch, wondering where I had gone, why I left her. The only conclusion she could possibly have reached is that I was too much of a pussy to deal with her brother, so I ran away without even a good-bye.

"Anyway, I understand," said Tristan. "If that had been me getting beat up by Alistair, I would've run away too."

"I didn't run away because Alistair was smacking me around."

She seemed confused. "Then why did you?"

"Because of this," I said, lifting up the phone.

"Is that Alistair's phone?"

"Yup."

"But what about the hard drive?"

"Oh I got that too," I said, patting the bulge under my shirt. "But this is so much better." Then I lifted the phone for her to see, and showed her the two messages.

"Wow," she said quietly, almost as if she wasn't sure what to think of this new development. "What are you going to do with it?"

"I don't know yet," I said. "I need to talk to Jesu—" But then I stopped myself. "I mean, Henry. I need to talk to Henry. He has the rest of the evidence, so…"

"Right," she said. "But, I mean…that still doesn't really prove anything, does it?"

"It proves that Alistair was lying. That he was there. That he was doing drugs."

"But it doesn't tell us anything about what happened *after* that. What happened with Ryan? Didn't you find anything? A message to Phil about what happened? A voicemail from someone he told? Anything?"

"No, nothing like that." I sighed. "Not that it matters, though. I mean, what we need now is just something to take to the cops. We know, basically, what happened with Ryan and Alistair."

"We don't know anything!" she screamed, in an outburst of emotion. "Nothing! And these stupid text messages don't tell us a damn thing." Then she began to sob.

"Hey now. Hey," I said, trying to calm her down a bit. "It's alright. We're not done yet. We can still find out more. We can still investigate. It's not over."

She took a deep, shuddering breath. "I just have to know…. I just have to know."

I guess it hadn't occurred to me before that Tristan's motives in this thing could be different from mine. I was searching for a way to get Alistair on the hook (however I needed to do it), but Tristan was still trying to figure out if he was even guilty. But I let it go, figuring that it was only because she hadn't seen everything that I saw back in those woods.

"Anyway," I said, as gently as possible. "We should probably get going." I began to shift myself up to get out, but she tugged me back down.

"Let's just hang out a bit," she said. "Do you mind?"

"In here?"

"Yeah." She wiped the tears from her cheeks. "It's kind of nice in here."

"Okay," I said, settling back down. "Okay.

Only then did I remember that Tristan had been "investigating" as well, so I asked her if she managed to learn anything from Alistair. But she just shook her head, staring down at the dirty floor. "Nothing," she said. "Nothing that I didn't already know."

And so we stayed in that little plastic house for maybe an hour, barely saying a word. Every so often I would catch her staring at me, a few tears running down her cheek, as if I were the one who had caused her all this pain. And after a little while she took my hand and she held it until we left. Sure, it seemed strange…but, I don't know, I just figured she was sad, like I was sad, and sometimes when you're that sad and it's late and dark and you're sitting Indian-style in a little plastic house in a stranger's backyard, you do strange things.

Thirty

Things were turning around for me; I could feel it.

I could feel it with the first waking breath I took at the crack of dawn the next morning: a sense of possibility, of everything getting faster and realer, of revenge within reach, of hope. I hopped on my skateboard, and headed straight for St. Soren's. Saturday football practice got going at seven, so if I wanted to have any chance of talking to Jesus I'd have to get there fast.

I nearly killed myself, but I made it in record time—bombing down the hills and shooting through intersections with nothing more than blind faith in the absence of cars—arriving at three minutes past six. And to my surprise and relief, Jesus Jackson was right there waiting for me, lying in the fresh dew, his hands behind his head, staring at the sky from the fifty-yard line—and without a scratch on his body or a bruise on his face.

As soon as I saw him there I quickened my pace, breaking into a full run by the fifty-yard line. When I reached him I had to pause, heaving for air to catch my breath.

"What...the fuck...happened to...your bruises? Your... black eye?"

He brushed me off with a wave of his hand. "Oh, you don't need me to have those anymore." Then he looked me over, seeming concerned. "What happened? You seem so excited?"

"I got it!" I said proudly. "The proof. I got it!"

Jesus propped himself up on his elbows. "Really?"

"I stole Alistair's phone. There are messages from him and Ryan making plans to meet in the woods."

"Well that sounds promising."

"And Alistair practically confessed everything, too," I said, sitting beside him in the grass.

Jesus furrowed his brow, and swung up into a seated position, face-to-face with me. "What do you mean, 'practically?'"

"Well, he didn't give any details, of course, but he did say he knew why I was snooping around, and then he smacked me a few times and told me to stay away from his sister."

"That's hardly a confession."

This annoyed me. "What the hell else could it mean?"

Jesus shrugged. "In court, quite a lot of things…"

"Well that's why it's a damn good thing I've got the phone."

"Damn good thing for what?"

"For going to the cops," I said, honestly astounded that he hadn't reached the same conclusion already.

Jesus jumped to his feet and began pacing. "Now just hold on a minute, you don't need to do anything rash here."

I climbed to my feet slowly, warily. "What do you mean *rash*? Alistair pushed my brother off a fucking cliff! Between the phone and my testimony about the coke and the fight and Alistair threatening me, the cops have got to arrest him."

"Look," Jesus said, lowering his voice a bit. "Eventually, you're going to have to bring this thing to the police. There's no doubt about that. But, if you bring it to them too soon, without the proper evidence…Well, it may wind up doing more harm than good."

"How? Ryan's dead! What more harm could possibly be done?"

"What are people saying, around school, was the cause of Ryan's death?"

"He fell off a cliff."

This was annoying. "Right," Jesus continued. "Now let me ask you this, has anybody at school—anybody—mentioned the word cocaine? How about drugs? Or suicide?"

"No."

"Of course not," said Jesus, placing his hand on my shoulder. "It was an accident. Ryan fell. Now he's a hero to the whole school. What do you think's going to happen if you go in to the cops with your whole story about drugs and fights and murder, but they don't believe the murder part?"

I shrugged, though I knew very well what was coming.

Jesus went on: "All they're going to have left is a story about fighting and drugs."

I nodded, silently.

"And those cops are going to take this murder thing *very* seriously. They'll be in this school before you leave the station, asking questions, talking to principals, searching lockers. Ryan's quiet, noble death will turn into a huge, awful spectacle."

He had a point, of course. The last thing I wanted to do was drag Ryan's name through the dirt. And besides, if they knew that Ryan was all coked up, they might think he fell off in a drugged stupor or worse. "Alright," I said. "Fine. So I'll leave out the cocaine."

"Then you'll have to leave out the phone. And then what do you have left? A scrap of cloth?"

"And the fight and Alistair threatening me and the foot-prints—"

"You need more," Jesus interrupted.

But I was too fed up to listen to him. Clearly Jesus didn't give a crap about justice or the truth or making sure Alistair got what he damn sure had coming to him. Hell, all he probably cared about was that I wound up accepting whatever spiritual bullshit he was going to lay on me so he could collect the rest of his money…and I was seriously starting to doubt he'd have much success at that.

So I turned and walked as fast as I could off of the football field, silently cursing Jesus Jackson and the day that I met him. I resolved to go to the cops that very day. As I hopped back on my skateboard and sped away from the school, I heard Jesus yell, off in the distance, "You need a confession! A real confession."

I didn't care, though. I was already gone.

Thirty-one

An hour and half later I was staring at the bland brick façade of the police station, with Henry by my side and the phone in my hand, nearly paralyzed with anticipation. This was what it all added up to; this was where I would prove my case, get my revenge, or lose it all forever. I just couldn't take that step: what if I didn't have enough evidence? What if there were holes in my story, what if they just plain didn't believe me? It took Henry finally placing his hand on my shoulder, and saying, "Are you sure about this?" before I finally put on a brave face, brushed him off, and took those few steps up to the door.

As we walked up to the front counter, Henry was sweating and twitching and his eyes wouldn't stop darting crazily around the room. From the look of him, any decent detective would have assumed that he was the murderer. Luckily, though, he lagged behind a few paces as I approached the officer on duty: a pretty young woman with a demeanor I considered a bit too sunny for a cop.

"Can I help you?" she asked with a smile, like she was working the counter at an ice cream parlor instead of a police station.

"I need to speak with Detective Conrad," I said.

"Oh, I'm sorry. He's usually not in on Saturdays," she replied.

I guess it spoke to my lack of experience with such matters, but it never occurred to me that the detective would be anywhere but at his desk, poring over a file of some murder case. "Oh," I said. "Well I really need to talk to him."

"You can leave a message, if you like. Or else come back on Monday after nine."

This was clearly unacceptable. If I put it off, I'd lose my nerve. "No," I said firmly. "It's an emergency. I have some evidence about a murder."

"A murder?" She nearly started laughing.

"Yes. Ryan Stiles was murdered and I have evidence to prove it."

Her face changed, became ever so slightly more concerned. "And what did you say your name is?"

"Jonathan Stiles. His brother."

The second these words left my mouth, everything changed. The nice, smiling police lady became instantly and incredibly serious. Her left hand snapped at a phone and within seconds she made a half-turn on her chair and started whispering intently into the receiver.

She hung up. "Follow me."

She led us back to the same white waiting room where I had been after Ryan's death. Although she didn't say a word, I assumed that we were waiting for Conrad to come all the way in from home. And by the sour and disheveled look of him when he arrived, I was sure that we had woken him up.

He grimaced as he approached the two of us, his unshaven face sagging and wrinkling like a rotten tomato. "So are you really doing this?"

I nodded. Henry froze.

"Well come on in, then." He opened the door to his office, straddling the threshold so we had to squeeze past his gut just to get into the room. We sat down in the two chairs facing his desk as he took the seat across from us. At first he just glowered, slurping his coffee and tapping his fingers on his computer keyboard. Then, as if he'd finally woken up enough to remember me, a look of recognition came into his eyes, and, almost with a note of sympathy in his voice (but not quite), he said, "So what's this all about? "

"Ryan didn't just fall into the ravine behind St. Soren's. He was pushed."

The detective appeared neither surprised nor concerned. "And what makes you think that?"

"I happen to know that he got into a fight with Alistair St. Claire right before he died."

"Now how would you know that? You told me that the last time you saw him was before school on the day he died."

I took a deep breath, glanced over at Henry (who may not have actually breathed since we arrived at the station), and began my story—the story I'd conceived and rehearsed a hundred times in my head since the night before. "Well, officer, that was lie. I did see Ryan right before he died. Henry and I had wandered into the woods behind the school by chance, when we came upon Alistair St. Claire, Michael Murphy, and Philip Shea doing cocaine in a little clearing just about fifty feet inside the tree line."

"Wait a second," broke in Conrad, scribbling notes on a pad in front of him. "You said it was Alistair St. Claire, Michael Murphy, and who?"

"Philip Shea, sir."

"Right." He paused. "And Ryan wasn't there? He wasn't doing drugs with them?"

"No, sir. Just those three."

He jotted down one more thing on his pad, leaned back in his chair, and squinted at me skeptically. "Continue."

"Well, as soon as we saw them, we turned around and started to head back to school, but they ran after us and Alistair tackled me, while Mike and Phil went after Henry."

Conrad raised an eyebrow. "It took two of them to take on this kid?"

I felt my heart beating faster "I'm just telling you what happened. Anyway, they pinned us both down while Alistair screamed about how if we told anyone we saw them they would kill us."

"Kill you?" echoed Conrad.

"Well, yeah. That's what he said. But I didn't think he was being serious at the time. You know...I just thought he meant that he would beat us up or something."

"Right. Sorry. Go on."

"Anyway, right about then Ryan came running up out of nowhere, dragged Alistair off of me, pushed Mike and Phil away from Henry, and told us to run."

"And did you?"

"Yeah, we ran away, but as we were leaving we saw Alistair and Ryan fighting...and it looked like it was getting really serious."

"And what time did all this take place?"

"Well, they let us out early that day...so probably like one o'clock."

"Okay, and then what happened?"

I swallowed hard. "And then Alistair followed Ryan to the edge of the ravine and pushed him in."

He leaned in. For a brief moment, he actually seemed to be taking me seriously. "And you saw this happen?"

"Well…no."

"Did you see anything after the fight?"

"No….I mean, not technically. But we do have evidence that backs up what we're saying."

Conrad raised an eyebrow. Henry, sensing his cue, pulled three big plastic bags out of his backpack: one containing the piece of fabric from the prickle bush, one containing a few dozen pictures of footprints and feet, and the other containing the phone. I launched right into a huge explanation of the significance of each piece, how we went about finding them, what we thought they meant, and how the detective could go about using them to convict Alistair.

Just as I was finishing my explanation, Conrad excused himself from the room, saying he needed to check something.

"How do you think it's going?" I whispered to Henry.

Henry shrugged, still too scared to speak.

"Well, I think we're making progress," I said. "He seemed skeptical a first, but I think he starting to come around."

A few unbearably long minutes passed, and then Conrad came back into the room, sat back down, and told me to go on. It took about five more minutes for me to finish (I didn't want to leave anything out), and as soon as I brought the story up to that very morning, I said, "So what do you think? Do we have enough to arrest Alistair?"

Conrad leaned back in his chair, rubbing his temples with the middle finger and thumb of his left hand. Leaning forward again, he stared hard at Henry.

After a little while, he said, "Henry—It's Henry, right?"

Henry nodded.

"Henry, can you give me and Jonathan a moment?"

Henry nodded again but didn't move.

Conrad paused, and then waved him to the door. "Just go ahead and wait for us out there, okay?"

Henry finally got it. He nodded a third time and nearly sprinted from the room. Just then, Conrad's phone rang. He picked it up, mumbled something like, "Yeah, okay," and placed the receiver back on its cradle.

Then Conrad turned back to me, his entire demeanor changed. He seemed sad, almost human. He said, "I had a cousin, an older cousin, named Jeff." He stared wistfully out the window. "Jeff was about four years older than me and when I was growing up he lived with my aunt and uncle right down the road, not a hundred yards from my front door. Now, I was an only child, and Jeff had nothing but sisters, so as we grew up we were about as close to brothers as we ever knew. I mean, I looked up to him for everything—he taught me how to fish, play ball, gave me advice on girls, how to dress—everything. Anyway, I was probably just about your age when Jeff got drafted into the army. This was back in '73, so that meant he was going to Vietnam. Now I remember like it was yesterday, the day a young man in uniform came to my aunt's door with a telegram—"

"Excuse me," I broke in. "But what does this have to do with arresting Alistair?"

Conrad shook his head. He stood up, came around the desk, and put his hand on my shoulder. "Never mind," he said. "Come on."

I got up, unsure of where he was taking me, and followed him to his office door. He opened it. And I understood immediately what was happening, what he'd done. There in the waiting room, looking more like they were there to bail me out than back me up, were both of my parents, sitting beside a truly mortified Henry.

"What the hell is this?" I demanded.

Conrad leaned down. "Look, this is going to be hard for you. But the sooner you accept things the way that they are, the sooner you can start to get better."

"But what about all of the evidence? What about our story?"

Conrad seemed truly concerned, but I was too angry to care. "Look, Jon, I know that, to you, it all makes sense, but it doesn't add up." He leaned down further, almost whispering. "We talked to Alistair. And Mike and Phil and the whole football team, and their families. Those guys were nowhere near your brother when he died." Then he paused, as if unsure if he should continue. But he did: "Jonathan, Ryan tested positive for cocaine during his autopsy. But I think you knew that." My face went crimson, showing Conrad just how right he was. "Okay. I'll let your parents explain the rest."

And with that, Conrad exchanged a knowing glance with my father, gave me a little push across the waiting room, and retreated back into his office. I was speechless. All the progress I made had disappeared; it was gone. And as my parents ushered me into my mother's car, I felt myself retreating from everything: the police station, my family, Ryan's death. It all faded to a white hum on the periphery of my consciousness as I spent the drive home in silence, staring placidly at the trees and their newly colored leaves.

Thirty-two

My parents didn't offer me any further details of Ryan's death. And I didn't bother to ask. In my mind, I'd heard enough: The coroner, or whoever, had tested Ryan for cocaine, and he came up positive, thus making me a liar. Furthermore, Alistair and his boys had gotten together on a story that was good enough to convince the cops, thus making my story implausible, at best. Whatever credibility I thought I had, whatever chance there was of convincing anybody of anything—it was all gone. What else was there to know?

So my father took off with Henry (who seemed irritatingly relieved, almost smiling as he carried the bag of useless "evidence" by his side), while my mother drove me home. A few times on the ride she tried to start a conversation, first pointing out that there was a sale at some department store and then moving on to more pressing subjects like whether or not I was hungry and if I wanted her to rent me a movie. I didn't answer a single one of her questions, just like I didn't respond to her knocks for the next three days. I just remained locked in my room, accepting the occasional meal, while avoiding even the smallest bit of pointless conversation.

It's hard to describe my state of mind over those three days. I didn't feel numb anymore, as I had since Ryan's death, but I didn't really feel sad yet, either. I just felt beaten; utterly defeated.

And no one really seemed that worried about it. My mother left meals and clean clothes outside my door. My father left me pamphlets about Krishna and bought me one of those Zen gardens where you make lines in a little box of sand with a tiny rake. I barely ate the food, and I couldn't bear to read a word of the pamphlets. But the Zen garden was actually quite nice.

On Tuesday, after about three hours of raking tiny circles in the garden, I heard a knock at my door.

Breaking my silence for the first time, I said, "Not now, Mom. Come back tomorrow."

"Jonathan?" It wasn't my mother. It was Tristan.

I stared deep into the swirls of sand, deciding stupidly that she could do no harm, and walked over to unlock my door. "It's open," I said finally, as I went back to my position on the bed, raking my garden.

Tristan gently pushed open the door and came in. She squinted a bit as her eyes adjusted to the dark. "Jonathan?"

"Hey."

I mustered an effortful smile as she shuffled over, taking a seat beside my little Zen garden. "That looks very calming."

"It is."

Neither of us said anything for a minute or two; we just stared at the swirling sand. Finally she put her palm on my hand, stopping me. "So, what's this isolation act all about? Your mom said you've been in here for days."

"I don't know. I just haven't felt like doing much since Saturday."

"Why," she asked. "What happened on Saturday?"

I paused. "Wait. You don't know about anything that

happened since Friday night?" I found this hard to comprehend, though of course it made perfect sense.

"Um...no."

"Henry didn't say anything to you about it?"

She chuckled nervously. "I've tried to ask him about you
five times, but he always runs away when he sees me coming."

"And my mom didn't either?"

"No. I mean, I only talked to her for a minute before coming
up here. What happened?"

I lay back on the bed, staring at the ceiling. "I went to the
cops."

She gasped. "You didn't!"

"I did. I took the evidence and Henry and I told the detective all about everything."

"I never thought you'd really go to the police," Tristan
whispered, seemingly more to herself than to me.

"Well, I guess you were wrong there."

"And you told them what you think about Alistair?"

"I did. I gave Detective Conrad the whole story...or a version of it, anyway."

"What do you mean a version?"

"Well, I sort of left out the part about Ryan doing coke."

"And what did he say?"

"He said that he knew Ryan was high. He said Alistair and
his friends all had alibis. He said my theory was impossible.
And then he called my parents."

Tristan lay down next to me, on her side, propping her
head up on her hand. "Oh, Jonathan."

"I ruined it," I said, feeling the weight of the words as I
spoke them. "I ruined my one chance." And then, for the first
time since Ryan's death, I felt my eyes well up with tears. I
swallowed hard a few times and tried to hold them back. "I

can't go back to the cops now…no matter what I find. They'll never believe anything I say."

Tristan took my hand and gave it a squeeze. She was almost smiling. "But why would you have to? The detective said it was impossible. They must just know that it was an accident. You should be relieved."

I turned to face her. "Impossible? Relieved? Tristan, they lied to the cops. Alistair and Mike and Phil, they told a bullshit story about some alibi. They got away with murder! And because I lied about the coke, I don't have a chance at proving any of it. That's not a relief!"

"But, what if you're wrong?" she said pleadingly, squeezing my hand even tighter. "I mean, what if it *was* an accident? And yes, they lied about where they were so they wouldn't get in trouble, but that doesn't mean they killed Ryan. They just didn't want to get kicked off the team, or suspended, or whatever. You don't *know* that it was Alistair. You weren't *there*. You don't even know that Alistair is capable of doing something like that."

"I was there two minutes earlier, and he looked damn near capable enough."

"He was angry. He was high. I'm sure he was acting crazy, but that doesn't mean he's a murderer."

I sat up. "What the hell is this, anyway? Why are you defending him?"

"I'm not. It's just—"

"It's just what?"

"It's just that this is all insane," she said, jumping off of the bed and pacing in front of me. "You really think that Alistair is a murderer? A murderer? Really? He's just a kid. A regular kid that goes to our school. I went along with the idea for a little while, but if the police say he's innocent, then he's innocent."

I got up, fuming, and stood just inches away from her. "And what? It's all just an accident? A meaningless accident? Nothing that happened in those woods has anything to do with it? Just a total fucking coincidence?"

She was fighting the tears, and losing. "Yes! Or no, not a total—but yes, it has to be—at least…or mostly…or…."

"Or what? What the fuck are you saying, Tristan? You don't think it was an accident. You don't think Alistair did it. Then what? Do you think he jumped off that cliff?"

Then she smacked me. Hard. I didn't even really see it happen. I just heard it, felt the pain slice across my face, and then I was on the floor and she was running down the steps and out of the house. And then I was alone.

I stayed in bed, staring at the ceiling, for a very long time. From a logical point of view, I was having a hard time understanding what had just happened. From an emotional point of view, however, it was crystal clear: I was angry. Furious, in fact.

Now don't get me wrong, I wasn't so much angry about the slap. The slap was fine. I was pissed about everything that happened right before it. Tristan didn't think Alistair killed Ryan…or at least that's what she said. The question was: Did she really believe that? Or did she think that Ryan killed himself? Or did she actually buy that it was an accident? I went over her words again and again in my head: You don't *know*. You weren't *there*. You don't *know*. You weren't *there*. You don't *know*. You weren't *there*. Where the hell does she get off? No, I wasn't there when it happened, but I could damn well see where things were headed right before it happened. Ryan was outnumbered three to one, they were fighting, they were all coked-up out of their skulls, and besides, how else can you explain the way Alistair has been acting since it happened? Did she think that was normal? To be threatening the brother of your friend who just died? Didn't any of this matter to her? Didn't she see it?

I played out this imaginary argument with Tristan, alone there in my bedroom, for hours. I sat a make-believe version of her right down in my desk chair and laid out the evidence, the logic, the reasoning—piece by piece, hour after hour. We went over the events as I witnessed them: an explanation of the effects of cocaine on the central nervous system, the height of the ravine and its distance from the running path; we examined the characters of both Ryan and Alistair: their grades, behavior, social standing, and church attendance; I explained the physical evidence down to the minutest of details—the fabric, the footprint, the jersey, the phone—even making up expert testimony (which, I believed, was probably quite accurate) about the certainty of the correlation between what we found and the events on the day that Ryan died.

My mother knocked on my door at least two or three times throughout the process, but I just ignored her and continued the deposition, assuming she was just trying to feed me, or something equally insignificant. It was about a four-hour ordeal, all told, and by the end of it I was thoroughly exhausted and utterly convinced that I was right about everything.

Thirty-three

It was two o'clock on a Tuesday, just three days before Ryan was to start at St. Soren's (and three years and three days before he died in the ravine) when our mother drove Ryan and me to Saint Christopher's for our counseling session. I remember that she was wearing a stark white pantsuit, and that we were both freshly showered, our hair combed and parted, our penny loafers shining, and both of us dressed in matching khakis, blue dress shirts, and clip-on green ties.

Once in the rectory, a girl not much older than Ryan asked us to please sit and wait, and told us that the priest would be with us shortly. I slouched down into one of the hard wooden chairs and stared at the crucifix on the wall. This was a definitively mild crucifix, with Jesus' wounds represented by only a few small red nicks, and his crown of thorns looking more like a tennis headband than an instrument of torture.

To my great relief, the priest had my brother and me come in to see him at the same time, and told my mother to wait for us in the lobby. Initially, I had assumed we would each be going in alone, outnumbered by my mother and Father Kevin and a few other inquisitors thrown in for good measure. So this was a welcome development.

Inside his office, Father Kevin had arranged three chairs in a semicircle around a small table, on top of which was a large, leather-bound King James Bible.

"Please," he said, smiling warmly. "Sit, sit. Make yourselves comfortable."

We did as we were told, making our way to the two chairs that sat closest to the door. "Oh, no. No," said Father Kevin. "Please. I'll take the middle chair."

Divide and conquer, I thought.

When all three of us were sitting, Father Kevin spent a minute or two just looking us both over, a serene sort of calmness on face. Finally, he came out with it: "So, you two boys have been having a hard time with your faith, then, is that right?"

We both shrugged. Then Father Kevin asked us if what our mother said was true, and if we really believed that God was not real.

I was about to agree, but Ryan broke in too soon. "Actually, Father, it's really just me. Jonathan listens to me talk about it sometimes, but that's all."

"I see," said the priest. "And do you believe your brother, Jonathan? When he tells you these things?"

The truth, of course, was that I believed him completely; that Ryan could have told me the world was made of string cheese and that God looked exactly like a pepperoni pizza, and I would have bought it completely.

But of course, I had to be a bit more noncommittal if I was going to get out of this thing alive. "I don't know. Maybe a little."

Ryan clearly picked up on my discomfort, and came to my rescue. "Actually," he cut in. "The real problems with your theology are a bit over little Jonny's head."

Father Kevin raised his eyebrows sharply. "Oh? Problems, you say?"

"Well of course," Ryan said, growing bolder. "Don't get me wrong, there are a lot of really nice things about Christianity, but your whole theology just has so many holes, that it's basically useless."

These words smacked the patient expression right off Father Kevin's face. He leaned forward in his chair, glaring. "Now, I don't know what you think you've figured out here, but I can assure you that—"

"Hold on there," Ryan said, growing calmer as the priest got more flustered. "Take a breath. Let me explain."

Father Kevin huffed a few times and then relaxed a bit. "Please," he said. "Enlighten me."

Ryan smirked. "Sure thing." Then he turned to the great big King James Bible and opened up to the book of Exodus, Chapter 20. "You recognize this, Father?"

Father Kevin squinted at the page. "Of course. The Ten Commandments."

Ryan pointed at a verse. "What's this one here?"

"Thou shalt not kill," read the Father. "Are you going to tell me you have some kind of problem with 'Thou shalt not kill?'"

"No, no." Ryan chuckled, turning a few pages. "That's a good one." He pointed to another verse, in chapter 32. "Now what's this one say?"

Again, Father Kevin squinted down at the page, and read, "Put every man his sword by his side, and go in and out from gate to gate throughout the camp, and slay every man his brother, and every man his companion, and every man his neighbor."

"Now that's a whole lot of slaying," said Ryan. "Especially since God told the people—like, a few pages earlier—that they 'shalt not kill' anybody."

Father Kevin rolled his eyes. "Now Ryan, just because you find a passage that seems to contradict, doesn't mean—"

"Please Father," broke in Ryan. "Indulge me for another minute."

The priest stared at my brother as if he'd already seen every passage that Ryan was about to show him…and, who knows, maybe he had. But he seemed to make some sort of calculation and nodded anyway. "Okay, Ryan. Please, continue."

And so Ryan continued for maybe a half-hour, or more, flipping around the King James Bible, showing contradiction after contradiction. Father Kevin just sat there, stone-faced and unimpressed. I, however, was riveted. Sure, after a whole year of critiquing religions with Ryan, I didn't put much stock in the Bible, but I never thought it could be shown to be so incredibly flawed, so ridiculously inconsistent.

At last, Father Kevin had heard everything he needed to hear. He shut the Bible before Ryan could turn to another page. "Enough," he said. "I get your point."

"Good," said Ryan. "I'm glad."

"However," said Father Kevin, rising to his feet. "You have to understand that this is a book written by men, and it's not meant to be taken literally word-for-word."

"There are quite a few people who would disagree with that."

"Yes, there are, and if you've shown anything here it's why they are wrong in doing so. Because in actuality, the Bible is a collection of parables and metaphors that must be interpreted, meditated on, prayed about. That's why you have clergy like myself to help you to understand the truth—God's truth— that lies beneath all of these words on paper. And for that you need faith."

"Faith?" said Ryan.

"Yes, faith…God asks us to believe in him even though there is no scientific proof of his existence, and even though his Holy Word may seem to be a little inconsistent in some places."

Now Ryan stood as well. "You know, I'm glad you brought up this idea of faith, Father. Because this is really where the whole thing breaks down for me."

"Oh? How so?"

"Well, it just seems to me that your god has gone to great lengths to throw peoples' faith off the trail of his truth, don't you think? I mean, science points to evolution and the big bang, his book is full of holes, and there are so many other religions to choose from…."

"Now, now," said the Father. "You're getting confused. It is the devil, the father of lies, that deceives people from the truth, that creates these…distractions."

"So then why doesn't your god just open up the sky, fly on down to Earth, and show everyone the truth? He can do that, right? He is a god, after all."

"Of course he can, but he wouldn't. Because then the people wouldn't need faith."

"But what about all of the people who believe the 'lies,' as you call them? People like that are dying every day. What happens to them?"

"Well, without Jesus, they…"

"They go to hell? Because your god wanted to play some game with them?"

"Now it's hardly a game, you see—"

"And here's the point, Father, the biggest contradiction of them all. God cannot simultaneously be good, loving, and all-powerful, if the world he created dooms millions upon millions of its souls to an eternity of torture. Something has to go. Either he's not all-powerful, or, if he is, he's a major league asshole. Or, or, or—and here's a wild idea—the whole story is just a steaming pile of horseshit, made up by a bunch of black-robe-wearing freaks who thought so little of the people they were shoveling it to, that they figured they could sell them any old load of crap, just so long as they threw in a few scary statues and some stained-glass windows."

Father Kevin, as you might imagine, was not amused. He turned, and walked over to the window, looking out at the rectory courtyard. He took a few deep breaths and said, "Jonathan, will you leave us alone please?"

But by this point, I didn't want to go anywhere. I would've much rather stayed and listened to how this whole little show-down was going to play out, and who would prevail in the end. But I knew better then to tempt my own fate by defying the priest in his current mood. So I just suppressed my smile, stood from my chair, and headed out into the lobby.

Then, as I was closing the door behind me, I caught Ryan's eye for a second, and he winked. And it was only then that I realized what the priest had already seen, and why he had asked me to leave: that Ryan had won the showdown before it even began.

Ryan came out of the rectory almost an hour later, seeming quite content and at ease. Smiling, actually, as if the whole thing had gone even better than he expected. When I asked him what happened, he just told me that he and Father Kevin had a good talk and that everything was fine. He never told me any more than that, and the following week he began his freshman year at St. Soren's without so much as a whisper of protest. He joined the football team, made a few friends, and went quietly to mass every Sunday with our mother. And we never spoke about that day, or about gods, or religions, or anything like that again.

The effect of all this on me was profound. After the first Sunday mass in which Ryan didn't let loose even so much as a single snicker, I decided that I would never find a god I could believe in, so I would simply be an atheist for the rest of my life. We grew further and further apart over those next few years, and if I'm being honest with myself, it wasn't until I started looking into his death that I finally understood how little, by the end, I actually knew about his life.

That might be the saddest part of this whole story.

Thirty-four

The next morning, there was a note for me in the kitchen: "Cassie stopped by last night. I knocked on your door three times to let you know, but it sounded like you were busy. Anyway, she left you something."

It was early in the morning, and I had barely slept, so it took me a moment to recall the night before, and put it all into context. I read the note over again, and then noticed that underneath it there was an envelope baring my name written in purple, glittery pen. I tore it open, having no idea what Cassie would want to leave for me.

It was a picture from the party on Friday night, of Cassie and me dancing—her wrists were draped round my neck, my hands were on her hips, and we were staring into each other's eyes. But what was most striking was the look on my face. I looked happy. Just happy, like a high school kid should be, dancing with a pretty girl on a Friday night.

It stopped me so abruptly because that look, the person in that picture and that feeling he was experiencing, seemed so incredibly foreign to me. He seemed like someone I'd never met, who lived in a time, a town, and a country I'd never been to.

Then I flipped the picture over, and found the note that
Cassie had left for me. It said, simply:

> Jonathan,
>
> I get it. I probably would have left too. Every-
> body at school has been talking about how cool
> it was to hang out with you on Friday. I know
> you're probably going through a lot right now,
> but if you need to talk just call me. I miss you.
>
> Love,
>
> Cassie.
>
> PS. Homecoming is this Saturday, and they're
> calling it the Ryan Stiles Memorial Homecom-
> ing Dance. Anyway, I'm sure you don't want to go
> or anything, but I've already told everyone that I
> won't say yes to anyone but you.

Of course, the fact that they were holding the dance in
Ryan's honor was a bit nauseating. But it was the last part
of the note that really got me—that she wouldn't say yes to
anyone but me. I sank down to the floor, pulling my head into
my knees, leaning my head against the cabinets. What am I
doing? What's happening? Ryan is dead and Tristan fucking
slapped me and Ryan is dead and my father's a Buddhist and
Ryan is dead and my mom won't stop smiling and Ryan was
probably killed, but I'll never get to prove it, but that doesn't
even matter because Ryan is still dead and to top of it all off,
this sweet, innocent, beautiful girl is clearly in love with me.

Well, there was only one place I could go, only one person
I could see. I just hoped I could sneak out onto the football
field in the middle of a school day without being noticed.

As it turned out, sneaking up to the football field didn't prove to be a problem at all. A thick fog had rolled in off the ocean, and visibility around the campus was slim. I just skated right up to the front gate and strolled out onto the fifty-yard line.

But Jesus wasn't there.

I waited for about twenty minutes, and he still didn't show. I searched all around the football field for him, and then behind the bleachers, up by the street, in the parking lot. But he was nowhere to be found. A half-hour ticked by, and then another, and another.

My first thought was that he had another run-in with the guys who had beat him up before. Or then again, maybe he just took off and left town—it wouldn't be that surprising, considering the way that everything else had been going with me lately.

I climbed about halfway up the stands and lay down on one of the benches, hanging my head over the end so that the whole world inverted. With the thickness of the fog, it didn't even seem to make that much of a difference: the sky was a little darker and the Earth a little lighter, but other than that, it all looked just about the same—hazy and blurred and completely out-of-focus.

After another few minutes, I noticed a glint of white begin to distinguish itself from the pale gray of the fog, coming toward me from the spot in the woods where I last saw Ryan. I held my breath. I squinted as the white glimpse grew more full, until Jesus Jackson himself came walking out of the whiteness, heading straight for me.

When he finally made his way to the bleachers, he took a seat next to me, chuckled, and said, "So is it really that bad?"

"Worse. I thought you took off to Mexico with my twelve dollars."

This made him laugh even harder. "No," he said. "Tempting as that may be, I think I'll stick this job out."

"I was almost ready to go report you to the police."

He rolled his eyes. "Police? I think you know how much good that would do."

"Wait a minute," I said, pushing myself up to a seated position. "Do you know about…everything?"

He let a mysterious grin creep across his face. "You mean, do I know that you went to the cops, that they didn't believe you, called your parents…all that stuff?"

"Yeah! How the hell do you know all that? Did you talk to Henry?"

Jesus shook his head. "It was a guess…though, of course, a well-educated one."

"Oh…well, I wish you could have guessed it before it all happened."

"I did, remember? You just weren't listening."

He was right, of course, and this just made me feel worse. I leaned back against the bleachers, staring up into the gray void of fog. "So what do I do now? The cops won't listen to me. All of my evidence is gone, or useless, and I don't even have anyone to help me anymore."

"Why not?"

"Henry is probably too scared to talk to me after going to the cops, and Tristan left my house in tears last night after she decided to smack me in the face."

Jesus gave me a sidelong glance, frowning. "Why did she do that?"

"I don't know. Because she's fucked up? Because she wants to believe it was all an accident? At any rate, I'm pretty sure she's done trying to help me."

"Well," he said. "You're right and you're wrong."

"How do you figure?"

"You're right that you're alone. Even if Henry or Tristan do come back around, this is ultimately your quest—for better or worse—no one can finish it but you."

"Yeah, whatever. There's nothing left to finish. It's over."

He cocked his head to the side. "Do you really believe that? That it's over?"

"I don't *believe* anything. It's the truth. It's reality. I might as well accept it."

With that, Jesus Jackson hopped to his feet and began to bound up the steps to the top of the stands.

"Where are you going?" I called after him.

"Come with me," he said, without even turning his head.

"Where? Why?"

"Just shut your mouth and come with me. Now."

I really didn't feel like doing anything. In fact, I was starting to wonder why I even bothered getting out of bed. "Do I have to?"

"Yes."

So I slowly rose to my feet, and followed him up to the top row of the bleachers. "So now what?" I asked.

Jesus climbed up on the railing behind the last row. "Come up here," he said. "I want to show you something."

I looked up at him warily. It was a hell of a drop off the back of those bleachers—not enough to kill you, but probably far enough to break an arm, or even a leg—and the railing didn't look so sturdy. "I don't think so," I said.

"Come on," Jesus prodded, shaking the rail a bit. "It's perfectly safe."

"Fine." Cautiously, I grabbed the top bar of the railing, hoisting my feet onto the lowest bar. "What am I looking for?"

Jesus pointed through the fog toward a far line of trees past the baseball diamonds and soccer fields. "Can you see that?"

"What?" I asked, seeing nothing as I squinted harder, trying to make out what he was pointing at.

"Climb up one more," he said. "It's just over that big pine tree."

Frankly, I couldn't even make out the pine tree, but I did as I was told, climbing up one more bar, so that my kneecaps were pressed against the very top of the railing. The bar beneath me shook a bit. I tried hard not to look down as I tried to distinguish the shapes through the mist.

"I still don't see anything," I complained, and just as the words left my mouth, I felt Jesus' hand press into my back, and push me hard over the rail.

I screamed, but it was too late. With my knees pressed against the top bar, my whole body just tilted straight as a board over the edge. Almost in slow motion, I watched the world turn upside down again. I felt the blood rushing to my head, and just as my body started to accelerate toward the ground, it all stopped with a great and painful tug—I was suspended, my head still far above the ground. And Jesus was above me, holding my ankles and grinning like an idiot.

"What the hell are you doing?" I screamed.

"Just relax, would ya?"

"Relax? Are you crazy?"

"Maybe. I've certainly been accused of worse, but that's hardly the point now. You *have* to relax. We're going to have a conversation."

I looked past my feet to the gray sky above. I tried to breath a bit more slowly, to calm myself. "What are we going to talk about?" I asked.

Jesus smiled. "Faith."

"Oh, Christ," I said.

"Jackson, actually."

"Very funny. Can we start talking now, please?"

"Okay. The way I see it, you're having a crisis of faith."

"I never had any faith to begin with. Haven't you been listening to anything I've told you?"

"I have, and you said that you don't believe in God, not that you don't have any faith. There's a big difference."

"Fine. Whatever. Just get on with it."

"Right," said Jesus. "So, here you are, living your life while you're having this crisis of faith, which is kind of like flying a plane while having a crisis of fuel—all it really means is that you're running low…or in your case, nearly empty, you know?"

"Um…sure."

"Now, tell me: What happens when you run out of fuel in a plane?"

This was getting very annoying. "I don't know. You crash. Can we move this along a little faster?"

"Exactly," Jesus replied, clearly unmoved by my plea. "You crash." And with that, he let go of my ankles.

The ground smacked into me like a brick in the face. I yelped in pain, tasting mud and grass on my tongue and in my teeth. I rolled over, my body aching, and saw the silhouette of Jesus' head leaning over the railing, a big ridiculous smile on his stupid face. "What the hell did you that for?" I screamed at him.

He chuckled. "To prove a point."

"What, that you're an asshole?"

"No," Jesus said. "That whether you believe in God or Buddha or Krishna or nothing at all, sometimes you just have to take a leap of faith."

I struggled to my feet. "Are you crazy? You dropped me! What the hell does that prove about faith?"

"Look at you," he said. "You're standing, you're talking, nothing's broken—you're fine. We leapt and we landed."

"Yeah, but what if I wasn't fine? What if I fell badly and broke my leg, or my freaking neck? That could have just as easily happened."

"Yes, it could have."

"So what the hell would you have said if it had?"

"Well," Jesus said, leaning over the rail, looking me straight in the eyes. "I would have said that it was worth a shot. That taking a leap of faith is always worth a shot. After all, whether you land on your feet or fall on your face, at least you'll know what's on the other side. At least you'll know the truth."

And just like that, he was gone.

I struggled to my feet and made way back to the bleachers, where I remained for the rest of the day. I sat through the gym classes, and the kids coming out to smoke, and the practices, where Alistair and his boys played scrimmages, and Tristan and her girls practiced their cheers out on the far field over by the woods. A breeze began to blow as the day wore on, clearing out the fog and making the whole world seem so crisp and clear by comparison. No one seemed to notice me, up there in the stands, with my hood pulled down tight around my face…or at least if they did, no one bothered to interrupt my quiet pondering, to disturb my secret planning.

Thirty-five

Now I have to stop here for a second to talk a bit about *inspiration*. As an atheist, I don't believe in *divine inspiration*, exactly....Or at least, I don't believe that there's any divine god or mystical whatthefuck out there to do the inspiring. But inspiration itself? That mysterious, unexplainable, baffling burst of insight that somehow manages to tie everything together in a neat little knot? Well, that I believe in. That, I know is true because it's exactly what happened to me as I was sitting in those stands, watching the football team practice. And the whole rest of this story—its entire sad and unfortunate ending—would have been impossible without it.

So there I was, sitting high up in the bleachers watching the players run back and forth and back and forth, when I caught sight of Alistair, sprinting headlong down the field. He was being chased by a bevy of his teammates, and they were gaining on him fast. He bore down and tried zigzagging to lose them, but it didn't work, and then finally this monstrous linebacker (he must have weighed 250 pounds, at least) came barreling at him from the side, diving into Alistair's path and taking him right out at the knees. Alistair instantly was in the air—high in the air—doing a full frontal flip about four feet off the ground, and right then, right in the middle of the tackle, there was this moment—an instant, really, like a frozen tableau in time—where Alistair just seemed to hang there, upside down, dangling, suspended immobile over the ground.

And at that moment, it all just washed right over me: the plan. Seeing Alistair dangling there in the air, I knew exactly what I had to do. What I had to do *to him*. Sure, it took me a few hours of pacing around behind the bleachers to work out the details, but the plan itself was there; the inspiration, the method, and more importantly, the final result: a public confession at the Ryan Stiles Memorial Homecoming Dance.

After working out some more of the details, I came up with two things that had to get done right away if I was going to have any chance of putting this plan into action: make up with Henry, and start acting like a relatively normal, slightly-sad-but-not-psychotic Dead Kid's Brother.

I figured that making up with Henry would be as simple as going over to his house and apologizing for being such a lunatic for the past few weeks. Getting him to help me with one last stunt to prove Alistair's guilt—well, that would probably be impossible. My only hope was to convince him that I *didn't* want to do the whole detective thing anymore, and then somehow trick him into playing his part in the plan. I doubted the first part would be hard; the second, though… well, I'd just have to work that one out on the fly.

Wanting to get started as quickly as possible, I skated over to his house, rang the doorbell, and hoped like hell one of his parents didn't answer.

If there was in fact a god, he clearly wasn't on my side at this point, because Henry's mom answered the door, breaking down instantly into a convulsion of whiny-voiced, eyebrow-raised, hand-wringing empathy.

I tried to block it all out, but the parts that got through sounded something like this:

"Oh, Jonathaaaaaaan. How aaaare you? Are you all riiiiiiiiight? Oh my goodness, you poor soooooooul."

I'd learned by then that the best response to such a display was no response at all. The less you fed into them, the more they just assumed that you'd rather be left alone.

It worked all right with Mrs. Sun. She only kept it up for about two or three minutes before getting the hint. She told me Henry was "in the basement with his computer" in a mildly disapproving manner that seemed as if it would be more appropriate if he were down there with a bag of weed or a stack of dirty magazines.

When I opened the door to the basement, the computer was off, and Henry was staring at the top of the steps, waiting for me.

"I heard my mom," he mumbled. "Sorry."

"It's okay," I lied. "It doesn't bother me so much anymore."

He nodded, and as I walked down the steps and sat on the ratty little couch they kept next to his desk, I noticed that he appeared to be even more uncomfortable than usual. So I just jumped right into my apology, hoping for the best: "Look," I said. "I'm sorry. Really sorry. About everything—the police station, of course, but everything before that too. This whole *ordeal*. It's just…well, it's just something that I think I had to do to deal with Ryan's death. Just some crazy thing. But I'm over it now."

Henry looked at me like I was speaking another language. "You're what?"

"I'm over it," I repeated, trying to sound as convincing as possible. "I don't think Alistair killed my brother, or anything absurd like that, and I recognize that I only really thought that as a way of coping with my loss."

"Really?" he said.

"Really."

"Okay. I mean, if that's what you really think."

He seemed far less excited than I imagined he would be. "What's the matter?" I asked him. "Isn't that what you think?"

"Actually, no. I don't think that at all. I'm even more positive than ever that Alistair had something to do with your brother's death."

"What?" I couldn't believe what I was hearing. "Are you crazy? Why?"

Henry paused, seeming to appraise my true intentions. Then he said, "Take a seat. I want to show you something."

I lowered myself into the chair. "What's this all about?"

Henry opened the top drawer of his desk, pulled out the hard drive I had retrieved for him from Alistair's house, and plugged it into his laptop.

"Was there actually something on there?" I asked. "Did you find anything?" To be honest, I had all but forgotten about the hard drive once we had Alistair's phone. It just seemed so much less likely to be useful.

"Here," said Henry, clicking open a window that seemed, at first glance, to contain nothing but line after line of gibberish and computer code. "I just found it last night."

I moved my face closer to the screen. "What am I looking for here? This all looks like nonsense."

"It's a chat session from sometime less than a week before we copied the files. Most of it is still encoded, but this part is readable." Henry moved the mouse, and highlighted a few lines right in the middle of all the gibberish.

...789:8;@AHKOU$null'%angeÄÄÄÄ><>
Stop worrying!</><>I can't.</>A few more
months and everyone will forget</><>Maybe. I
just wish I could forget.</><.fl.agsYdestR&%
58e6ef ___ZN21T & eÄÄ...

"Jesus," I said, after reading them over a few more times.

"Right?"

"Any idea who the other person is?"

"No. I tried everything, but there's no identifying informa-tion. Do you think we should take it back to Detective Conrad, see if it makes him change his mind?"

"It won't," I said.

"But clearly Alistair's lying about something. Won't that matter to him at all?"

"No. We're going to need a lot more than this to make him change his mind."

"But we have to do something, right?"

"Right."

"What though?"

"Well, I have a plan—if you're willing to help."

"Of course, of course. What is it?"

I smiled, glad that I didn't have to trick Henry into going along. "We're going to get Alistair to confess."

"Confess?"

"Yup."

"But how?"

"Simple," I assured him. "We'll give him no other option."

Thirty-six

When I think back on it now, it amazes me that Henry, given how good he was at pointing out the technical flaws in my plan, never seemed to notice the fundamental ones. After all, it barely took him a moment of consideration before he tossed out all of my ideas, worked out his own plan, and then labored night and day with different designs until he got it right.

But I guess I can't blame Henry. The technical side, for the most part, went off without a hitch.

When Saturday night—homecoming night—finally arrived, my anticipation and anxiety had become almost too much to bear. Henry had taken care of all the preparations at school, so I hadn't set foot at St. Soren's since I left there on Wednesday. And by the time I skated up to the gym, freshly washed and wearing my best school dance clothes (once again pulled from my mother's picks of previously disregarded fashion), I had thought through my plan a thousand times, trying to predict and prepare for every possible glitch or snag.

The one thing I didn't prepare for—couldn't have, really— was Cassie. I knew I would see her. I knew, of course, that she would take my coming to the dance as an acceptance of her invitation. But I never expected that the moment I stepped into that gym she'd break away from her little gaggle of girlfriends, make a beeline across the dance floor, and grab the back of my head, pulling my face into hers, pushing her tongue into my mouth, and pressing every possible centimeter of her body into mine.

When she pulled away, I just said, "Wow. Thanks."

She smiled. "I knew you'd come." Then she took me by the hand and led me into the dance.

Now let me tell you: That was the only time—from the moment I thought of it to the second I passed the point of no return—that I ever doubted my plan.

And it wasn't just because Alistair was her brother—that didn't really bother me so much—it was more that I knew that as soon as I went through with it, this feeling would end. And because her last name was St. Claire, I knew that it would never come back.

But all of that was for the future…at least an hour more down the road. First, though, I just needed to act normal: dance, laugh, talk, have a good time (but not too good), and put on the perfect picture of the Dead-Kid's-Brother.

So I did. I went out there and I acted as normal as I could. I danced, I joked around, I complained about teachers and homework and uniforms and rules. And at more than one point during that hour, I really wished that it could just stay that way. That this was just how high school was working out for me: friends, a dance, a girl, a normal Saturday night.

But then the reality sank in that this was never how high school would be for me. That the only reason Cassie even knew who I was, the only reason I ever talked to her, the only reason we were there together at that dance at all, was because my brother was dead—and her brother had killed him.

So I began to get mad. At everything, everyone. At first it

was just this twinge in the back of my mind, but then it started to grow, becoming more present and encompassing. I got mad at Alistair, of course, but also at Ryan (he was hanging out with Al, after all; he was snorting coke in the back of the school), and I got mad at myself and my mom and newly Buddhist dad, and I got mad as hell at Jesus Jackson for not following through on his promise of complete and total faith, because Lord knows I could've used it, in that sparkling gymnasium, with that cherry-lipped girl—maybe even to stop me from what I knew I was about to do.

I got so angry at one point that I had to leave the dance floor, take a breather in the bathroom. I locked myself in a stall and put my head in my hands. The thoughts were just going too fast: *Am I really going to go through with this and will Alistair really confess and what if he doesn't and what if I accidentally kill him or paralyze him or worse, and what if Cassie never speaks to me again, and what are you crazy of course she'll never speak to you, and is that worth it, and of course it's worth it, 'cause he killed your fucking brother he killed your fucking brother he killed your fucking brother.*

And then I heard it, my cue. They were about to announce the homecoming king and queen.

I sprang into action, my body moving as if on autopilot. I'd rehearsed it all so many times in my mind that I didn't have to think at all. I stumbled zombie-like out of the bathroom and began making my way toward the front of the stage.

About halfway through the crowd, though, I was stopped by a hand on my shoulder. It startled me, and I jumped as I turned around. But it was only Cassie, smiling and perky in her black velvet dress.

"Oh," I said. "Hey."

She caressed down the length of my arm, finally taking hold of my hand in her own. "Let's get out of here," she said. "We can break into the teachers' lounge, try out the couches....You now, there's a rumor that Mr. Cooper keeps a bottle of vodka stashed in the freezer."

If I'd have let my body have its way I would have collapsed right there on the floor, or just followed her like a puppy wherever she wanted to take me. But my mind's will was strong; it had rage and anger and hatred on its side. And in the end my mind won.

"I..." But I didn't know what to say. I wanted something good, something that wasn't a lie, something that would pardon what I was about to do. Unfortunately, I don't think those words existed. "I can't. I just...can't. I have to go."

"Okay," she said, seeming confused, but not upset. "Well maybe later then."

I couldn't respond. I just started to walk away but stopped after a few steps. I turned and met her big blue eyes, still filled with something like hope. "I'm sorry," I said. Then I turned quickly and pushed myself the rest of the way to the stage.

―――――

Once right at the front, I stared up at Ms. LaRochelle at the podium, the heat of the lights making her thick, orange cake makeup run in rivulets down her face. Beside her was Mr. McDuff, the associate principal, holding two rhinestone-bedazzled crowns. And right behind them both sat a pair of elaborately decorated wooden chairs covered in tinsel and glitter and lights—the homecoming thrones. One for the queen, and, of course, one for the king.

She gave some kind of introduction, but I couldn't hear it over the blare of my heartbeat throbbing in my ears. It just sounded like buzzing, or like someone screaming under water.

There was applause. The crowd parted, and Tristan came walking up to the stage. She gave me a sad smile as she passed; I averted my eyes. I had hoped she wouldn't win (it would be easier without having her so close), but I wasn't surprised that she did. Who else could it have been?

What happened next was nothing I even considered, not for a second. The plan, of course, was for Alistair to win. According to Henry (who, in retrospect, was probably not the best source for such information), he was a shoo-in. But instead of Ms. LaRochelle calling out a congratulations to Alistair, she yelled up at the catwalk, "Can someone turn the projector on please?"

I noticed then that behind the podium, just to the right of the giant crucifix, was a large white projection screen, about ten feet high and twenty feet across. And a moment after I saw it, that whole great big screen was filled with Ryan's face.

A moment of hushed silence spread across the gymnasium. I knew the picture well. It was taken by the school photographer the previous year, just after the last football game of the season. Ryan was sitting cross-legged on the fifty-yard line after everyone else had left the field—exhausted, dirty, and happy. The photographer must have crouched down as well, because the perspective of the shot is looking up, just slightly, toward Ryan's face, and in the background you could just make out the glimmer of lights reflecting off the goalposts. His eyes were gazing right at the lens, right at me, and they were so easy and so forgiving and so kind, as if to say: *Don't do it, Jon; don't do it.*

But I didn't listen. Instead, I understood instantly that this was my one window of opportunity—emotions were running high, Ryan was already on everyone's mind, and Alistair, if he had any soul at all, would be half-broken already.

So I summoned every last ounce of courage I had. I climbed up onto that stage, turned, and faced the jury of my peers.

The timing was, in fact, perfect. No one resisted my taking the podium at all; Ms. LaRochelle actually smiled as she shooed Mr. McDuff off the stage. After all, what more perfect climax to their homage to Ryan than for his previously silent, brooding younger brother to make his first public speech in thanks of their kind and warmhearted efforts?

This was, of course, exactly what I wanted them to think. I played into it as best I could, flashing a sad and thankful smile both to Ms. LaRochelle and Mr. McDuff. Tristan seemed nervous, but calmed a bit when I touched her hand, and whispered, "It's okay," before stepping up to the microphone.

I took a deep breath and peeked to my right, confirming that Henry was right there in the wings, right where he was supposed to be: sweating and worried and miserable, standing right beside the pulley system for the light bars. I turned to the crowd. Though the lights were shining in my face, I could still make out most of my classmates, smiling through their sympathy, wishing me the best, grateful for my presence, and ready to witness a truly heartfelt moment. Even Alistair, standing right out in front, completely oblivious to the peril that was about to befall him, was staring at me with a look of honest hope in his eyes.

For a moment, I thought about how easy it would have been to have just given them the speech that they wanted—thanking them for their sympathy and their prayers, telling them of my heartache and sadness, offering my assurances that even though we'd never see him again, I could just tell by the depth of their love that Ryan was *right there in that gymnasium with us.*

But of course I could never give that speech...for the simple reason that I just wouldn't have believed a word of it.

Jesus Jackson had clearly failed at his endeavor to instill in me a faith of any sort in anything, because as I stood up on that stage, I didn't have the slightest idea whether Ryan was in heaven or hell or purgatory or nirvana or being reincarnated or even resting peacefully in some atheistic nothingness. All I knew, for sure, was that Ryan was in the ground. That's all. And Alistair had put him there.

So began my speech:

"Hi...everybody. I'm Jonathan Stiles." I took a breath. It was the only sound in the whole gymnasium. "And, well... this guy on the screen behind me is my brother—was my brother—Ryan. As I know you are all aware, he died about three weeks ago, on my very first day as a student here at St. Soren's. Now, I probably don't have to tell you, but starting at a new school is hard enough, but when something like this happens, well, it just really makes it almost impossible to have a normal or a positive time of it at all." I took another deep breath to compose myself. I could feel my stomach clenching in on itself in spasm after spasm. A few girls in the first row seemed to see my anxiety as an abundance of emotion, and they began to tear up, practically in unison. "Anyway, I just, really, wanted to get up here and tell you how great you've all been in trying to make this a little bit easier for me, and how much I know Ryan would appreciate this whole night." I glanced again over at Henry one last time before making the big leap..."But you know, there's one person who has just been so great to me, and I know he was one of Ryan's closest friends. He was one of the last people to ever see Ryan alive, and I just really want to honor him in a special way tonight... Umm, Alistair St. Claire, could you come up here, please?"

I looked right at Alistair, right in his eyes, and gave him the most sadly affectionate face I could muster. He seemed taken aback, and a bit scared. But then the crowd started to clap, and he had no choice but to smile, climb up onto the stage, and take a place beside me at the podium. "Thanks for coming up, Alistair," I spoke into the mic, though I could no longer bring myself to look at him directly. "I asked you up here because I want to give you something. It's something that was very special to Ryan, and I know that, after everything you've done, he would really like the fact that I'm giving it to you."

Alistair smiled nervously. I took a few steps toward the throne, and picked up the crown. "Ryan would want you to wear this. After everything you went through together, he'd want you to be the king."

The room erupted into applause. Alistair smiled in relief as I placed the crown on his head, and motioned for him to sit down in the throne beside Tristan. It was, by all measures, a truly touching moment.

It was also, of course, a trap. While everyone else was dancing, Henry had attached one end of a light-pole wire to the back of the king's throne. The wire ran down to the stage floor and disappeared behind a curtain, where it rose to a pulley high above the stage, before ending at four hundred pounds of counterweights that Henry was about to drop from a height of about forty feet.

As soon as I gave the nod, Henry would let go of the rope, escaping out the stage door while the counterweights sent Alistair flying into the air, hanging at a height roughly similar to that from which Ryan fell to his death. I would then grab the bottom of the wire and threaten to unclip it if Alistair did not confess immediately to his crime.

"Thank you," Alistair whispered, seeming honestly touched.

"Take your seat," I whispered back. "You've earned it."

"I would be honored to," Alistair replied, stepping over to the throne and smiling at the crowd before finally sitting down.

"Hold on tight," I whispered.

Alistair gave me a quizzical look, clearly confused. But he did as he was told, and as soon as I saw his hands grip the armrests, I gave Henry the nod.

For a half-second, the faces of the crowd went blank with confusion as a loud metallic screech rang out from sound of the counterweights tearing toward the floor. By the time I turned back, Alistair was forty feet in the air, gripping the chair with all of his might, swinging back and forth across the stage, from Ryan to the crucifix and back again, screaming.

A chorus of gasps leapt out from the crowd. Tristan jumped up from her chair, and sprinted to the edge of the stage. Mr. McDuff ran up to stop me, but before he could climb the steps I grabbed the support wire, and pulled it out for everyone to see. "Stop right there." I shouted. "Come any closer and Alistair falls."

Mr. McDuff froze. A few girls screamed and ran for the door (maybe they thought I had a gun, or a bomb). Above me, I could hear Alistair begin to cry.

Then, precisely as I had asked him to, Detective Conrad entered the back door of the gym.

"Thank you for coming, Detective," I shouted back to him. "This will all make sense in just a second."

Detective Conrad stared at me quizzically. Then he followed the gaze of the crowd up over my head to where Alistair was dangling in front of the cross. Instantly, he seemed to understand the whole situation. "Now just hold on there, Jonathan," he yelled, raising both of his palms and approaching the stage. "Just don't move. Don't touch that wire. This is not how you want to do this."

I jerked the wire. Alistair screamed and tried to pull his feet up on the seat of the throne. "Just stay right there detective." I looked up at Alistair. "Just tell this detective the truth, and I'll let you down nice and easy. Okay, Al?"

"What?" he cried. "What truth? What are you talking about?"

I jerked the wire again, causing the whole gym to erupt in a single scream. "The truth about Ryan, about what happened out in the woods behind the school three weeks ago. You can start with the pile of cocaine I saw you snorting with your asshole friends….And then you can tell us all how you pushed Ryan into the ravine."

Alistair stared at me in shock. Then he stuttered, "Th…th…the…there was no— You what? Y…y…y…you think I pushed Ryan, are you fucking crazy?"

I yanked the wire hard. A distinct cracking sound came from somewhere in the throne. "There was no what, Alistair? You're gonna tell me there was no coke? That it was just sugar on that textbook? Or were you going to say that you weren't trying to beat Ryan into a pulp right before he died?" I yanked hard again. Again, another crack.

"Okay!" He yelled "Okay! There was coke! We did a few goddamned lines after practice! But I didn't kill him! Jesus, Jonathan…"

I turned to the crowd, satisfied that things were starting to go my way. *Another few seconds up there,* I thought, *and he'll spill everything.*

And it was then that I saw Cassie. I was hoping that I wouldn't notice her at all…or at least if I did, that I wouldn't be stupid enough to make eye contact. But I was. And I did. And the look she gave me—so hurt, so betrayed—wiped the self-satisfied grin right off of my face.

But I had to go on. So I swallowed my shame and checked

to see if Conrad was at all swayed by Alistair's admission. But Conrad was still just staring straight at me, approaching slowly, showing nothing. "So what do you make of that?" I asked him.

"Now I need you to listen to me, Jonathan, okay?" His voice was calm and even. His eyes wouldn't leave mine...not for a second. He kept on approaching. Slowly, slowly. "Alistair did not kill Ryan. He was nowhere near that ravine when Ryan died. Dozens of witnesses—many in this room, I imagine—can attest to that."

"Well, they're lying!" I screamed at him. "I was there. I saw Alistair trying to beat the crap out of Ryan right before he wound up at the bottom of that ravine. Tell him, Alistair. Tell him how I found you all there, and how you were so fucking scared that I'd tell a teacher about your damn coke that you started to beat on me and Henry, and when Ryan came to defend me, you took it all out on him, the three of you beating him until you pushed him into the ravine." And then I gave the wire the hardest jerk yet.

Alistair screamed. Tears were covering his face. "Okay, yeah, we fought, okay? We fought, but when Ryan ran off into the woods, he was alone. Jesus, just ask Tristan, she was right there with me."

And this is when it all started to fall down on me. Everything slowed. I turned to find Tristan, standing by the wings, clutching the curtains and silently crying. "Tristan?" I said, though too softly for her to hear. "What...what is he...?"

But she wouldn't even meet my eyes, much less respond. My hand loosened on the wire, sending Alistair swinging though the air. The cracking and the gasps grew louder in unison.

"Christ, Tristan," Alistair screamed. "Just tell him. Who cares what he knows. It's not your goddamned fault. None of it is your goddamned fault, already! Just tell him."

My eyes were still on Tristan, waiting for a response. But she just stood there, staring at the floor like a coward.

After a moment more of swinging, Alistair said it all for her: "She broke up with him, okay? Tristan and me had a thing and so she broke up with him. She tried to give him his damned school ring back and he freaked out and ran off into the woods. But that was way after you and your friend took off." He paused to catch his breath. "I mean, we tried to go after him, but he just disappeared. And Tristan's been going crazy about it ever since, because she feels so freaking guilty and because she's been so afraid you'd find out about us. But Jesus, Jonathan, no one fucking killed him. Now just please let me down!"

I hadn't even begun to process any of this when Conrad spoke up again, still moving closer with every step. "Listen to me, Jonathan," he said, his voice clear, articulated. "Listen to me very carefully. You're confused, and upset, and that's okay. But listen: What you think happened is impossible."

I didn't have the strength anymore to argue. "But…"

"You told me this all happened right after you got let out early that day, right? About one o'clock?"

"Yeah…"

He stepped closer. "Ryan made three phone calls between two and three o'clock. Two to Tristan, and one to your mother. He left messages, Jonathan. He could not have fallen into the ravine before four o'clock."

"What are you…?" I began, but I couldn't finish the question…My mind was searching back, dizzy and confused: *It doesn't make sense. Ryan died right after I left. Hadn't someone told me that? Did I just assume it? Did I really…?Could I have?* "It doesn't make…why was he…he should've been home…. or somewhere…."

"Listen to me, Jonathan," Conrad repeated, now at the foot of the stage, keeping his hands at the ready and his eyes on me. "Listen to me closely. Ryan had a fight with Alistair about his girlfriend—long after the whole thing with you and Henry—and then Ryan ran off into woods. Alistair followed him, and came back a few minutes later. Lots of people saw him come back—teachers, coaches, bus drivers—lots of people—but Ryan didn't die until almost two hours later. Both Alistair and Tristan were long gone by then. Look Jonathan… Ryan probably just got too close to the edge and lost his balance. Maybe it was the wind, maybe it was just bad luck, but it wasn't murder." He put his foot on the first step leading up to the stage. "I should have told you this when you came to see me last weekend, but I thought it would be better coming from your parents. It's my fault that I didn't tell you, and I'm sorry. But I need you to let Alistair down now, okay? Nice and easy, okay?"

I turned again to look at Tristan, and the sorry, pathetic expression on her face told me everything I needed to know: She knew that Alistair was innocent all along; she was just trying appease her own guilt, or sadness, or something. I turned to Alistair, swinging above me, and suddenly felt so sorry for him. Sure, maybe he stole Ryan's girlfriend, but he didn't deserve this. He didn't deserve any of it.

So I began to let him down. What else was there to do? Inch-by-inch, nice and easy, just like Conrad said. But before I had lowered him all the way back to the stage, that cracking sound returned, louder and harder. With at least ten feet left to go, the wooden bar where the wire attached to the chair gave way. And Alistair fell.

What happened over the next few minutes is kind of a blur: I heard the unmistakable crack of wood breaking against the stage. I heard Alistair yell out in pain, and then a general panic erupted in the room. I don't know exactly when I made the decision to run, but I know I didn't wait long. I just remember bursting through the stage doors into a torrential downpour, feeling the rain soak my clothes as I ran across the parking lot, under the bleachers, and collapsed on the fifty-yard line of the football field.

Now, I'm not going to lie to you. It would have been really nice if Jesus could have swung by right about then. I could have used the friend. But he didn't. I whispered his name: "Jesus? Jesus Jackson? Jesus Jackson? Jesus Jackson?" But nothing happened. And after about five minutes I began to see the flashing lights from the police cars and the ambulance as they came driving up to the gym, and I decided that staying on school grounds was probably a bad idea. I had to find someplace to hide.

So I cut through yards and parks and woods, avoiding all the major roads and even most of the minor ones, until I finally reached the radio tower. It had already stopped raining by then, and I found a dry patch of pine needles at the base of the tower where I could rest until morning. Despite everything, I fell asleep almost instantly. And as I began to nod off, I stared up at the spot on the tower where Cassie and I had first spoken. At that moment, I had more regrets about her than about anything else from the whole ordeal...the way she stared up at me while I was on that stage, finally aware that I had been using her the whole time. Of course, it was never that cut-and-dried for me—and the real tragedy is that she didn't even know how hard I fell for her, or the simple, pretty truth that in the midst of so many questions and contradictions, she was the only thing I was ever certain of at all.

Thirty-seven

I woke up just before dawn, and there was no question of what I had to do next: I would go to the football field, I would sit on the fifty-yard line, and I would wait for Jesus Jackson. I was sure that half the police in town were looking for me by that point (not to mention my parents). I was going to have to deal with them eventually—I couldn't hide forever. And besides, I was going to get my goddamned twelve dollars back.

Thankfully, there didn't seem to be anyone waiting to snatch me up at the school. They probably figured, quite logically, that St. Soren's was just about the last place I'd turn up. I tried to keep myself as hidden as possible, though, so I had to sneak through the woods before making a dash to the football field.

To be honest, I really didn't expect to find Jesus Jackson there at all (and I was starting to think that I might never see him again). But to my surprise, there he was: just how I first found him, standing on the fifty-yard line, playing a game of imaginary football with no one.

I stopped at the edge of the field and watched him for a minute before he noticed that I was there. He seemed to be having a grand old time with his pretend tight-ends and invisible opponents, and I couldn't quite tell if it was infuriating or hilarious. It just didn't seem to matter to him at all that he was alone, that none of it was real, that nothing about his game— not the winners or the losers, not the moments of glory or embarrassment of defeat—would ever matter at all to anyone but him, or even exist outside of the confines of his mind.

When he finally saw me, he smiled and waved as if greeting an old friend after a long time apart. "Jonathan! There you are. I was wondering when you'd show up."

I walked out onto the field, trying to decide if I should plead with him for help or punch him in the face. In the end, though, I decided on a more practical approach.

"I want my twelve fucking dollars back," I said.

Jesus frowned. "I was afraid you might say that." He sat down on the field, patting the grass beside him. "Sit down. Tell me what happened."

I sank to the ground, glaring into his eyes. "Alistair is innocent. Tristan was lying to me the whole time. Cassie is never going to speak to me again. And I'm probably going to jail. If that isn't proof that my leap of faith was a failure, then I don't know what is.'

Jesus seemed to have been expecting me to say precisely that. "Interesting, interesting. So Alistair didn't confess, eh?"

"No!" I yelled. "He didn't confess because he didn't do it! He's innocent! Ryan died hours after their fight."

"Oh," Jesus said, with a furrow in his brow. "Did you at least find out how Ryan really did die?"

"No. Tristan dumped him for Alistair, they fought, and then he ran off on his own. A couple of hours later he was dead. Maybe he jumped. Maybe he fell. Maybe a goddamned alien threw him into the ravine."

"Well, you're still going to find out what really happened, aren't you?"

"Whatever..." I said. "It doesn't matter anymore. I don't even care how it happened."

"But...you do care, don't you?" he asked, his voice softening a touch. "You *need* to know how he died, right?"

"No," I snapped back. "I really don't. Knowing how he died is not going to bring him back. Knowing how he died is not going to give me a brother again. That's not the fucking point. That's not the question I care about."

"Then what is the question you care about?"

"I want to know where he is now!" I screamed. "Right now! At this moment! Dead! What the hell happened to him *after* he died, not before. What happens to everybody, what's going to happen to me? And I don't want any of your stupid 'constructions' or my school's stupid god or my father's lame-ass pamphlets, I want the truth! A truth I can live for, and die for. An irrefutable truth about what the hell it means that Ryan is dead and that someday I'm going to die too! I want proof, not faith. I want to know!"

Jesus reached into his pocket and pulled out a crumpled wad of money. "Here's your twelve dollars," he said. "I can't help you."

I stared at the money in his hand. "You can't?"

"I can't give you the truth," he said calmly. "I don't have any to give. That's not really what I do."

I sighed. Of course it wasn't. I wanted to snatch the money from his hand, but I just couldn't bring myself to do it. "So what the hell were you doing for me all this time, anyway? What was the point of all this?"

"Look," he said, "I don't build *real* gods or invent real religions. I can't give you knowledge, or proof, or anything like that. The best I can do is to help you get to a place where you're ready to take a leap of faith, to make a decision, to find some version of reality that you can believe, and *then start believing in it.*"

"Yeah, well then you clearly didn't get the job done," I said. "All I found out for sure is that there are no answers, and no matter how hard I look for them, there never really will be."

I reached my hand out to take the money from Jesus, but he snapped it back just as I was about to grab it. "Now hold on one second," he said. "How sure are you, exactly, that you can never find these answers?"

"Excuse me?"

"You said that you are sure that there are no answers, and that there never will be, no matter how hard you look for them, right?"

"Yeah, so?"

"So I just want to know *how* sure you are about that statement."

Now he was just getting on my nerves. "Completely sure," I said. "Not a doubt in mind." I reached out again for the money, and again he pulled it away from me.

"Would you say, for example, that you're one hundred percent sure?"

"Yes!" I yelled. "One hundred-freaking percent! Now give me my goddamned twelve dollars!"

"Sorry," he said, hopping to his feet and placing the money back in his pocket. "I'm afraid I can't do that. One hundred percent faith is what I promised, and one hundred percent faith is what you have. Technically, you still owe me thirty-six dollars and seventy-five cents, but we'll just call it even at twelve."

"But you were supposed to give me faith in *nothing*. Not faith in the fact that there's nothing to have faith in!"

"Well now you're just quibbling," he said, quite pleased with himself. "And besides, I made no such promise."

"And what, exactly, am I supposed to do with this crappy faith? Just be happy that I don't know anything?"

"You can do whatever you like with your faith," he said. "Be happy, be sad, be anything you want. But my job here is done."

And before I could protest, I heard the sound of a siren somewhere behind me. I wheeled around to see if I had been spotted by the police, but thankfully they seemed to be on the other side of the school.

When I turned back, Jesus was gone.

I stood there, frozen, for a few minutes (or maybe more) just thinking about what Jesus Jackson had said: that he had succeeded, that he had fulfilled his end of the bargain. That I now had faith: one hundred percent.

And I had to laugh, because he was right, just as he had been right all along. In the end, you can't be so concerned with *reality*. Sure, there has to be a real truth out there, somewhere. But if Jesus Jackson taught me anything, it's that you can never *really* know the truth. Not about life, not about God, not about what's in another person's heart, or even your own. All you can ever really know is what it *feels* like. What it feels like to laugh and cry and hate and hurt and hope and fear and love; what it feels like to live.

Thirty-eight

Having no place left to go, I just started walking back toward home, figuring that I would be found at some point before I got there, but not caring enough to hide anymore. After just a few minutes of walking, though, I found myself passing by the entrance to Saint Christopher's, and decided to step inside.

The chapel seemed empty, so I wandered slowly toward the altar, just taking it all in, and thinking back on all the Sundays I had spent there when I was a little kid. I was almost at the first row of pews when I heard a voice say my name.

"Jonathan? Jonathan Stiles?"

I turned to my left, and there was father Kevin, kneeling just a few feet away. "Oh," I said. "Hi."

"Please sit down," he replied, almost in wonderment. "What brings you here so early?"

Thankfully, he did not seem to know about the previous night's events. But I had to give him some kind of answer, so I brought up the only possible topic I could ever want to discuss with him. "I want to talk about Ryan."

He smiled at me gently, as if he was expecting this very answer, and then motioned for me to sit down beside him in the pew.

"What about Ryan would you like to talk about, exactly?" he asked.

Of course, I really didn't feel like talking about Ryan with anyone, much less a priest. And yet, there was one question that I always wanted an answer to. "Three years ago, when Ryan and I came to talk to you, what did you say to him after you sent me out of the room?"

He looked a little surprised by the question (I imagine he was anticipating a more general inquiry about death, or heaven, or something like that), but he didn't let it faze him much. He folded his hands across his stomach and nodded slowly in recollection. "Ah, yes. That was a long time ago. Why come back here after so long, for that?"

"I just…Well, I think Ryan changed after that. A lot. And I just need to know why."

He nodded some more, apparently accepting my reason. "I didn't have to say much, really. I figured out pretty quickly that his fervor was for your benefit, so once you left the room, I just asked him to explain to me again why he didn't believe. The next thing I know, he's telling me a very long, involved, and personal story about not believing in Christianity, but still needing there to be a god." Then his eyes flickered into a smile. "And if I recall, he said that he had researched just about every god that ever was, and couldn't find any evidence to support any of them. Is that right?"

"Yeah," I said. "That's right."

"And when I told him it was impossible to find *proof* about something that you're supposed to have faith in, he told me that it was impossible for him to have faith in something without having any proof about it."

I had to chuckle a bit. "Yup, that sounds like Ryan."

"And so I told him that he had reached an impasse. He

couldn't believe in any god without evidence, he couldn't find evidence about any god at all, and yet he still felt like he just *needed* to believe."

I felt the bottom drop out of my stomach. It sounded quite familiar, this dilemma. "So, what did you tell him?"

Father Kevin shrugged. "I told him that it didn't matter how many gods he read about, he would always come back to the fact that believing in God—in any god—requires faith. And faith means believing in something you cannot prove. If he really needed God to exist, then he would just have to accept that he existed, despite any evidence he found to the contrary. If he couldn't bring himself to do that, then he would just have to go through life without a god. It's really very simple, when you think about it."

"And what did he say?"

"Nothing," said Father Kevin. "He just thanked me for my time, and said he should get going."

"What…that's it?" I asked. "That's all? He just got up and left?"

"Pretty much," he said. "Although he did ask me for a favor first."

"What kind of favor?"

"He asked me to not meet with you again, unless you really wanted to meet with me. He was worried that he had already influenced your ideas too much, and if anyone else tried to influence them, you would wind up just as confused as he was. I guess he thought you'd be better off figuring out what to believe for yourself. I generally don't meet with people who do not wish to meet with me, so I had no trouble agreeing."

"But did he *ever* tell you anything about what he believed?" I asked. "Even years later, did he ever tell you what choice he made?

Father Kevin shook his head. "No, he never did. He came to church, took Communion, he may have even gone to confession a few times, but I never knew what he truly believed in his heart."

"Of course," I said, mostly to myself. "Only Ryan could know that."

"And the Lord," added Father Kevin.

"Right," I said. "Him too."

And with that, I thanked Father Kevin and walked out into the dawn.

Now, I won't lie to you, this all put me in a mild state of shock. Not so much because Father Kevin didn't know what Ryan chose to believe about God (how could he, after all?), but rather because Ryan was able to make a choice at all.

And then again, maybe he didn't. Maybe he was pretending the whole time and that's what led him to the edge of that ravine behind the school. Or on the other hand, maybe he just accepted the whole God thing, became an honest, contented Catholic, and had the best three years of his life. Of course, these are just more and more questions that I'll never be able to answer.

But what I do know is that I could never follow the same path that Ryan did. Whether his faith was real or an act, he jumped on the bandwagon—he played along, he joined the club. And that's just not in me; it's not who I am. I could never *pretend* to believe like that, and I could never *decide* to believe like that. Even if I wanted to.

And as I stepped out of that church, it occurred to me that I didn't have to make that choice at all. That you don't need to choose between accepting someone else's faith and going without faith altogether. That you can choose to have faith in anything you want, in anything you *feel*. You can have faith in science, or your favorite comic book, faith in the stars or faith in the Earth, faith in your job or your family or your best friend or your dog. You can have faith in the sweet face of a pretty red-haired girl who just wants to be close to you because she thinks that you just might want to be close to her too....

And so I made my choice. Right there, on the front steps of Saint Christopher's. I made my choice and I ran down the steps and then clear across town, as fast as I could, until I found myself stumbling and panting on the St. Claires' lawn.

Cassie must have heard me out there in the yard, because she appeared at her window before I even had the chance to toss a pebble at the glass. She looked angry at first: her face hard and hurt. But then I saw her eyes focus on something in the distance. I turned to see what it was, though I already knew: it was a police car, making its way slowly past the house, searching for me.

I collapsed onto my knees—out of exhaustion, or desperation, or emotion, or all three—and Cassie softened, a little bit. Then she smiled, climbed out her window, and joined me on the lawn.

And after all of it was over—after the cops and the apologies and the wrath of my mother, after Henry and I got kicked out of St. Soren's for good (which really wasn't much of a punishment)—after all of it, the only thing that still mattered was the fact that I had finally made a choice. I chose to believe in what I feel. I took a leap of faith, and landed.

And sure, I still don't know how Ryan wound up in that ravine, or where he is now, or if he's anywhere at all. But it doesn't bother me anymore. What matters is that I have faith in where *I am*, now. And I am right here. And I am alive.

To receive a free catalog of Poisoned Pen Press titles, please contact us in one of the following ways:

Phone: 1-800-421-3976
Facsimile: 1-480-949-1707
Email: info@poisonedpenpress.com
Website: www.poisonedpenpress.com

Poisoned Pen Press
6962 E. First Ave. Ste 103
Scottsdale, AZ 85251